# Sign Me Up

## Dulcie Dameron

© Copyright 2023 Dulcie Dameron

All rights reserved.

No part of this book may
be reproduced in any form or by any electronic mechanical means, including
information storage and retrieval systems, without written permission from the
author, except for the use of brief quotations in a book review.

Author's note: This is a work of fiction. Names, characters, places, and situations, while possibly inspired by real life events, are a product of my imagination. Any similarities to real people, places or things are purely coincidental. Character mentions of celebrities do not necessarily express the author's personal beliefs.

Cover Design done by: K. Leah

Edited by: Jennia D'Lima

# KISSING A KENT BROTHER

♥

*Sign Me Up*
*Spoke Too Soon*
*Flirty Little Secret*

# Dedication

*To my sister, Jamie, who I promised to name my future child after.
Here's to hoping you'll accept a fictional character as a namesake instead
of one of my real-life kids.
Because that ship has sailed.*

# A NOTE FROM THE AUTHOR

Dear Reader,

Thank you for picking up this book! I'm humbled and honored that you've chosen to take this journey with me.

I feel it's important to note that our MMC, Parker, is a deaf man living in a mostly hearing environment. As an author, I've tried my best to research and do my due diligence to make his character as nuanced as the deaf community itself, but I'm sure I've probably fallen short somewhere. As a hearing person, I can't even begin to understand what it's like to have a sensory difference like this, so inevitably, I won't get it all right.

This book was read by sensitivity readers who are immersed in deaf culture or have deaf relatives, so just know that I've taken their thoughtful insights and suggestions into consideration for this story as well.

There are many interactions between Parker and Jamie, a hearing person, where I don't explicitly mention her or him signing to each other. Just know that Jamie is always trying to communicate with Parker through what Sign Language she knows as well as speaking (unless otherwise noted), while Parker's dialogue will be in italics. It would have become extremely redundant to the reader if I had to continuously use dialogue tags such as "she said/signed" or "he signed." So for flow of the story, I've added this note to help you during those interactions.

I hope you love Parker and Jamie as much as I do!

XO,

*Dulcie Dameron*
ROMANCE AUTHOR

# 1

# JAMIE

*FOR THE LOVE OF all that's good and green in the world, please make it stop.*

How many more times can I offer up this silent prayer while being held prisoner by none other than Les Jenkins, the *Treemont Gazette*'s very own encyclopedia of useless things?

A hundred? A million? Is there a limit?

Waiting for the copies of the press release I just completed to be printed out, I brace myself against the corner of the office copier while Les drones on and on. You'd think with a name like *Les* the guy would understand the concept of *less being more*. But nope. He doesn't get it. Not even a little bit.

I'd like to think I'm a patient person, but this is the fourth time Les has trapped me at the copier this week. And it's not that he's a bad guy, but if boring was a person, it would be him. Not to mention his brown suit and pale yellow tie combo mixed with his signature fried bacon smell remind me of the interior of a Waffle House. *Ew.*

Doing my best to resist taking a deep breath lest I inhale the scent of dirty diner, I bolster my mind for the rest of this titillating conversation. If this is anything like Tuesday's copier meetup, I'd better settle in and buckle my seat belt because this guy has proved he can go on for a surprisingly long while. Last week, his riveting discussion on the mating habits of marmosets lasted so long my coffee got cold. Today, it's bird calls—or something like that.

Finally, as if God Himself has smiled upon me, a tall, dark, familiar figure saunters up behind Les, bringing with him a whiff of expensive, delectable cologne that subtly overpowers the lingering smell of fried bacon.

Parker Kent, my work bestie and now lifeline, gives me a smirk with one eyebrow raised. His light green eyes sparkle with a hint of humor that I can't fully appreciate while being held captive by Les.

As usual, Parker's the perfect blend of cozy and professional, with his mussed-up hair and baby blue dress shirt that's open a bit at the collar—so much so that I have to pump the mental breaks when my mind begins to romanticize his effortless good looks.

He's my *friend*. We're *friends*. It's platonic.

Les hasn't noticed Parker's presence and keeps spinning some tale about a bird that lives in the northwest region of the state.

I widen my eyes and blink dramatically at Parker, telling him without words to please sacrifice himself on the copier conversation altar for the sake of my sanity.

"So, you see, Jamie," Les says, snagging my attention as he swipes the back of his wrist across his glistening forehead, "Avian vocalizations are a grossly understudied subject in general, therefore, you can't just assume that every two-syllable call you hear is your average warbler. It could very well be a titmouse." He smiles as if he just imparted some earth-shattering secret.

With as wide a closed-mouth smile as I can manage, I give him one slow nod, then lift my eyes back to Parker, silently begging him to help me. He shakes his head with that boyish smile I've come to crave, then signs, *OK, but you owe me.*

I purse my lips and give him an almost imperceptible nod before he blessedly taps Les on the shoulder to get his attention.

When the compendium of worthless facts himself turns to my friend, I bolt in the opposite direction, mentally reminding myself to thank Parker later. He's always so willing to take the figurative bullet for me in this office. I really should buy him a plant or something.

I hurry past the line of cubicles as fast as my size nine feet will take me, eager to escape any more talk of avian communications. I shake my head as I think of how my boss, Stefan Sanders, praised Les just last week for his exceptional editing skills in the obituaries. If only Les could edit his copier conversations just as efficiently, we'd all be better off. Those interactions should be strictly limited to the harmless, superficial topics of the weather and other office pleasantries. In those brief interactions, less is almost always more.

I reach the sacred blessed quiet of my cubicle just as Stefan, our editor-in-chief, strolls up. He's impeccably dressed, as usual, in a three-piece suit. A decent looking man in his late forties with salt and pepper hair, Stefan's presence exudes power and leadership. If only keeping up employee morale ranked as high as his personal fashion sense. In his typical way, Stefan drapes his arm over my small cubicle wall, rapping his knuckle on the top.

"Jamie, you got a minute?"

I smile, but inwardly grimace. Stefan's "talks" seldom involve giving us praise. Usually when he wants to chat, it's because we've disappointed him in some way. "Sure, boss. What's up?"

I keep my tone as light and breezy as possible. In almost every interaction with my boss, I sense he can hear the nuances in my voice to the point where he'd give me more work if I sounded exasperated, or he'd withhold an exciting project if I seemed too eager. The man is known for putting people in their places—and keeping them there. Thankfully, I don't seem to be in his line of sight this month, but one conversation could change that.

"I was hoping I could talk to you about your highlights on the Little League game from last Saturday," he says, peering over his dark-framed glasses at me.

"Oh, sure."

Again, I do my best not to sound *too* happy about the assignment, using only the smallest amount of inflection in my voice. Almost like I'm bored. Like I fulfilled my obligation with minimal enthusiasm.

"Your latest story was good, Jamie, but don't you think you went a little overboard with this one?" Stefan pauses as if waiting for a reply, but I'm rendered momentarily speechless. *What is he getting at?* "I mean," he continues, waving his coffee cup with his other hand, "you didn't need to add that part about the tall kid. *A sixth-grade Goliath?* Really?"

Understanding dawns when he mentions my addition of Barrett Andrews, the six-foot-two sixth grade pitcher who played for the home team on Saturday.

"Oh, don't worry about the nickname," I say, ready to explain myself. "I asked the parents if that would be all right to use in my story. They loved it. Said they would get him a T-shirt made with it on the back, even." I smile, hoping to drive home the air of nonchalance I'm going for.

Stefan frowns. "You're not writing stories, Jamie. You're filling up space in the sports section with statistics and facts. It's not your job to entertain the masses with your dry sense of humor. It's your job to report the news."

*Why, thank you for mansplaining that to me, Stefan.*

"But," I hedge. "I thought it was pertinent to the game, sir. A six-foot-two, twelve-year-old kid is kind of a big deal." I chuckle nervously.

"The height of some middle-school pitcher isn't *pertinent* information, Miss DeFreese. If you can't recognize that, then maybe I need to put Lucas back on sports for a while."

My spine involuntarily stiffens as Stefan eyes me with a judgy raised eyebrow like he's assessing my worthiness as a person.

"No, sir, that be won't necessary. From now on, I'll focus on sticking with the *statistics* and *facts*. Message received." I offer him a stiff smile and a completely unnecessary finger gun pointed at his chest. Of course, I pull my thumb trigger with a sly wink to add to the awkwardness of this moment. *What is wrong with me?*

Stefan's lips pull into a thin line as he gives me a firm nod and steps away from my cubicle. "Good. I'm glad we understand each other."

Without another word, he moves past me down the aisle, leaving me to retreat to my desk and bury my face in my hands. I rub the heels of my palms into my eye sockets, thankful I was running late this morning and didn't have time to apply eyeliner and mascara. Smudged eye makeup would only add to my growing frustration.

I'm not surprised Stefan didn't appreciate that I wrote about the tall kid pitching for the home team and the way he towered over his teammates. Stefan was right. I did add embellishing details to my article in an attempt to entertain the reader. Just because it's a kids baseball game doesn't mean the article should be boring, it should be full of fun additions that keep the reader engaged.

And besides, at 5'9", I'm a tall kid myself. Growing up I frequently felt out of place being a head taller than most of the girls—and even boys—in my class. And seeing how some of the players on the away team jeered at the kid, I bet Barrett Andrews feels some of my pain. He deserves to be *praised* for the thing that makes him special, not put down because of it.

I raise my head and stare at the same screensaver I've had since my first day at the *Treemont Daily Gazette*. My grandma Nonie's wrinkled face smiles back at me, as if she'd just handed me one of her signature chocolate hazelnut cookies.

*It'll be all right, James Gang. You can't win them all.*

Her familiar words of comfort echo in my mind in the low, gravelly voice she often used during our late-night kitchen conversations. She was always so careful not to wake up Grandpa after nine p.m., claiming he needed his beauty rest. *A beautiful man like him with a full head of hair at age seventy needs all the sleep he can get*, she'd say with a conspiratorial wink and a smile. If only she were here to wrap me up in one of her lung-crushing hugs and give me a real-life pep talk.

I sigh and lean back in my chair, knowing I need to get back to work. These sports stories—er—*stats* won't write themselves. Just as I drag my computer's mouse across the pad, a soft, flying object pelts the side of my head. I swivel around, knowing exactly who I'll find.

Sure enough, Parker peeks his dark-haired head over the side of my cubicle wall, his vivid green eyes crinkling at the corners. I lift my hands and sign, *What's up, Superman?*

Okay, so he's not *exactly* Superman, but his last name *is* Kent and he's tall and broad enough to be considered a more svelte version of the famous Clark Kent, minus the glasses. Parker isn't lanky, but he's naturally thin and can eat whatever he wants without gaining weight. *The jerk*. And he frequently comes to my rescue in this office like my own personal version of a superhero.

When I first laid eyes on him walking into the *Gazette* to replace Mr. Tinkles (yes, that *is* his predecessor's real name), I legitimately thought that one of the background dancers from Shania Twain's "Man! I Feel

Like a Woman!" music video had gotten lost and wandered into our office. He was just so tan and had the most striking eyes that stood out perfectly against his unruly dark hair.

Thankfully, when Parker started, he wasn't wearing black eyeliner or leather pants like the models in Shania's music video or that would have been really awkward. Probably.

His eyes lock on mine and he jerks his head in the direction Stefan went, as if to ask, *What'd the boss want this time?*

I sigh and roll my eyes before lifting my closed hands and dragging them outward to sign the word for *nothing*.

Parker cocks his head and lowers his brows. He drags his thumb under his chin while simultaneously shaking his head *no*. Clearly, he's not buying my line.

"Oh, you know," I say in a hushed voice no one else would hear while trying to sign the rest. "He just came by to commend me on writing such a moving piece on the Little League game from last Saturday. He said it was my best work."

Parker's mirth-filled eyes dance and his lips twitch. Though he can't hear the sarcasm lacing my tone, he knows me well enough to detect it in my words and facial expression. I wish I knew more Sign Language to be able to convey the discussion with our boss word for word to Parker, but I am not as skilled as I want to be.

As much as I've learned from the ASL class our boss paid for the *Gazette* employees to take, plus independently studied on my own by binging YouTube videos, I still struggle sometimes. And since I've never personally known another deaf person before Parker, I'd never realized the importance of learning the language. For the hundredth time in the last year of knowing him, I wish I'd taken the American Sign Language elective in college.

At once, Parker's eyes soften, almost like he can sense my thoughts. Or maybe it's not so much my thoughts he's reading as it is the conversation he witnessed with Stefan. Parker can read body language better than any person I've ever known.

He points at me, then signs the words for *story was great*. Next, he spears me with a look that says, *go ahead and try to argue with me. You know you won't win.*

I smile and say, as well as sign, "Thank you, Parker. You're a good friend."

A muscle in his jaw twitches before he smiles and makes the sign for lunch, tipping his head in the direction of the employee break room.

"I thought you'd never ask," I say, rising from my desk.

He follows me to the large break room where the drab gray countertop lining the wall topped with a mediocre toaster that burns things just as much as it under toasts them and a fire engine red microwave greet us.

After we grab our lunches from the fridge, I settle in beside Parker with my delicious fall-inspired salad topped with toasted pecans, dried cranberries, diced apple, and roasted turkey breast. I can't wait to dig in.

Lifting my fork, I peek at my handsome friend. His eyes are closed, head bowed in prayer, and his brow is furrowed so deeply, I'm tempted to press my fingers to his forehead and smooth away the offending lines.

But that would be weird, so I won't.

Even though Parker is more touchy-feely with people than the average guy, I'm not super big on physical affection. Plus, it kind of feels like something inside of me knows that if I were to reach out and touch him, I wouldn't want to stop.

Attraction can be a tricky thing, especially when it's your *friend* you're attracted to. It doesn't feel wrong, per se, but having romantic wonderings about Parker is bound to get me into trouble and I refuse to do anything that might risk our friendship or make it weird.

Been there, done that with my high school boyfriend, Tyson. We were friends all through elementary and junior high, until one day he asked me to be his girlfriend. After that, everything was great...until it wasn't. We broke up right before our junior prom and never spoke again for the duration of high school. Every time he saw me, he'd dodge me or pretend I didn't exist. There were no more secret inside jokes, late-night study sessions or eating off each other's plates. And to make matters worse, our friend group chose him over me. His popularity won out in the end.

My senior year was miserable because of it.

So I can never allow Parker to be another Tyson. Not when he's my one light in this dark office with his funny antics, superhero personality, and overindulgence in sweets.

Speaking of which, I look down at the lunch he's packed for himself and shake my head. It's his usual. A peanut butter and jelly sandwich, a bag of classic potato chips, and an oatmeal cream pie for dessert. Oh, and last but not least, a twenty-ounce bottle of Coke and a bag of M&Ms. Because he just has to wash down a salty yet also sugar-laden lunch with a healthy dose of liquid sugar. It's really a medical marvel that he stays as fit as he does.

Parker bites into his sandwich and narrows his eyes at me like he senses my silent judgment. I narrow my eyes right back. He knows how I feel about his less than stellar eating habits, but he doesn't seem to care. It's the only sore spot in our relationship.

Male laughter from the hallway gets my attention and I drop my head back in exasperation. Parker knows that sign as well as any. He nudges my shoulder and spells out L-U-C-A-S with his fingers. I nod and his lips pull into a tight line.

If Parker is my light in the office, Lucas Whitwell is the purveyor of darkness. He's the most annoying man-child I've ever met. Not only has he *relentlessly* flirted with every female in the office, he's also been known to make passive-aggressive comments to anyone who makes him feel inferior. Parker being one of them. And let's not even get into how he sucks up to Stefan.

When Lucas walks into the break room and sees us, he stops midstride and raises a skeptical brow. "Well, well, well, aren't you two a lovely couple." He saunters over to the cabinet and pulls out a can of round spaghetti noodles in sauce. I smirk, thinking that's the perfect lunch for this man-child. I last ate those when I was ten.

"We're not a couple," I mumble before stuffing another forkful of salad into my mouth. Parker watches our interaction closely and I can feel his entire body stiffen beside me.

Lucas gives me an overly bright smile as he pops the top of his can and dumps its contents into a microwave-safe bowl. "Whatever you say. Though you might be interested to know Jordy's got quite the crush on this big guy." He tips his head toward Parker with another sickeningly sweet smile, and I grimace.

An uneasy pit forms in my stomach, but I shrug it off and go back to my salad. "Parker and I are just friends." But saying it doesn't ease the uncomfortable feeling inside me.

Lucas makes a sound in his throat like he's not sure he believes me, but thankfully he doesn't press the issue. Instead, he leans back against the counter, facing us. "I hear the boss has some big announcement he's going to give today." I immediately perk up at the word *announcement* and glance at Parker. His gaze bounces between Lucas and me.

"What's it about?" I ask.

"Stefan doesn't tell me *everything*, Jamie." Lucas chuckles like he made a joke, but my frown only deepens. "All I know," he continues, "is that it's *big* and it involves *all* of us."

Parker taps my shoulder and frowns. *An announcement?* he signs. I dip my chin in a solemn nod. His brows knit together like he's thinking over a problem.

I desperately hope Stefan isn't going to start laying people off. I know times are getting tough, but what would that mean for those of us who rely solely on our jobs here to make a living? My mind then goes to Parker. His job is on the lowest ladder rung of all, meaning he might be one of the first ones let go.

"But I'm sure it's nothing to worry about," Lucas says with another fake smile. "He's probably just switching up our assignments for the quarter or something." *Yeah, or something.*

I finish eating in silence, waiting for Lucas to turn around and wash his bowl, then face Parker. I'm guessing dread is written all over my face because he lifts his "sword finger"—as he likes to refer to it—and cocks his head. My eyes widen as I shake my head, silently pleading for him not to use it. It's the weapon he wields whenever I'm feeling down, the one sure-fire way to make me laugh.

A slow, sinister smile takes over Parker's face as he curls his finger a few times, waving it over my body. "Don't you dare," I mouth, holding my hands out in a protective gesture.

He completely ignores me and tries to jab it into the ticklish spot on my side, but I twist away before he can make contact. That only spurs him on. Quicker than a blink, he brings his hand down onto my thigh and squeezes the fleshy part just above my knee. I squeal out a laugh as I grab Parker's hand, trying and failing to get him to stop.

Lucas spins around with a scowl directed right at us. "What's so funny?" Parker's hand stills on my thigh, his warmth seeping through my skin. I'm thankful Lucas can't see it from his vantage point.

"Oh, nothing," I lie, not wanting to give him any more ammunition about Parker and me being a couple. "Just had something in my teeth and Parker was making fun of me for it."

Lucas narrows his eyes like he doesn't believe me for a second. He dries his bowl and sticks it back in the cupboard. "You two enjoy your long lunch. Some of us have *actual* work to do around here."

When he leaves the break room, I roll my eyes dramatically and make a face at Parker. He laughs, then goes right back to tickling me. I manage to wedge my fingers in the crook of his neck where he's most ticklish, and he eases up just enough for me to hold my hands up in surrender.

"Okay! Uncle!"

He leans back, a satisfied grin curling his lips upward. *You needed to laugh,* he signs.

I shake my head. "I'm just concerned, that's all. Announcements from Stefan are seldom a good thing."

Parker's expression tells me he knows exactly what I'm talking about. Maybe he's worried about layoffs too. Parker is the paper's one-man data division. His job mainly consists of recording all the real estate transfers and property sales for our county. Where I at least sometimes get to cut out early to travel to and attend some mediocre—*at best*—sports events, Parker is stuck here in the office, glued to his desk all day, every day. I write about sports statistics and winning/losing teams, adding my own unique flare, much to the chagrin of my boss, while Parker is forced to write about the most mundane facts known to man, day in and day out.

My mouth turns down into a frown just thinking about it because, deep down, I know that Parker is destined for something more meaningful than a job like this. He doesn't ever complain about his work, but I can still sense his dissatisfaction here. Whether it's his deafness that mentally holds him back from pursuing something more or something else altogether, I don't know, but I'm not brave enough to ask him about it.

Having a hard-of-hearing friend is still relatively new to me and I wouldn't want to be insensitive by bringing it up. We've become close throughout the past year, and I figure if it's something he wants to talk about, he'll bring it up on his own.

As if sensing the dark turn of my thoughts, Parker pokes me in the side again, and I yelp. He waves his sword finger around in a silent threat, but before he can reach me, I stand and gather my things.

"Come on. *Some of us,*" I say, using air quotes, "have work to do today."

# 2

# Jamie

Technicolor rainbows unfurl in my chest as I sit at my desk and sip my third cup of coffee. It's doctored to perfection with a splash of half and half and a sprinkling of coconut sugar. It tastes like liquid hopes and dreams so I'm counting on it working its magic any minute now.

I stifle a yawn and resist the urge to drop my head onto my forearms. I didn't get home until late last night after attending a soccer game I was designated to report on. It was notably entertaining. I watched in awe of how uncoordinated five-year-olds could be. All except for one boy who seemed to carry the entire team. Of course, his dad was the coach.

Coach Dad would run the entire length of the field with his son's team, hollering out what to do, play-by-play. It was annoying, yes, but also a little sweet. It made me wonder if I'll ever have a home and family of my own one day—the white picket fence kind of life. With kids and a husband and soccer games of our own to attend.

At the rate I'm currently going, it doesn't seem likely.

My last boyfriend, Mike, who I'd foolishly thought might be *the one*, was charming and beautiful, but after seven months of dating, he just didn't seem as into me as I was into him. After multiple times of him leaving me out or blowing me off, I ended it. That was almost two months ago now, but my heart is still a little sore. Probably more so from rejection than anything, but still...even that hurts.

And coming out of yet another failed relationship has me wishing there was someone who could give me more than what my career can offer.

From the time I was little, the only goal I truly clung to was to grow up and be a writer. I was the girl in third grade who carried a pencil behind her ear and a notepad in her back pocket, ready to jot down anything that inspired her. From the way Nonie's blueberry pancakes melted on my tongue to the playground drama at school, it had all found its way onto my little notepad. I just *knew* I was destined to be a writer.

That's why I pursued a degree in journalism and also why I started up *Just Read Jamie*, my blog dedicated to reading and reviewing my favorite fiction books. But lately, it all doesn't feel like enough.

It's not that I'm ungrateful for my work, because I truly am thankful to be where I'm at, even though writing sports *statistics* and *facts* while blogging about fiction on the side isn't what I had envisioned a writer's life to be. I realize, though, that this may be just a small, first step on the path toward what I really want to do—become a writer whose stories are worth reading.

So, I'm content to bide my time and pay my dues like the rest of the world in order to accomplish my end goal. But every time I've thought of that end goal lately, it seems hollow without someone to share it with. Maybe it didn't while Nonie was alive and Pops knew who I was, but now that she's gone and he doesn't, it all just feels...empty.

I pinch the bridge of my nose, remembering it's time to pay for Pops's care center bill. Thankfully, he checked himself in when things started to get bad with his mind... things like forgetting what basic household items were used for, wandering outside in the middle of the night, forgetting my name... It breaks my heart thinking of how fast he's declined since

Nonie died. The sudden tightening of my chest has me rubbing the spot over my heart, trying to ease the sting of loss that threatens my composure.

*Deep breaths, Jamie. Take deep, cleansing breaths.*

The therapist I briefly saw after losing Nonie recommended I do deep breathing exercises when the pain seems unbearable, so I lean back in my swivel chair, close my eyes, and focus on my breathing. Dr. Weeks, the aforementioned therapist, tried to diagnose me with grief-induced anxiety and shove meds in my face, saying my *episodes,* as she referred to them, sounded like panic attacks.

I wasn't interested in being prescribed meds or being slapped with a label like that in the midst of my grief, so I kindly ignored her and never went back. I do, however, take the advice she gave me about the breathing exercises. I figure it couldn't hurt.

After a few silent minutes, I open my eyes and see a very handsome, very *masculine* face looming over my cubicle wall. It scares the living daylights out of me, and I fall backwards in my chair, tipping it over and landing flat on my back.

My legs flail straight into the air as my skirt hikes precariously up my thighs, most likely exposing the revealing lacy, pink underwear my roommate Daria convinced me to buy last week. My eyes shoot to Parker's, whose are blown wide. A lump of regret hits me hard in the stomach.

I squeeze my eyes shut and will this embarrassing situation into oblivion, frantically trying to pin down my skirt. I have a sudden flashback to first grade when Bobby Hauck lifted my skirt in front of the whole class, showing off my bright red undies with Minnie Mouse on the front. I vowed then and there to never wear brightly colored undergarments again for as long as I lived.

See what breaking a vow gets you? Absolute mortification.

I toss myself to the side, trying to extricate myself from my compromising position, but the chair's arms are holding me hostage. The next thing I know, Parker is at my head, lifting behind my shoulders, trying to maneuver me to my side.

Finally, we succeed, and I rest on my knees, breathless. He kneels in front of me, but I can't raise my face to look at him. And, to add insult to injury, my cheeks flame hot and probably match the shade of the underwear he just glimpsed.

Why couldn't I have just told Daria to eat dirt when she suggested I needed to add a pop of color to my wardrobe in the form of lacy underwear? What nonsense! Don't get me wrong, I like girly things from time to time, but the color pink should be relegated to cute coffee mugs, planters, and my Hello Kitty robe, *not* my underthings.

Maybe I'm just a prudish grandma at heart—I mean, I was raised by one—but I'll stick with buying the black, comfortable unflattering granny panties that completely cover my rear-end from now on, thank you very much.

Parker taps the top of my knee, urging me to meet his eyes. When I don't, he tips my chin upward with his finger and forces me to make eye contact. *You OK?* he signs with a look of concern.

I roll my lips together and give him a curt nod. My body may be fine, but my pride is most *definitely* not. Parker has seen the barely-there lacy, pink underwear and is probably scarred for life.

His finger lightly grazes the bottom of my chin, trailing upward to my cheek, and a tingle courses through me. If it weren't for the fact that I just flashed him, I might lean into his comforting touch. But as it is, I'm still too embarrassed about what I know he saw.

A throat clears from behind Parker, and I peek around him to see Stefan staring at us with raised brows. "Am I interrupting something?"

Parker turns, sees our boss, then gently pulls me to my feet. He looks a little sheepish but starts using his hands to mimic what exactly happened. I force myself to speak, thoroughly embarrassed now.

"I was an idiot and fell backwards in my chair," I explain to our boss.

Stefan looks between us, unconvinced, but quickly changes the subject. "I need you two in the conference room in five. I have an important announcement to make." With one last look between Parker and me, he stalks off, leaving us awkwardly alone again after my little impromptu tumbling act.

"Thanks for helping..." I start to say, but then realize Parker is turned away from me and can't see my lips. I grab his arm to get his attention. "Thanks for helping me," I reiterate.

He smiles, then signs, *Sorry I scared you*.

I let out a self-deprecating laugh. "The fault was all mine."

His eyes crinkle at the corners and he hooks his thumb over his shoulder, indicating we make our way to the conference room. I smooth down my skirt as we walk, my mind going over multiple worst-case scenarios. I have no clue what this meeting could be about, but even the notion that Stefan may be switching up our assignments for the quarter makes sweat bead on my upper lip.

As much as I resent the fact that I'm only covering local sporting events, I would hate to have to relinquish my role to someone else. Someone like Lucas, the boss's pet.

Once we make it to the conference room, the only two seats available at the long table are side-by-side in between Lucas and Les. On one hand, I'm elated that Parker and I will be able to sit together. On the other, I'm frustrated that we'll be sandwiched between the world record holder in longest, most boring copier conversations ever, and the man-child who puts people down with his expertly crafted back-handed compliments.

Mercifully, Parker walks toward the chair beside Lucas. I know he's taking another bullet for me, so I hurry beside him to the seat next to Les, the *lesser* of two evils in this instance.

Les gives me a self-assured smile, and we all face Stefan. He's standing at the head of the table and behind him is a board covered up with something resembling a sheet. Are we about to witness some kind of surprise presentation? The uneasiness that plagued me before walking into the room doesn't let up once I'm seated.

The Sign Language interpreter comes in and sits off to the left of where Stefan is standing, ready to do her job. She must work as a freelancer, because she's only here for meetings and things of that nature. I wish I knew enough ASL to be able to sign for Parker. Then he'd only have to look at me and not the pretty petite interpreter. An unbidden surge of jealousy rises to my surface like an ugly pimple needing to be popped and I'm not sure why. I shove it back down before I'm tempted to dissect it and focus my attention on Stefan.

"I called all of you in here today to address something that has come to my attention, but also to share some good news," Stefan says to the group. My eyebrow raises slightly. *What* has come to his attention? And *good* news? That's unexpected.

Our editor-in-chief stuffs his hands in his pockets and jingles his keys, which I've learned is a sign of nervousness. "I've been made aware that our office environment lacks a certain...*friendliness*. Camaraderie, if you will."

Parker knocks my knee with his and I meet his surprised expression. Others look around too, appearing completely baffled by our boss's words. Stefan has never tried to bring the employees together, in *friendliness* or otherwise. The atmosphere here is more closed-off than any job I've had before.

Suddenly, I'm struck with the realization that this meeting must have something to do with the employee survey he e-mailed to everyone last week. The e-mail stated that it would be completely confidential and anonymous, plus we'd receive a five-dollar gift card to the local sub shop if we completed it. Naturally, I did the thing because only a fool turns down a discount on a sub sandwich from O'Malley's Subs.

But now I distinctly remember there being a question on the survey asking us to rank the overall friendliness in the workplace on a scale from one to ten. I *may* have been a little hangry that day and rated it a one, then left a quip in the comments section about how I could have easily rated it a zero, but they didn't give me that option.

Now I'm regretting not eating that candy bar Parker offered me a few minutes before opening that survey. If only I'd known an entire meeting would be based on my lousy rating, I'd have snatched that baby up and devoured it, curing my hunger while also saving the rest of us from having to endure this awkward meeting.

Hindsight is twenty-twenty, folks.

"That's why," my boss continues, startling me from my thoughts. "I've decided to include some mandatory morale-boosting activities into your work assignments for the next few weeks. Things like trust building exercises, out-of-office field trips, that sort of thing."

Surprisingly, Lucas raises his hand first. "Are you saying we're going to have to spend time with each other *outside* of work?" His face contorts with disgust, and I suppress my urge to laugh.

Stefan gives Lucas a pointed look. "Most of the activities I have planned will happen in the afternoons during work hours, but yes, some will be scheduled outside of regular work hours. In those cases, you will not be forced to attend, but I will *strongly* encourage it." Stefan's gaze roams around the room, looking each of us in the eye to drive home his point.

I hate the term *strongly encourage*. Basically, he's manipulating us without looking like an overbearing ogre of a boss and saying we *must* comply.

*Lovely.*

I try to gauge Parker's reaction to the news, but his attention is focused on Lucas. With the way Lucas is low-key scowling at his co-workers you'd think we ate his moist-maker sandwich for lunch. I let out a chuckle thinking of that *Friends* episode where poor Ross has that happen to him, which only makes Lucas scowl in my direction. His outward disdain surprises me. Lucas's rudeness is usually sugar-coated but leaves a disgustingly artificial taste in your mouth at the end, yet right now, he's not even trying to disguise it.

"Personally," Stefan continues with a smile that appears almost painfully uncomfortable for him, "I'm looking forward to these little excursions we'll be taking together. Which brings me to our first one." He turns and grabs the "sheet" on the poster board behind him and whips it off, unveiling a poster of a...pumpkin patch?

My gaze swings to Parker as I squeeze his thigh in a death grip. His muscles twitch under my palm and I immediately release him, wondering what the heck I was thinking touching him like that. But I can't help it, I'm just so...so shocked by this random turn of events. When I drag my gaze up to meet his, his brow is scrunched low, a hundred questions in his eyes.

*Me too, buddy. Me too.*

"This is Corny Acres Pumpkin Patch where we will be having our first employee adventure." Stefan's voice cracks on that last word, forcing me to stifle a giggle. Seeing my boss this far out of his comfort zone is wildly entertaining. "Since this will be our first camaraderie exercise, I expect everyone to be there with bells on."

Who is this person and what has he done with my boss, Stefan Sanders? The no-nonsense, gruff, impeccably dressed man who has the knack for making people feel the need to impress him—and always acting underwhelmed even if they do? I expect that any minute now Ashton Kutcher will be popping out from under the table yelling, "You've been *punked*!"

Unfortunately for those of us around this table, Ashton doesn't make an appearance. And this workplace disaster train that we are all stranded on is heading full force toward a cliff without any sign of slowing down. I look around the table once more, wondering what's going on in everyone else's heads.

Beside me, Les starts rubbing his hands together like he's about to start in on a riveting lecture on the lifecycle of some obscure insect none of us have heard of. On the other side of Les, Gladys Mullins taps her bright red fingernails against the table, eyes narrowed, lips pursed, appearing none too pleased.

Jordy, a girl fresh out of college who started working as Stefan's assistant six months ago, simpers on the opposite side of the table from Parker, waving to get his attention, then pointing to the poster board like he can't see it for himself. *Gee whiz, back it up, Jordy!*

Parker's eyes are locked on me with a look that says *Please save me.* Meanwhile, the rest of my co-workers look as dazed and confused as I feel, like we really are in some kind of hidden camera scenario.

Stefan steps forward and passes out a brochure to each of us. "I'll be sending out an e-mail this week with all the details, but plan to keep your afternoons open next Friday." When he's finished with his task, he says, "Now that we've got that covered, it's time for the good news."

Right. Because none of what he just said was good news. My eccentric co-workers and me spending bunches of time together outside the office? Worst. News. Ever.

"The famous YouTuber, Paris Dawson, has returned to her small hometown, just a few miles down the road from Treemont. There have been numerous rumors circulating about her and her movie producer ex that she'd like to put to rest. Since she's leery of tabloids and most national news sources, she's agreed to give the *Gazette* an insider's interview, in exchange for us printing the truth. And with her recent rise to popularity, I expect this article to go viral."

My ears perk at this revelation. An exclusive interview with *Paris Dawson*? The most down-to-earth yet insanely gorgeous lifestyle and beauty blogger ever? Um…yes, please! Sign. Me. Up.

Then another idea sprouts in my mind like a brand-new baby plant. Paris recently wrote a book about her almost instant rise to YouTube fame. If I'm able to interview her for work and it goes well, there might be a chance she'd meet with me again and allow me to quote her on her new book. My blog subscribers *love* when I do author interviews, but if I was somehow lucky enough to be able to sit down with Paris or even get some fiction recommendations from her? They'd absolutely eat it up!

That's it. It's decided. I *have* to score this interview.

"But Miss Dawson has made it clear she doesn't want to sit down with just anyone," Stefan continues. "She wants to give her side of the story to a reporter she can trust…someone with empathy, morals…someone devoted to writing up the truth—in its entirety."

My stomach sinks to the floor when Stefan's eyes graze over me briefly. Does he think I *don't* do that? That because I add my own unique flair to the sports section, I somehow lack morals?

Like he's already guessed which way my thoughts have run, Parker loops his foot behind mine and tugs it toward him. The sudden warmth shooting up my leg makes my midsection quiver. I can't meet his eyes with the physical sensations his touch delivers but I'm guessing he means to offer me some form of silent support. And for that, I'm grateful.

But holy cow, when he reaches under the table and runs his knuckle along the top of my thigh, my whole body threatens to convulse in a shiver. It's incredibly distracting. I bat Parker's hand away as discreetly as I can and he stops, turning to face our boss.

"I haven't decided which reporter will get this opportunity yet." Stefan grabs the back of his chair and leans forward, making it creak under his weight.

"You mean, it's up for grabs?" Another co-worker, Eric, a beach-bum lookalike in his mid-fifties, asks the question with a cocked eyebrow. He may insist on wearing Hawaiian shirts and flip flops in the office, but Eric takes his job seriously. The only person Eric's style really bothers is Lucas. Something about not wanting to see the man's hairy toes. And I've got to agree with him on that one.

"There are still some things I'll need to discuss with Miss Dawson, but let it be known that if you're vying for the interview, I expect your full participation in the employee morale-boosting project."

Again, my stomach dips. He's basing his decision on whether or not we gladly sacrifice our free time to participate in this ridiculous social experiment? My hands tighten on the sides of my chair as I scream internally. Especially when I see Lucas plaster on a smile that could rival some of the clowns from my nightmares.

I don't like things I can't control. Everything in my life is purposefully organized because I thrive on living within a certain set of parameters. That's why I eat healthy, work out regularly, and stick to the same, solid routine I've cultivated over the past few years. Because it limits the amount of things I can't control.

But this weird co-worker kiddie field trip thing we're being forced into just to be considered for an exclusive interview with Paris? It has me feeling like I'm spinning off the rails into outer space.

There are only four people who would qualify as reporters on our small-ish staff: me, Lucas, Gladys, and Eric. While I'm relegated to the sport's section, Gladys does the community bulletin board, Lucas writes up the breaking news reports, and Eric takes most of the lifestyle stories from in and around the area. At first glance, Eric would probably be the best choice for the interview since it's within his wheelhouse and he's got seniority, but it's clear that Stefan wants us to work for it.

"That will be all for now," Stefan says. "You're dismissed."

At his last word, I scamper from the conference room, needing to make it back to the safety of my cubicle where there is no Cyborg Stefan making his employees go on field trips to boost morale. Where we don't have the prospect of a promotion in the form of an exclusive interview with a well-known celebrity riding on whether or not we play his childish games.

I can't even believe this is happening. I'm so rattled, I'm contemplating making myself a fourth cup of coffee. Just as I'm about to reach my safe zone, there's a gentle tug on my arm.

I turn and face Parker. *You OK?* he signs.

Sometimes, he's so considerate it turns my insides to mush. "Yes, I'm fine."

I motion for him to follow me into my cubicle, then sit in my chair. He leans back against my desk in front of me, waiting for me to explain. "This whole thing just weirds me out," I say, keeping my voice as low as humanly possible while still making sure Parker can read my lips along with my broken Sign Language.

He quickly signs something back, but I don't understand all of it. "I didn't catch that last phrase."

He nods and grabs the notepad and pen from my desk to begin writing. I'm thankful he doesn't get irritated with me for not understanding him all the time. As usual, he's the picture of patience as he scribbles away on his notepad, then shows it to me.

*This is my fault.*

My brow wrinkles in confusion. "Your fault? How so?"

As he continues writing, my eyes are drawn to the way he bites his lip in concentration. I know I shouldn't find that action so attractive on my friend, but I can't help it. Before I can slip into a daydream about how I want to tug it free from his teeth, Parker flips his notepad around for me to see again.

*I was the one who gave the overall friendliness of the office a poor rating.*

I burst out laughing at Parker's admission. Apparently, I wasn't the only one who was hangry the day we got the email. "That's hilarious," I say between laughs. "I did too. Then I said I would've rated it a zero, but it didn't give me that option."

Now both of us are laughing, him more loudly than me. The guy has no volume control when he laughs, and I love it. I also love that Parker has no clue how deep and manly his voice sounds, because if he did, he'd probably be using it to sweet talk all the ladies. Instead, the rich, warm sound is mostly reserved for me when I'm gifted the opportunity to make him laugh.

"All right," I say with a sigh. "It's time for us to get back to work."

Rising from his seat on the desk, Parker nods, then signs *Later* right before his hands quickly form the letters P-I-N-K-Y.

*Wait...did he just...?*

My mouth falls open and Parker laughs again before sauntering back to his side of the wall. That infuriating man just gave me a new nickname based on the color of my unmentionables. If my face wasn't turning every shade of said color right now, I might have the gumption to slug him.

Looks like I'll be hiding myself away in my bubble of safety for the duration of the day. A girl can only take so much shock and embarrassment in one morning.

# 3

♥

# Parker

Today was supposed to be monumental. A springboard for change. A day to trump all other days. At least, that's what I built it up to in my mind. But now that I'm alone at my desk staring at the computer screen in front of me after Stefan's announcement, I'm feeling a bit on edge.

Extracurricular employee *adventures*? It almost seems like someone put our boss up to this because there's no way he'd willingly subject himself to spending time with those he deems beneath him. Stefan isn't a terrible boss, but he's also not the greatest. And he never goes out of his way to give one of his employees a kind word. Yet now we're just supposed to believe that he suddenly wants to boost employee morale?

*Yeah. Okay.*

I'm not about to say anything about it, though. I can't afford to get fired. At least not until my dream of becoming a best-selling author comes to fruition. As a deaf man in a hearing society, my work options can be limited. You'd be surprised at the number of jobs where you have to actually be able to use your sense of hearing. Plus, there's no way I'd relinquish the perfect excuse to get to be with Jamie every single day.

It's been exactly six weeks since she dumped that poor excuse for a boyfriend, Mike, and I've patiently bided my time. These past few weeks have felt like an eternity as I've watched her get over him.

Am I being dramatic? Possibly. But I've been in love with Jamie almost since the day I met her. So having to watch her go on date after date with a guy who didn't appreciate her ate me up inside.

I knew Mike didn't deserve her from the moment she shared one of their text conversations with me, asking my advice. Apparently, Jamie had asked if he wanted to hang out with her one night, and he'd blown her off in the worst way ever, saying he couldn't because he had to give his cat a bath.

*Really, dude? Give your cat a bath?*

I sigh and lean back in my chair, lacing my hands behind my head. I should've asked Jamie out the second I knew she was single a year ago, before she started dating that tool, Mike, but my own insecurities and the fact that we're co-workers kept me from speaking up. I've never been in a serious adult relationship. Never even had a girlfriend, unless you count Ella, my first love. But we were only in junior high and that was a long time ago.

As a twenty-four-year-old deaf guy who's never been really and thoroughly kissed, I wouldn't exactly classify myself as prime boyfriend material. But Jamie just *gets* me. Not only has she been relentless in trying to bring me out of my shell since I started working at the *Gazette*, she's also been equally committed to learning ASL on her own time. She works at communicating with me like no one ever has.

Sign language may not come naturally to her, but that she puts so much effort into learning how to interact with me speaks volumes. Out of all the *Gazette* employees, she and Stefan were the only ones to attend the ASL class he paid for. She still doesn't think she's good at it, but she understands way more than she gives herself credit for.

Plus, she's hilarious and we share a similar sense of humor. I knew very early on in our friendship that she needed a friend in the office as much as I did as a newbie. Since I started working here, we've shared countless inside jokes and enjoyed laughing at the ridiculousness of our co-workers on the regular.

Basically, we have a blast together.

And that's why I worked up the courage and decided that today would be the day to tell her how I feel. My older brother, Dane, insists that three weeks is enough time to wait to ask a girl out after she ended her previous relationship. And since he's a serial dater with way more experience than me, I listened.

But now that Stefan dumped this weird employee socialization thing on us, the timing doesn't feel right. And I can't even bring myself to replay the awkward moment when Jamie went flying back in her chair. I was honestly more concerned for her well-being than with what I saw, but now the pink and lace image has a hold on my mind, and I can't shake it loose. Nor could I pass up the opportunity to tease her about it.

Then there's Jamie and Lucas's exchange in the lunchroom... *We're not a couple,* she'd said. Even though it's the truth, I can't deny that her words stung. It didn't seem like she put much force behind them, but still. She did grimace after Lucas said it, which doesn't seem promising.

Did that admission mean that she doesn't *want* us to be a couple? *Ever*? That the very idea disgusts her?

My mind is working double time, trying to convince my heart that I should wait to confess my feelings, at least until I'm more sure she'll reciprocate. I run a hand through my hair, frustrated. A day that was supposed to be epic has now dwindled to a big disappointment.

A light tap on my shoulder startles me and I whip around to see a wide-eyed Jamie staring down at me. "I'm sorry," she says with a frown. She knows I hate when people come up behind me unawares, but sometimes it can't be helped. Like right now when I'm so lost in thought about *her* that I wasn't paying attention.

*It's OK*, I sign back to her with a smile. I want her to know that she's not the one at fault.

"Ready?" she asks as she pulls her purse strap higher onto her shoulder. I sign *yes* before turning back to my desk and powering down my computer for the day. I grab my jacket from the back of my desk chair and follow Jamie toward the exit.

This is, by far, my favorite time of day. The two of us walk out of work together every day that she doesn't have to leave early on assignment. It's a habit I hope we never break.

Lucas eyes us as he leaves his own cubicle, but I ignore him. Who cares if he thinks we're a couple. Maybe with any luck, one day we will be.

As I follow Jamie out to the elevators, it's hard not to focus on the gentle sway of her curvy hips or the way her cropped jacket hits right at the top of her waist. But I don't. Because my mom raised me to be a gentleman. Full disclosure, though...Jamie *does* bring me to distraction.

Her strawberry blonde hair falls past her slender shoulders, and her bluish-gray eyes constantly beckon me to get lost in them. Her perfect nose with a little bump in the center is peppered with freckles that get more prominent as she spends more time in the sun. And most distracting of all is her mouth.

And, ironically, it's the one part of her that I'm forced to stare at. All. The. Time.

I've always been a good lip-reader, being the only one of my family with a sensory difference, and have relied heavily on the skill to understand what people are saying since I've been a child. But Jamie's lips have me thinking about way more than just what she's saying.

Her mouth is a bit downturned with a full bottom lip and a very prominent cupid's bow on top. She has this little freckle that lives just above her top lip, and it drives me absolutely crazy. It doesn't help that she usually wears dark, moody lip colors that accentuate every delicious nuance of her lips.

I could easily go into heavy detail but I won't since those thoughts aren't exactly rated G. I would wager that they're more of the PG-13 variety. That is, assuming there's making out with your best friend in PG-13 movies. I wouldn't exactly know since I was banned from watching anything over PG growing up (to say that my brothers and I were sheltered would be an understatement). Besides, I'm more of a reader, so my TV watching is limited to the romcoms that Jamie forces me to watch when we have the occasional movie night.

We make it to the elevators, and I hit the down button as we slide inside. In seconds, we're on the lower level of our small business complex, headed outside. As I hold the door open for her, the late afternoon sun instantly warms my face. When we make it to Jamie's car, we stop and face each other.

Her hair shines in the late afternoon light, drawing my eye, as does her pleasantly upturned mouth. Everything about her makes her beautiful to me, but her beauty goes way beyond what a person can see on the surface. She's sweet and thoughtful underneath that mildly grumpy exterior, and her sass keeps me in stitches. I can tell she feels things deeply and gets a little anxious sometimes. Every once in a while, I catch her biting her thumbnail or wringing her hands, a sure sign that she's experiencing anxiety. On those days, I make an extra effort to lighten the mood and make her smile.

"So," she starts, looking up at me with her stormy eyes and drawing me away from my thoughts. "What do you think of Stefan's announcement?"

I shake my head and shrug, signing, *I think he's been possessed.*

It looks like she snickers as she signs, *What?*

*Possessed*, I sign again, then convulse and roll my eyes back in my head, acting out something taking over my body. When she slaps my arm, smiling, I stop.

*I don't like it,* I sign. *But I'm glad it wasn't something worse, like layoffs.* Her eyes widen and she nods. "Me too."

Neither of us make a move to communicate for almost a minute when the urge to tell her what I'd planned to at the beginning of the day grows rapidly within me. I hadn't envisioned telling her while we're in the parking lot at work, but with the way the sun is hitting her hair, the moment feels right.

Just as I'm about to bring my hands up to speak, she steps back and opens her car door. "See you tomorrow?" she signs.

Disappointment clamps around my heart like a vice, but I dip my chin and offer her a one-handed wave. She smiles and slips into her car's front seat and just like that, the moment is gone.

Once again, I'm questioning if I'm the right kind of guy for Jamie. If I can't even work up the courage to tell her how I feel, do I really deserve her?

I turn and head for my truck, second-guessing everything.

---

"How did it go?" Dane signs almost the moment I step through the door. I shrug off my jacket and hang it on the hook by the door, then remove my shoes. My brother is anal about tracking dirt around the hardwood floors of our shared studio-style apartment in historic downtown Treemont. If I even take two steps with my shoes on, he's waving his hands and chasing me around with his little Swiffer mop.

I ignore his question and go straight for the kitchen. If he's going to poke and prod at the sore spot I'm nursing, and I already know he will, I'm going to need something cold to drink. Sometimes I wish his job as a senior commercial pilot didn't allow him so many days off to annoy me.

Opening the fridge, I grab a Pepsi and pop the tab. I'm mid chug when Dane pushes on the arm that holds the drink to my mouth. Soda drips down my face onto the floor and I glare at him, wiping it away with my arm.

"I said, '*How'd it go?*' he signs again with an exasperated look. I take a step back and point to the mess he made on his precious wood floor. He rolls his eyes as he grabs a dish towel, wets it, and cleans up the soda he made me spill. When he straightens, he crosses his well-defined arms over his swole chest. He's not as tall as I am, but I can never get the kind of definition that he gets from the gym. Still, his muscles don't intimidate me.

I'm not ready to talk about Jamie yet. Especially when there's nothing to report.

"You didn't tell her, did you?"

Dane's question makes me wince. How can he always guess what I'm hiding? I'm convinced that reading people is one of his secret superpowers. Unlike me or our older brother, Logan, he can size a person up within the first two minutes of meeting them and his first impression is usually spot on.

I shake my head as I sign *no*. Telling her today just didn't feel right. *I don't know if I can,* I tell him honestly.

"What? Why?"

I look away, grinding my teeth. Dane doesn't understand what it's like to be me. He dates all the time and never lacks feminine attention. And though my appearance might interest some girls, as soon as they realize it's harder to communicate with me than an average hearing guy, they retreat. Jamie is the first person since high school who's gone above and beyond to be able to speak to me in a way I relate to. The first one who doesn't treat me like I have a *disability*.

I don't see my deafness as a disability at all. My mom and dad taught me to see it as a sensory difference, nothing more. True, I process things differently than others, but I am in no way disabled. And yet, that's how I feel around most girls.

But Jamie hasn't retreated and in the last year, we've grown close, but asking her for more brings up all the insecurities I've struggled with since high school. What if she doesn't see me as boyfriend material?

I can't say all that to Dane, though. He would do his brotherly diligence to reassure me I'm some great catch and have a lot to offer Jamie. So instead, I shrug one shoulder and sign, *Not the right time.*

I cross my arms, signaling that I don't want to keep conversing with him, but that doesn't deter my bull-headed brother. "Did something happen at work today?"

There he goes, reading between the lines yet again.

Reluctantly raising my hands, I sign, *A co-worker referred to us as a couple and she denied it.* I raise an eyebrow and harden my expression, daring Dane to come up with an alternate explanation for that one.

"I see," he says as his gaze drops to the floor. His brow furrows deeply and I take that as my cue to finish the rest of my Pepsi. As soon as I crush the can and toss it in the trash, vibrations through the floor have me looking back at my brother. Stomping is just one of the ways my family uses to get my attention.

"Don't read into what she said," he says as well as signs. "You guys *aren't* a couple. Not yet. She probably didn't mean anything by it."

I turn away and head for the couch, ready to pull out my laptop and get to work on the one thing I can control—my fictional characters' lives. I may not be able to convince Jamie that we could be great together, but I can at least give my characters their happy ending.

When I plop down on the couch, the other end sinks too. I twist my head to the side and give my brother a deadpan look. I don't appreciate the way his eyes soften at the edges. His sympathy isn't welcome.

"I still think you need to tell her," he says.

I roll my eyes, face forward, then grab my laptop from under the couch. Powering it on, I pretend like he's not there. Of course, he's not letting it go and taps my shoulder.

"You deserve to be happy, and Jamie sounds like a great girl," he signs.

*She is*, I respond immediately because it's true. Jamie is special. But what if I tell her how I feel, and she doesn't feel the same? What would happen to our friendship? Would it be awkward between us? I couldn't stand the thought of not having her to hang out with at the office.

Besides, I'm almost positive there's some sort of unspoken rule at work about employees dating each other. I think that's why Lucas keeps insisting that we're already a couple, just so he has some fabricated dirt he can feed Stefan when his need for it arises.

Dane taps my shoulder again until I look at him. "Don't let fear hold you back. Honestly, it sounds like she's into you too."

I don't respond because I don't know what to say. Dane's only met Jamie once and it was in passing as he picked me up from work when my truck was in the shop. He's only going off the things I've shared with him. There's no way he can know for sure.

"Just think about it," he signs before punching me hard in the arm. I try to kick him, but he hops up from the couch just in time with a growing smile. He makes his signature immature *nah nah nah boo boo* face and I throw the pillow at him while he goes back to the kitchen.

I click open the document I've been working on for the better part of the last six months and try to focus on where I'm at in the story. Dandrick has just rescued Lady Elyse from the evil King Volkien's men. He's doing his best to soothe her, but she's still terrified.

As I consider how this pivotal moment in the story should unfold, Jamie's mortified expression after she fell out of her chair flits through my mind. She was so embarrassed I witnessed her fall, but she shouldn't have been. I was the one who scared her half to death. When I forced her to look me in the eye and her embarrassment melted into gratefulness, warmth spread through my chest. I'd like to think that my help and reassurance did that for her, that maybe me being there for her meant something.

If only I could get her to see me like that all the time. To give me a chance to be the one who catches her anytime she falls.

# 4

♥

# Jamie

"So, you've got a new nickname, huh?" Daria sputters a laugh as she stretches up into cobra pose. Ignoring her, I school my expression and face forward, planting my hands on the mat and lengthening my spine. Briar, our friend and yoga instructor, helps a guy in the front row who pretends he can't get the hang of it. I hate assuming the worst about people, but the smirk I saw on his lips a few minutes ago tells me he just likes Briar's hands on him. I mean, come on. It's *cobra*.

"You can ignore me all you want," Daria says, a smile in her voice. "But I still think it's hilarious."

"It was mortifying," I hiss, trying to block out my friend, and lean into the pose. This stretch normally feels so good on my back, but right now, I'm too irritated to enjoy it.

"Come on, Jamie, it's just Parker. Who cares if he saw your undies?"

I shoot her a withering glance before turning forward again. "It was literally the brightest pair I own. The ones you *insisted* I add to my mostly black wardrobe." Her giggling now garners the attention of Briar. Our instructor's lips flatten into a thin line as she heads back up front to get everyone started on the next move.

"You know," I whisper-yell, "I feel like you should really be the one taking responsibility here. If it wasn't for you and your over-bearing fashionista ways, he would've seen the plain, black ones that thoroughly cover all my...assets."

At that she snorts and drops her head forward into her hands. I glare at her, wishing for once she'd give me a little sympathy. Daria's unfairly lithe and stunning, with long dark hair and golden-brown skin. She's probably never had to endure an embarrassing incident in her life.

"You're not allowed to go shopping with me anymore," I demand.

"Now, don't say that," she says with a pretend pouty frown. "You know my fashion sense is impeccable. Just be glad it was the girly pink ones and not the black granny panties."

"I would have preferred the latter."

"All right," Briar says in her sweet falsetto voice with a clap of her hands. "Time for cat-cow."

All eight of us in the class move onto all fours, curling our backs up into the cat position. "Listen, I think you should just be glad it was Parker," Daria murmurs in a low voice so we won't disturb the rest of the class. "At least Lucas didn't find you in such a compromising position."

She's not wrong about that. If I'd flailed like that in front of my work nemesis, there's not a doubt in my mind he'd hold it over me for future blackmail. He might've even snapped a picture. I cringe just thinking about it.

"I guess you're right," I say with a defeated sigh. "I definitely don't need him dragging up any dirt on me with this exclusive interview on the line."

Daria shakes her head. "I still can't believe Paris Dawson has agreed to give the *Gazette* an exclusive interview. You have to promise me that if you get it, you'll let me come with you. I can hide behind a plant in the office or something."

I chuckle and bend my body more deeply into the pose, doing my best to rid my mind of the week's building anxieties. It's nerve-wracking enough knowing Stefan is going to choose one of us to interview a celebrity like Paris. But we also have to play nice and pretend we're loving these employee field trips, or we won't even be considered for the opportunity. It's clear he's not basing his decision solely on the merit of our work. And there's no denying my attitude at work has been less than stellar lately.

Then, to add a cherry on top of this messy and stressy sundae, I accidentally flashed my work bestie, earning myself a new nickname. I close my eyes and breathe deeply as sweat trickles down my body, collecting in places I'd rather not even think about right now.

"Is it wrong that I desperately want to be the one he picks for this interview?" I whine, sneaking a look at Daria.

"Girl. The fact that you have to ask me that says so much about you." We shift into the next pose Briar calls out, then sink into it, stretching our muscles. "You deserve that interview, Jamie. It's not wrong to want something you've worked hard for. You're an amazing reporter and if Stefan can't see that, it's not on you. Maybe it's time you moved on from the *Gazette* and found work somewhere your talents are appreciated."

My friend's words wrap around my heart in a soothing way. "Thanks, D. But I don't want to leave the *Gazette,* you know that. I enjoy what I do and Parker's there…" I trail off, not knowing how to finish that statement.

Thankfully, I don't have to because Briar rises to her feet and announces, "Great job, everyone. You all did amazing. Class is dismissed." She bows with all the grace of a gazelle as she flashes her perfectly white teeth our way. Daria and I start rolling up our yoga mats when Briar pops up in front of us.

"Okay, you two," she says, crossing her arms and raising an eyebrow. "What were you guys laughing at back here? Was it Brodie? Because I'm this close to kicking him out of my class." She holds the tips of her thumb and forefinger close together, mimicking just how close she really is.

"No, it wasn't him," Daria says, raising her eyebrows at me. "Jamie had a little...*incident*...at work today."

"Oh?" Briar looks between us, brow wrinkled.

"It was nothing," I lie. "I just fell out of my chair and flashed Parker."

Briar's eyes go wide, and she bites her lip to contain her smile. "Aw, that must have been embarrassing, I'm sorry." Ever the sympathetic sweetie, Briar reaches out and rubs a hand down my arm.

"It was, but I'm over it."

Daria shoots me a skeptical look which I dutifully ignore. "Anyway, we wondered if you wanted to grab dinner with us at The Fuze. Appetizers are half-off tonight."

Briar's angelic face lights up like the Fourth of July. "Yes, I'd love that! Let me just close up the studio and we can head out."

We mingle with a few of the other class members until one by one they exit through the studio's double doors. Of course, Brodie is the last to leave, hanging on Briar's heels like a lovesick puppy. But not like a cute puppy, more like one who's foaming at the mouth.

"Well, I'm gonna go ahead and change in the back," Briar says, sending a glance our way, begging us to help to make this guy take a hike. "It was nice seeing you again, Brodie."

She slips behind the beaded curtain that leads to the back room and Brodie's face falls. He picks up his mat and water bottle, then nods to Daria and me as he leaves. At least we didn't have to woman-handle him out of here.

"Ugh," Daria groans, "I thought that guy would never take the hint."

"Me neither," Briar says, coming out of the back dressed in the same matching lavender athletic clothes she wore during our class.

"You're not going to change?" I ask.

"No, I just needed him to leave." Her mouth turns down and my hackles instantly rise.

"Briar, if he's upsetting you, maybe it's time to cut him from the class."

"She's right," Daria agrees. "If you feel unsafe—"

Briar cuts her off with a laugh. "No, no, it's not like that. He's never even asked me out. I just feel like he's purposely not getting the moves right so I'll take the time to help him. And then after class, he usually hangs around until I shut off all the lights." She slings her gym bag over her shoulder and heads for the door. "I don't feel unsafe, I'm just"—she shrugs—"not used to a guy being so blatant in his advances. It's off-putting."

"I *so* get that," Daria adds. "I'm all about the strong silent types myself."

I can't help but laugh. "Strong silent types, D? Then how come every guy I've seen you with is flirty and outgoing?"

She opens the door for us to pass through, shaking her head. "Maybe I just realized my type isn't the guys I naturally gravitate toward? Just because we live together doesn't mean you know everything about me."

Her words make me mentally pause, but I keep walking toward my car. "You sound like you're hangry. Come on, let's go smash some tapas and tacos."

My friends laugh and we all pile into my little hatchback. I don't know about them, but I'm ready for a little girl time without having to think about any of the stressors at work. Or my embarrassing moment that I already know will keep me awake late into the night.

I'm still reeling from Stefan's announcement yesterday when my phone buzzes at my desk. As soon as I see the name on the screen, I glare at it like it just did me dirty.

**Mike**:  Hey, babe. Miss you. Can we talk?

What on earth brought on this little turn of events? And why is Mike calling me *babe*? He stopped doing that about a month before I broke up with him.

Tightness spreads across my shoulders and I stretch my arms back in response. I don't want to reply to Mike's text, but at the same time, I also don't want him to think that I'm bitter about our breakup by *not* replying.

Because I'm not. Honestly, I've thought very little about Mike Jonas since we went our separate ways. I mean, *maybe* I miss having a boyfriend...and *maybe* I miss some of the things that come with a romantic relationship...the good morning texts, the fun date nights, the random bouquets of flowers...But the more I think about those things, the more I realize I don't miss sharing them with Mike.

I spin side to side in my swivel chair as I run my fingers over my baby succulent Beatrice's soft leaves, mulling over what exactly I should do when my phone buzzes again.

**Mike**:  I know right now you're wondering if you should even respond. The answer is yes, you should.

I roll my eyes at Mike's attempt to make me laugh. He always thought he was hilarious, but I never got his humor. His second text does, however, prompt me to respond. Even though I have no fond feelings for him, I should still be cordial.

**Me**: Hey, Mike. What's up? I'm at work.

Almost immediately, another text comes through.

**Mike**: I know, babe. I just wanted to ask if we could talk later. Can I call you?

Instantly irritated with his continual use of the word *babe*, I send back another text.

**Me**: Please stop calling me that. We aren't dating. And I couldn't imagine what we'd even have to talk about.

I drop my cell in my purse, ready to be done with this little back and forth. He made it very clear where I stand with him when he started to blow me off and make excuses for why he couldn't see me. I know I'm no supermodel with a sparkling personality, but I at least have enough self-respect to know that I deserve more than that from a guy who claims to be my boyfriend.

And even more than that, I don't *need* a boyfriend. Sure, the idea of a dedicated guy doing sweet things for me and liking me *for me* might make my romance-loving heart go pitter-patter, but it doesn't mean I *need* to have that.

I'm perfectly fine on my own right now. Mike can go kiss his cat.

I begin to type away on my keyboard, ready to unleash all my frustration onto the little black keys, when something hard pelts the side of my head. When the small, colorful object falls on my desk, I pick it up and toss it in my mouth.

"Keep 'em coming, buddy," I mumble as I keep typing. "I could use a little something sweet right now."

Another jellybean hits my head but doesn't fall. I reach up, fish it out of my half-up hair, and hold it up to eye-level, inspecting it. It appears clean and non-hairy, so I pop it in my mouth. I'm not really in the mood for Parker's games right now, but I won't tell him that. He'll worry and whip out his sword finger to try and make me laugh. And to be honest, my pride's still a little sore after accidentally *baring all* to him yesterday.

I choose to ignore him and continue eating the afternoon snack he keeps throwing my way. After eating three more jellybeans without a word or glance at Parker, there's a tap on my shoulder.

I sigh and spin around in my chair, ready to face my antagonist. "Can I help you?"

Parker has one eyebrow raised like he's the Rock or something, and he has both arms crossed over his chest. He isn't signing a word, but I can read him like a book.

"What?" I ask, mildly annoyed. "I'm busy." I straighten in my chair and cross my arms in defense. I'm allowed to have a busy day at work. He, of all people, should understand, accept that as truth, and walk back to his cubicle.

But of course, he doesn't.

*What's wrong,* he signs before kneeling in front of me with both hands braced on the arms of my office chair, rolling me closer. The action is so unexpected that I inhale a short, quick breath as both my hands fly to his chest to stop myself from lurching forward.

When his muscles jump under my palms, I pull my hands back and tuck them under my thighs. Parker raises both eyebrows and tilts his head to the side, his light green eyes piercing through me.

I have no reason not to tell Parker why I'm irritated. But something inside me wants to shy away from telling him. Maybe it's because I know how Parker feels about Mike. He never liked the guy, especially when Mike started to act all shady.

But maybe I should tell Parker about his text. That way, I can get another guy's perspective on what Mike's end game is with me. If Parker can shed some light on why Mike is texting me out of the blue, it would be worth it. I have little patience for relationship games.

"Nothing is wrong," I say as I reach down into my purse and pull out my phone. "Mike just texted me."

I tap in my passcode and bring up the text thread that Mike started. When I open it, I notice he sent me another text.

**Mike**: Look, I'm sorry. I want another chance. Please let me call you.

I read the text, roll my eyes, then hand my phone over to Parker. Maybe he can help unravel the mystery that is attractive men in their twenties.

Parker holds my phone, and his eyebrows come together as he reads through the texts. As his eyes dart back and forth across the screen, his lips pull into a tight line.

Still holding my phone in front of him, he lifts his gaze to mine. Once again, he's trying to see inside of my soul, causing me to shrink a bit in response. What is he looking for?

He places my phone in my lap as he stands, then grabs the pen and paper from my desk, scribbling away at lightning speed. When he turns the notepad around for me to read, I'm taken aback by his strong reaction.

*Why are you even texting him back, Jamie? The guy is a jerk. I don't know what his reasons are for texting you now, but I can promise you they aren't good. He doesn't deserve you.*

I blink at Parker, his chest rising and falling like he just ran around the building three times. Why does he seem so upset about this? And why is he mad that I texted Mike back? We dated for *seven months*. I feel that gives me the right to respond to the guy's texts, at least.

"I only texted him back so he wouldn't think I was still mad that we broke up," I say, holding Parker's gaze. His face is riddled with annoyance, which is so out of place for him.

*Are you mad you broke up?* He signs the phrase to me so rapidly I almost miss the last words. His movements are clipped and careless.

"No, I'm not mad. That's why I *texted him.*" I pause, assessing Parker. His body language is so uncharacteristically defensive that I have the urge to laugh. "Are *you* mad?" I ask, already knowing the answer.

An audible scoff leaves Parker's lips as he plants his hands on his hips and looks toward the ceiling. I blink, confused. I don't get why he's acting like this. Is it because I ignored his playful taunting with the jellybeans?

After a tense moment, he grabs the paper and scribbles again. *Not mad. But you know better.*

I *know* better? What does he mean by that?

My stubborn pride wells up and I spin away from him to face my desk. I've never been mad at Parker before, but the bubble of exasperation I'm feeling can't be ignored. If I didn't know any better, I'd say Parker was acting jealous.

Before my hands can even touch my keyboard, Parker spins my chair back around and with an apologetic look, he signs, *Sorry. Please forgive me.* He droops a bit as he searches my face.

Seeing his regret, I realize my edginess with him is mostly from my initial irritation at Mike. I don't need to take out my frustration on Parker any more than I need to entertain Mike with a response.

"I forgive you," I say while signing. "I only showed you the texts so you could help me decipher their meaning. But it's not important. I have no desire to text Mike back."

Parker's eyes soften as he reaches for my hand. Holding it securely in his, he runs his thumb over my skin and little sparks of awareness skate across where he touches. My gaze falls to our joined hands as I purse my lips to the side.

Parker's touch has always been warm and comforting, but lately, it feels as if my body is working over-time to send pleasure signals to my brain each time we make contact.

He quickly releases my hand and snaps to get my attention. *Sorry. I failed as a friend.* A sheepish grin crosses his face.

"You didn't. You're just looking out for me."

Parker dips his chin and signs, *I always will.* Before I can swoon at his sweetness, he straightens and points to my computer screen. *Did you get the employee email?*

"Yes, I did. Can you believe it?" In the email giving us the details about the pumpkin patch, we were also given a heads up about next week's activity which isn't really an activity at all, but a first-grade class coming to tour the *Gazette*.

Parker shrugs one shoulder in an exaggerated way and shakes his head as he signs, *Don't know what they hope to see.*

I laugh because I thought the exact same thing. "I guess just a bunch of adults sitting in cubicles staring at the computer screens in front of them. I plan to bake some cookies to bring along with me that day. Kids like cookies, right?"

Parker smiles wide. *Yes, silly. Kids love cookies. Me too.* He waggles his eyebrows and pats his stomach.

Giggling, I wave him out of my cubicle. "Okay, okay, I get the hint. I'll make extra for you, too. Now get back to work, Kent."

He winks and saunters away, leaving me wondering what type of cookies he'd like best.

# 5

♥

# Parker

The days leading up to today, the day of our pumpkin patch *adventure*—and I use that term loosely—have flown by. Normally, I would be annoyed that our boss is forcing us to play nice by frolicking in a corn field somewhere, but the more I think about going with Jamie, the more I keep conjuring a scenario where I'm lost in a corn field *with her*.

I can see us now...laughing as we pick out the perfect pumpkin for her front steps—of course, she'd probably pick out the one she thought needed the most TLC—holding hands as we trek through the corn maze and I purposely get us lost so I can tuck her hair lightly behind her ear...maybe even steal a kiss...I let out a frustrated breath, knowing that probably none of those things will take place. But hey, a guy can dream, right?

I try my best to focus on my work the rest of the day, but it's hard knowing that Jamie is in the cubicle right next to mine. The more I think about it, the more I wonder if I should throw caution to the wind and admit my feelings.

Ever since her text exchange with Mike the other day, there's been an uncomfortable foreboding invading my chest. Mike's texted words *I want another chance* glare like a billboard in my mind. He's trying to win her back. And pigs will fly before I stand by and let him weasel his way back into her life.

From day one, Mike treated her like an afterthought. She was more of an accessory on his arm than a person to be cherished. But Jamie could never see it. She was all the time telling me about the sweet things he'd do for her, which to me were merely common courtesy.

Forgetting to call her while he was away for a week on a business trip, then showing up with flowers when he got back as an apology? Sure...nice cover, bro. Taking her to a fancy restaurant for dinner on their six-month anniversary? He could've come up with something more original, something that coincided with her love languages which I know are quality time and unexpected gifts. Plus, he always calls her *babe* and only ever compliments her physical appearance. His lack of effort has irked me from the beginning.

And then there were the constant mixed signals. Every time it seemed like they'd taken a step forward in their relationship, Mike would withdraw, and Jamie would be confused. She'd confided in me more than once about how Mike seemed distant and uninterested. She never really knew where she stood with him, even after months of dating.

The worst part about it all is that from what I've heard from Jamie, her past boyfriends weren't much better. It's possible she doesn't even know what being loved by an honest-to-goodness nice guy feels like.

With Mike upping his game to win Jamie back, I can't help but feel like it's time I revealed my hand. I can't continue to pine for my best friend and hope for the best. No. Now, it's time for action.

And capitalizing on these work excursions is the perfect way to do it.

If I could just show Jamie what it would be like if we were together, convincing her with my actions that things between us could be amazing, maybe she'd give me a chance to be more than just her friend. Smiling to myself, I determine to enact a plan. The *Make Jamie fall in Love with Parker* plan.

How I'll execute it remains to be determined, but I guess I'll figure it out as I go along. More than anything, I want Jamie to know how much she means to me. How special and wonderful I think she is. And knowing just how independent that woman can be, I'll have my work cut out for me.

---

When late afternoon rolls around, a steady stream of anticipation hums throughout my body. And it's all because I get to spend the next few hours with Jamie. Will my motley crew of co-workers also be there? Yes. But will I pretend they aren't? Also, yes.

Plus, I sent an email to Jamie earlier asking if she thought we'd be split up for this particular activity, and she confirmed that Jordy said we would get to be with whoever we wanted.

I did a little online research on the Corny Acres Pumpkin Patch this morning and found out it's not just any pumpkin patch and corn maze. It just so happens to be one of the most popular fall excursions in this part of Ohio, boasting a hayride, corn kernel pit, petting zoo, and a *haunted* corn maze.

Now, truth be told, I'm not one for spooky attractions, and that's probably because I startle easily. Not being able to hear someone come up behind you will do that to a person. So, I'm not sure how this night will go, but I'm still excited to get to hang out with Jamie outside of work. Technically.

I slip on my hoodie before meeting Jamie at her desk. *Ready?* I ask her through sign.

She smiles and rises from her desk, grabbing her jean jacket from the back of her chair. I gently tug it out of her grasp, and hold it open for her to slip her arms through. She shoots me a questioning glance, but does as I expect and puts her arms through the jacket.

We head out to our cars and Jamie tells me that she'll follow me over to Corny Acres. It takes us fifteen minutes to drive there and get assembled in front of the trailer selling freshly made donuts at the entrance, where we were told to meet.

My stomach rumbles at the tantalizing smell of fried dough. Hopefully Jamie won't think any less of me when I singlehandedly smash a dozen of those delicious-smelling donuts that are now calling my name.

Stefan steps to the front of our group dressed in a trendy leather jacket that makes him look like he's trying too hard and waves a hand in the air. Jamie sidles up next to me and folds her arms under her chest. When our eyes meet, she gives me smirk that says, *this ought to be good.*

I turn back to our boss and watch his lips as he speaks, intently trying to focus on what he's saying. I don't catch it all, but when he holds up three fingers, I can make out the phrase, "Groups of three."

I turn my head away and grit my teeth. Why is it important that we stay in groups of three? I thought the goal of these activities was to boost employee morale, not make us want to quit altogether. My dream of getting to be alone with Jamie is fading faster than the daylight.

I suppress a sigh and look down at her. She's listening to Stefan, so I wait for her to meet my eyes. When she does, her lips move so fast, whatever she said is lost to me as she darts off toward the edge of our group.

I puff out my cheeks and run a hand through my hair. As I look around at the small group of people surrounding us, I mentally run through our options.

There's Les Jenkins—a man who would probably be able to spout off random facts about corn the entire time we meander through this maze. I could simply turn away to avoid having to pay attention, but that would mean Jamie would be subjected to his incessant knowledge about corn.

There's Lucas—the man who believes he's God's gift to women. Or Jordy—the girl who I realize is locking eyes with me and giving me a little wave. I nod in her direction to be polite, then turn back around. I have no interest in engaging in a pointless game of charades with the girl who has spider-like fake eyelashes.

Harsh? Maybe. But I'm seriously terrified of spiders.

There's a handful of other people from the paper I don't know well, including some of the paper boys who have routes around town. Apparently, Stefan invited everyone associated with the *Gazette* to come on these little outings, not just the office staff.

Out of the corner of my eye, I see Jamie and Gladys coming my way, so I start toward them. I'm glad Jamie had the forethought to choose someone as benign as Gladys Mullins to accompany us. She may be nearing seventy and have hair that mimics a home for bees, but it seems like the woman almost always keeps silent at work, which is a plus in my book. In fact, I would probably say that Gladys is a loner. Maybe even a tad grumpy at times.

Thankfully, she doesn't look grumpy right now as I approach her and Jamie. The stark contrast between the small older woman with a pinched face and glasses perched high on her pointy nose in her velour jogger suit lined with rhinestones and Jamie's cool casual look of black jeans and denim jacket reminds me what an odd group we must make.

When I reach the two women, I point to the donut stand and sign, *Hungry?*

Jamie glances toward the small trailer where a man in an apron hands a freshly frosted doughnut to a young girl, then back to me. "Oh, yeah."

Our small group of three gets in line for doughnuts, and I can almost taste the maple frosting on my tongue. I have a serious weakness when it comes to sweets. Jamie knows it too.

One time at work, Jamie snuck into my cubicle and stole my canister of mini-M&M's out of my desk. Then she proceeded to replace the M&Ms with a celery stick and put the canister right back where she found it. When a craving for sweets hit me in the middle of my workday and I reached for those mini candies of goodness, I popped the lid and tipped the whole thing back to my mouth, only to be disgusted when a celery stick slid down my throat, almost choking me in the process.

Of course, Jamie made sure to watch and record the entire incident. She laughed her head off and made fun of me for a week after that. But that's okay because I got her back. I replaced the lemon water in her water bottle with Sprite. Not as creative or funny, but it still irked her. She doesn't like to overindulge in sweets like pop on a regular basis.

We get to the front of the line, and I sign to Jamie which doughnut I'd like. Ordering out can be a guessing game when the person taking my order doesn't realize I'm deaf, and since there's a long line behind us, I don't want to cause it to back up. She orders for the both of us, as is usual when we eat out together, then Gladys orders for herself, and I make sure to pay for all three orders. This isn't a date by any stretch of the imagination, but, as a gentleman, I'm still going to foot the bill when ladies are involved.

Jamie ordered us each a doughnut and a hot cider, and both taste delicious. Way better than I'd imagined. After relishing my second bite of the sweet fried dough, I open my eyes and notice Gladys watching me, her brown eyes wide over the rims of her glasses. I stop mid-chew and look at Jamie. She's biting her lower lip to keep from smiling as she puts her cider cup to her mouth.

It dawns on me that I must have been enjoying my donut a little too much for a public space.

*Oops.*

I sometimes make noises when I eat, but I can't help it. When something tastes this good, it's worth a satisfied moan or two. I finish chewing my doughnut in what I hope is silence and swallow down the rest of my cider.

After tossing my trash into the nearest can, I sign *sorry* to Gladys, hoping she'll get the message. She returns my apology with a blank stare as she slowly sips her hot cider. I guess the two of us won't be best buds by the end of the night.

When we finish eating, our group begrudgingly starts toward the corn maze. I think at this point, all three of us are dreading this experience. Jamie isn't a fan of anything horror related, and I don't know enough about Gladys to determine if this is her kind of thing or not. I'm assuming by her permanent scowl and the cigarette she's about to light that she's not looking forward to it.

We reach the entrance behind what appears to be a group of college kids. A worker beside us says something to Gladys and motions for her to put out her cigarette. *Right.* Because smoking in the middle of a dry field of corn probably isn't the best idea. Gladys reluctantly drops her cigarette and snuffs it out with the toe of her all-white tennis shoes.

We enter the maze, following a winding path that seems to go nowhere. The college-aged group in front of us is having fun already, shoving each other and laughing, and as they round the first corner, we lose sight of them.

When we reach a fork in the maze, I grab Jamie's arm, then sign, *Which way?*

She purses her lips, looks both ways, then asks Gladys what she thinks. Gladys's lips barely move as she says something unintelligible to me and shrugs. When Jamie turns back to me, I point left. Why not?

Taking the lead, I step down a path that's covered in down-trodden corn. After a few minutes of walking, we cross under an archway made of corn and fake spider webs. *Yay*, my favorite.

We're swallowed up in a foggy haze and can barely see where we're going. To my delight, Jamie moves in closer to me and clutches my arm for support. My muscles flex in response and I smile, thinking maybe this haunted thing might not be too bad after all.

As we take tentative steps into the fog, a frightening figure with stringy black hair and gray skin emerges from the corn. Whatever it is boldly approaches us with long fingernails outstretched, beckoning us closer. *Yeah, no thanks.*

Jamie and I sidestep the creepy person as much as we possibly can, while I sense Gladys following closely behind us. We continue to navigate our way through the maze when a zombie child on a mini tractor emerges out of a wall of corn in front of us with an eerie smile darkening its face.

I jump back, alarmed, tugging Jamie along with me. We bump into Gladys, who moves around us and scowls at the child. She boldly steps forward and starts waving her hands, saying who knows what to the poor child actor, causing the little one's evil smile to quickly fade. Before I realize what's happening, Gladys is chasing the now crying child back into the corn with her purse, stopping once the kid disappears.

Jamie covers her mouth with her hand and looks up at me with wide eyes, like she can't believe what just happened. I raise my eyebrows back at her because I have no clue, either.

The three of us head down another path and after a while, we come across an empty coffin in the middle of a clearing. Faux candles are lit in lanterns, and pumpkins with carved, frightened faces are scattered around the area.

Gladys marches right up to the coffin and peers inside like she's daring anyone to pop out and scare her. When no one does, she turns toward us with a smirk. Then, like a phoenix rising from the ashes, the most menacing Dracula I've ever seen slowly stands up behind the coffin, ready to scare an unaware Gladys. His fake fangs protrude as he leans over the coffin toward her.

Jamie's frozen in place, staring wide-eyed at the scene unfolding before us. Taking the initiative, I point behind Gladys, alerting her of her would-be scarer. She simply raises a skeptical brow at me, removes her purse from her shoulder, and swings it behind her with all her might. It makes direct contact with Dracula's face, and he staggers back, drawing a hand up to where he was struck.

My mouth falls open at Gladys's reaction. I have the urge to stop and see whether Dracula's alright, but I'm not ready to be labeled as an accomplice to maiming an actor in the Corny Acres' haunted attraction. Instead, I grab Jamie's hand and dart out of the clearing.

When I look back to check if Gladys is following us, I see her standing over Dracula, who's now cowering in the fetal position on the ground, and jabbing a bony finger at him. She looks like she's scolding a naughty pet for tinkling on her expensive carpet.

I laugh and shake my head as we start forward again. After a few steps, Jamie pulls me to a stop and says something, but it's getting dark, and I can't read her lips.

I lift my hands between us and sign, *I can't see your mouth.* To drive home my point, I gently brush my thumb along her bottom lip so she gets the message. She shivers and blinks up at me, her pupils wide in the dusky evening.

After a moment of us just staring at each other, she steps back and looks back toward where we came, probably wondering if Gladys followed us. I tap her shoulder and point down another path. After what we just witnessed, I'm positive Gladys can take care of herself, and I just want out of this stupid maze now that it's clear this will be the absolute last place a romantic encounter with Jamie will take place.

I grab Jamie's hand and lead her away. After a few minutes of walking with no one jumping out at us, I'm starting to feel more confident that we're nearing the end of this thing. I slow our pace and lightly drag my thumb along the back of Jamie's hand, hoping she'll take note of the tender touch without shying away from it. Before now, we've never really had a reason to hold hands, but I'm loving every second of it. Hopefully, she is too.

As we round a corner on our right, I take stock of our surroundings. We seem to be completely alone. I lightly tug Jamie to a stop, and she peers up at me with questioning eyes. Swallowing down my trepidation, I move a step closer, hoping she won't be weirded out by my odd behavior. I just want her to know that I think of her as more than a friend. That all I do is think about her and how amazing we could be together, if only we were bold enough to try.

And since anything I try to sign will most likely be lost in the darkness, I'm hoping my actions will say more than words could in this moment. I'm close enough now that I can see through the shadows to every beautiful nuance of Jamie's face. The way her bluish-gray eyes twinkle under the moonlight, the way the light sprinkling of freckles across her nose gives her a youthful appearance, the way her perfect lips part as I close the distance between us...

Suddenly, as if someone shook me awake from a dream, Jamie's eyes widen and she yanks on the front of my shirt, pulling me into a wall of corn, stumbling and tumbling down to the ground. I plummet forward with her but catch myself before I drop on top of her. When I look in her eyes, they're filled with fear, fixed on something behind me.

I hesitantly turn my head to assess who or what is lurking there when I'm startled by a larger-than-life two-headed rabbit wearing blood-spattered overalls and wielding a chainsaw. He's brazenly advancing toward us, and I don't like the maniacal gleam in his four glowing red eyes. On instinct, I rip a few corn cobs from the stalks around us and start whipping them at the two-headed rabbit as hard as I can.

He tries to dodge them, using his chainsaw like a shield, but he's no match for my quick throws. When one of the corn cobs pelts him in his left nose, he staggers backward. I haul Jamie up and we run, not caring that we just assaulted a paid actor and ditched our sixty-something-year old co-worker in the middle of the maze with Dracula.

By the time we reach the end, we're keeled over, out of breath. Surprising us, Gladys reappears on the path adjacent to us with a sly smile. As a group of three again, we pass under a sign that says, "You survived Corny Acres Haunted Maze," finally putting an end to the madness that was the last forty-five minutes of our lives.

A few yards away, I see a few of our co-workers, so we head that way. I only manage to take a few steps when someone grips my upper arm from behind. Startled at the unexpected touch, I turn to see a large man who could be Hoss from *Bonanza's* twin brother, dressed in a plaid shirt and overalls, scowling at me. In true hillbilly fashion, he spits out a string of tobacco and then addresses me. The only words I'm sure I read right from him are, *ask you to leave.*

Apparently, my reputation precedes me.

I start to respond in sign, but Gladys gets the man's attention and gestures wildly with her hands. She advances on him, poking her finger directly into his chest, much like she did to Dracula, but this guy doesn't flinch. I have no idea what she's saying because her back is to me, but it seems intense. I look at Jamie and she meets my eyes with raised brows, mouthing, "Go, Gladys!"

After Gladys finishes giving the man a lecture, he eyes the three of us with newfound disgust and I'm positive he says, "I'm still going to have to ask you to leave."

He doesn't have to tell me twice. Grabbing Jamie's hand again, we start toward the exit, but not before Gladys stomps off ahead of us. Jamie smiles up at me, eyes glittering in the dimly lit walkway that leads to the parking lot. I can't contain the smile that tugs at my lips in response. I pick a piece of corn silk out of her hair and toss it aside. Even after trudging through a haunted corn maze and falling into the corn, she still looks beautiful.

This night may not have been anything like I expected it to be, but you won't find me complaining. The entertainment alone was worth it. Scare factor: Slightly terrifying. Gladys factor: Hilarious. And the fact that I got to hold Jamie's hand for a good portion of the night ended up being the main attraction.

# 6

♥

# JAMIE

"Miss Fowler's class is being introduced to creative writing this year and asked if we'd like to show the kids what a successful functioning paper looks like," says Stefan with his arm draped across Parker's cubicle wall. As usual, he's the picture of power and authority as the rest of us stand around in an awkward not-circle circle. "I expect everyone to be welcoming and accommodating."

I shift on my feet, gripping my plastic-wrapped plate of chocolate chip and M&M cookies a little tighter. I don't know how touring the *Gazette* will be a help to Miss Fowler's first-grade class when it comes to creative writing, but maybe we can at least be an inspiration to some aspiring young writer.

I would've loved to go on a field trip like this in school. All we had the opportunity to do was tour historical reenactments in and around Ohio. So ya know, if you would've asked me how to churn butter at age eight, I could've at least told you the basics.

Lucas shoots his hand up in the air like we're the ones in Miss Fowler's class. Stefan bobs his head in Lucas's direction, prompting him to speak.

"Ah, yes, Mr. Sanders. Would it be all right if I personally showed the kids how we fold the papers? I think some hands-on experience would be fun and engaging for them." He smiles wide, revealing his perfectly white teeth, and I resist the urge to roll my eyes. He's just trying to win more brownie points with our boss. I'd bet all the money in my savings that Lucas hasn't rolled a newspaper in this office once.

"I think that would be very helpful," Stefan says, returning Lucas's smile.

*Ugh. Lucas, one. Jamie, zero.*

"I made cookies," I blurt, holding up the plate like an offering. "I...uh...thought the kids would enjoy something sweet after the tour." With everyone's eyes on me, I regret speaking up.

"That's nice, Jamie," Stefan says, his smile oddly warm. "Maybe you can set up a refreshment table in the break room."

I dip my chin, relieved to be given a somewhat meaningful task, but I don't miss the annoyed look Lucas sends my way. It's become a habit of mine to ignore him, though. If he can show the kids how to fold the papers, the least I can do is feed them snacks.

Just twenty minutes later, a large group of little kids descends on the office with marker-smudged hands and toothy grins. Miss Fowler is a tall, older woman with thick glasses, but she seems to have the kids well-in-hand.

After Stefan makes initial introductions, we're all asked to stand at our cubicles and wait for the kids to make their rounds. They start at the far end where Les works, and knowing they'll be there for a while, I mosey over to Parker's side of the wall.

His eyes are already on me when I turn toward him. "So, you think the kids will enjoy this?"

He rests an arm on the corner of his cubicle wall and half-shrugs before signing, *Time will tell.*

"What are you going to tell them about what you do?" I eye his messy desk. Stacks of colorful sticky notes, a plastic piggy bank full of pennies, and a small cup overflowing with pens, highlighters, and scissors sits on one side of his desk while the other boasts a potted plant with a small spritzer, his Star Wars coffee mug, a bottle of Pepsi and a weird-looking alien head.

In contrast, my desk has my one succulent, Beatrice, a small salt lamp, and my coffee mug that reads, "Wears Black. Loves Coffee. Avoids People."

Parker's lips tip up in an almost flirty smile. *I'm telling them I'm a superhero,* he signs. *During the day, I work at the paper, but in the evening, I'm a superhuman hero.* I can't help but laugh, but when he starts unbuttoning his shirt, all humor leaves me.

"Parker? W-what are you...?" Before I can finish my question, he tears open his shirt, revealing a giant *S* on whatever costume he's wearing underneath his shirt and tie.

I sputter another laugh. "You're serious right now?"

He can't hear me, but he's grinning so wide and proud, I think he already knows how amusing I find this little idea of his.

I grab his arm and meet his eyes. "You're not seriously going to do this are you? I doubt Stefan will find it funny."

He waves off my concern with a smirk, then reaches into his top desk drawer and pulls out a pair of his blue-light glasses. *To finish the look*, he signs, then puts them on.

Another giggle works its way to my lips. Parker mimics a superhero stance with his fists on his hips and it takes an enormous amount of effort not to gape at how handsome he looks in glasses. They accentuate his strong jaw and his wavy, dark curls. I have the sudden urge to twist my fingers in them and see if they look as soft as they feel.

He clears his throat, and my eyes meet his. His smirk grows wider. *Lost in thought?*

Heat charges into my cheeks at his signed question. The way he's looking at me says he knows just how *lost* my thoughts actually got. "Um, no," I say, trying to make a smooth recovery. "I just think you look...ya know...good with glasses. That's all." I lift my shoulders like it's no big deal, even though my blush probably tells a different story.

Thankfully, Miss Fowler's class chooses that moment to stride up to Parker's cubicle. I hang back and creep to my own before his handsomeness has any more chances to affect me. He quickly buttons his shirt's middle button and covers it with his tie before turning toward the class. Apparently, he really is going for the whole superhero act.

I shake my head at my friend's antics. Something about him feels different lately. Maybe it all stemmed from when he acted a little jealous over Mike's texts, or maybe it was when we got lost in the corn field together, I don't know. But either way, his looks and touches feel like...more.

Like maybe there's something he's trying to tell me beneath the surface of his smiles or the sparkle in his eyes. I'm too afraid to look deeper, though. What Parker and I share is special. It's not every day co-workers get along the way we do. I know that all too well. We actually *want* to be together during working hours and even after.

What if I read into the signals I think he's sending me and find out I'm mistaken? Am I willing to risk losing our easy friendship here at work on *what ifs*? Some days, it feels like he's my only ally here. To lose our closeness would be devastating.

I clear my throat and straighten my already tidy desk, convinced I'm out of my mind and Parker is the same as he's always been. Shoving those thoughts aside, I step to my cubicle opening when a red-headed little girl approaches, followed by a string of other kids. They're all so cute, I can't help but smile down at them.

"Hi, I'm Jamie," I say with a friendly wave. I'm not usually the gregarious, cheery type. Not like Parker. But it's impossible to keep a sour face with the wide, innocent eyes of this first-grade class staring up at me. "Would you guys like to know a little about what I do here at the paper?"

Nodding their little heads, some even clapping, they give me an audible *Yeah!* When Miss Fowler gives me the green light, I launch into the spiel I prepared the night before. It's not long, in fact, it only took two minutes to recite from start to finish. But I came up with some follow up questions to ask them and a little assignment they could take home and work on.

"So, what are some exciting things happening in your school that you think you could report on?" I ask, kneeling down to their level, excited to hear their answers.

The little redhead immediately pipes up. "Our gym teacher, Mr. Vlasik, got hit in the head with a dodge ball by Billy Brooks!" Her eyes grow wide during the tale. "And he had to go to the hos-i-ble because he kept falling over! They took him in an am-ba-lence!"

My gaze lifts to Miss Fowler, who winces. "I see. That definitely sounds newsworthy." I straighten and run a hand down the front of my top. "What about something good? Is there anything you could report on that would make people happy to hear about?"

I scan the hands that immediately go up through the small group. "Yes, how about you," I say, pointing to a boy with a buzzed head.

"The lunch ladies started giving us chocolate milk this year. That makes me happy." He shrugs his little beefy shoulders and I smile.

"Oh, that does sound like good news."

After I finish my questions and tell the kids to come up with their own mini articles and turn them in to Miss Fowler for me to read, she thanks me for my time. "You and that tall drink of water beside you were the most entertaining so far," she whispers, leaning close. At the words *tall drink of water*, her eyes drift to Parker's cubicle.

I suppress a grin. "Well, I appreciate that, Miss Fowler. And don't forget, when you're done touring the office, I'll have refreshments set up in the break room." I explain where that is and wave goodbye to the kiddos for now.

I'm so caught up in the warm, fuzzy feels that talking to them gave me, I don't even notice Parker standing off to my left until he nudges me in the ribs with his sword finger.

I jump and turn toward him. "She said we were the most entertaining!" I whisper-squeal as I clasp my hands under my chin. "Maybe she'll tell Stefan and he'll be impressed with our effort."

Parker's brow lowers, telling me he didn't quite catch everything I said. Must have been the whisper-squeal. I repeat myself through sign and when understanding dawns, he responds, *If the way you handled those kids doesn't impress him, I don't know what will.* The sincerity in his eyes warms me all the way through to my toes.

"You were watching?"

He nods, a big grin blooming on his tanned face. *I was and you were amazing. I couldn't take my eyes off you.* Parker's lids lower the slightest bit and I'm almost positive his eyes drop to my mouth. It's not unusual for him to stare at my mouth. It's how he's able to piece together what I say through my broken Sign Language, but the look in his eyes is different—more heated and hazy.

My lips automatically part under the imagined attention, and for the first time ever, I wonder what it would be like to kiss Parker Kent.

Realizing the ridiculous turn of my thoughts, I take a quick step back and run a hand through my hair. "I...uh...need to go and get the cookies and drinks ready."

*Want my help?* he asks, oblivious to my inner freak out.

"Uh, no!" I wince at my too quick response. "That's okay," I try again. "I'm just gonna pour some lemonade and set out the cookies. No biggie." I spin on my heel before I can see his reaction and hustle to the break room.

Maybe it's all in my imagination, but it feels like something charged and electric happened between us, and I was not prepared for the way my thoughts betrayed me. Parker is my friend, my co-worker. Nothing more. Maybe if I repeat that mantra for the rest of the workday, my misguided heart will start to believe it.

# 7

♥

# Parker

I don't follow Jamie into the breakroom right away. She seemed a little tense when I offered to help her set out the refreshments for Miss Fowler's class. I'm hoping she didn't notice the way my eyes zeroed in on her lips when she wasn't speaking...I'd like to think I'm more discreet than that, but maybe I'm not.

Instead of overanalyzing the interaction, I focus on getting some actual work done for a few minutes before I head into the breakroom to steal a cookie for myself.

Jamie and Gladys stand at the counter, passing out cups of juice and napkin-wrapped cookies. I hang back along the wall, watching Jamie smile at each kid that approaches her. Something about the way she genuinely seems to enjoy listening to them has me imagining her as a mom someday.

We've never really talked about our futures or if we want families, so I don't know if that's something she even wants, but it's hard not to imagine the two of us raising a family together when all I want is to be with her for the rest of my life.

I know I've got to take it slow, though. I'd probably freak her way out if I said such a thing to her right now—she doesn't even know how deep my feelings go. But hopefully, soon, she will.

When the last kid goes through the line to grab a cookie, I saunter toward her. *My turn*, I sign with what probably looks like a stupid grin. I can't quite rein it in after the turn my thoughts took while watching her with the kids.

She hands me a cookie with an almost shy smile. A tinge of pink blooms in her cheeks, but there's no time for me to wonder why when Gladys shoves a cup of juice in my hands, her bright coral lips curled upward. Ever since the pumpkin patch fiasco, my elderly co-worker seems to have taken quite the liking to me. Whenever I meet her gaze, she usually sends me a wink or a wave, which is more than she used to give me.

As I turn and take in the room full of little kids, some are seated at the break tables, while others have congregated in clusters around the space. One little boy in particular catches my eye. He's got glasses and dark brown hair, and something about the way he looks over his shoulder piques my curiosity.

He turns toward the wall and crouches directly in front of an electrical outlet. I take a bite of my cookie and step forward, trying not to make it obvious that I'm onto him. I don't know if he means to cause mischief, but I know what kinds of things I got into when I was a little kid out for trouble. But before I can even register what he's about to do, the glint of a small, metal object in his hands is the last thing I see before he shoves it toward the outlet and all the lights flicker and go out.

I can't hear the screams and shouts coming from the little kids surrounding me, but their faces say it all. Most have mouths open, panic radiating from their expressions, while some cover their ears, and others laugh with abandon.

I head toward the little boy who probably gave himself the shock of a lifetime to find him laid out on his back, staring wide-eyed up at the ceiling. I bend down and gently pull him up to a seated position.

Checking the outlet, I'm not surprised to see a paperclip still shoved inside.

*You OK?* I sign to the boy. He barely acknowledges my presence, just stares down at his blackened fingers with a horrified expression. There's a strong probability he's not going to understand anything I sign to him, so I carefully lift him to his feet and steer him toward Jamie.

The room is dim, but light streams in from the windows, making it easy to navigate through the frantic children. Jamie stands with arms outstretched in front of a group of three little girls, and it appears she's trying to get them to calm down, while Miss Fowler does the same with a cluster of kids at the opposite end of the room. Gladys is chomping on a cookie beside the counter like chaos isn't ensuing around her.

*I found the culprit*, I sign when we reach Jamie. Her round-eyed gaze drops to the boy's hands. Clearly horrified, she takes the boy by the shoulders and directs him to Miss Fowler.

Stefan and a few of our other co-workers choose that moment to charge into the room, but our boss's mouth is moving too fast for me to catch what he's saying. All I know is that his reddened face and puffed out cheeks make him look like a cherry tomato about to burst.

After depositing the boy with Miss Fowler where Eric steps in to help check the boy for injuries, Jamie heads toward our boss and describes what happened. She points to me, then the boy I caught trying to electrocute himself, as well as the outlet across the room.

Stefan places his hands on his hips with a furious gleam in his eyes. He says something that makes her face instantly fall. I start their way, intent on explaining that Jamie had nothing to do with this disaster, but Stefan stalks off before I can reach them.

When I tentatively place an arm around Jamie's shoulder, she immediately turns into me. I draw her away from the center of the room and bend down so I'm at eye level in front of her.

*What did he say?* I sign.

Her glassy eyes and trembling lower lip nearly break my heart. "That this was a lawsuit waiting to happen. He said it was a good thought, wanting to give the kids refreshments, but that I should've been keeping a better eye on them."

*That's ridiculous*, I respond, anger multiplying inside me at a rapid pace. *You weren't responsible.*

She shrugs one shoulder and looks back at the class. Miss Fowler has calmed the kids down, and they now sit with their legs crisscrossed in the center of the breakroom, holding hands and rocking back and forth. Their mouths move in-sync which has me convinced they're singing "Kumbaya."

When my gaze moves back to Jamie, she's swiping at tears and her chest rises and falls too rapidly, like she can't catch her breath. I gently take her hand and lead her out of the break room and down the hall. When we get to the storage closet, I lead her inside and close the door behind us, flicking on the light so she can see me.

Tears stain her reddened cheeks and she's squeezing her sides as she heaves in what looks like tight breath after tight breath. I skim my hands down her arms and meet her eyes, trying to get her to focus on me. Her eyes dart back and forth across my face, her rising panic clear. I'm not an expert by any means, but if I had to guess, she's spiraling into an anxiety attack.

I make what I hope are shooshing noises and skate my hands up and down her arms in slow, soothing strokes, only removing them to sign, *Look at me. Focus on my eyes.*

She does as I command with a shaky nod, and seems to breathe in deep through her nose, then out through her mouth. Over and over she does this until her chest begins to rise and fall in a more natural rhythm.

I cup her face and wipe away her few remaining tears with my thumbs. She looks so defeated, so dejected, as she raises her hands and signs, *I guess I can kiss the exclusive interview goodbye.*

I shake my head with more force than necessary. *No*, I sign back. *It was an accident. There's still plenty of time to get on Stefan's good side.* She doesn't look like she believes me, but she doesn't have to. All she needs is to be confident in her own abilities. *You've got this. Don't doubt yourself.*

I brush some hair away from her face to see a whisper of a smile curl the edges of her pink lips. Unable to resist, I poke a finger into her right dimple.

*That's more like it,* I sign. A full smile blooms on her face then, and I can tell she's giggling. Much better than seeing her upset and anxious.

Before we leave the room, I pull Jamie in for a long, lingering hug. Her body instantly relaxes against mine and I tighten my hold, unable to stop myself from taking an inhale of her fruity-smelling shampoo and running my hand down her silky-soft hair.

When we make it back to the break room, Miss Fowler approaches with a sheepish smile. She and Jamie face each other, so I step back and let them talk. I hope the woman is apologizing for her little student with the death wish, not that she could have foreseen the incident happening either.

Don't get me wrong, I know what it's like to a be a precocious kid, but letting Jamie take the rap for something she had no control over has me running my hands through my hair repeatedly to try and calm down.

While Miss Fowler walks her class out of the breakroom, Jamie offers them a small wave, her smile wobbly. Again, I step behind her and wrap an arm around her shoulders. She leans into me, probably still somewhat rattled.

I wish I could whisper words of reassurance in her ear. Tell her she was doing a good thing by trying to entertain the kids with cookies—even Stefan thought so at first. Accidents happen, that's just life. And she wasn't the only adult in the room.

When an idea hits, I spin Jamie to face me. *I'm going to talk to Stefan. I saw the kid first. Tried to stop him but wasn't fast enough.*

She gives me a sad smile. "I doubt anyone could've stopped him. Kids are fast."

I give her shoulders a reassuring squeeze before heading toward Stefan's office. If I can make this right for her and somehow improve the way Stefan sees her, I'll sit in his office all day without an ASL interpreter and write out her defense until my hand cramps.

---

I never got the chance to speak with Stefan after the lights out incident because he personally went to the school and met with the principal and the child's parents. He must have been *really* worried about covering all his bases.

I did, however, leave a note on his desk explaining what I saw happen and vouching for Jamie. I'm not sure how much good it'll do since he was pretty perturbed when he stormed out, but it's worth a shot to save Jamie from having this interview stolen out from under her on a technicality.

Since all the power went out on the entire floor, me and all my co-workers essentially dismissed ourselves from work. If Stefan wanted us to stay and twiddle our thumbs while he sucked up to the parents of the kid who caused mayhem in the office today, well…he's bound to be disappointed.

I'm tossing the last of the food from the thawing fridge into the trashcan before it stinks up the entire office when Jamie walks in and gets my attention with a wave. "Want to grab an early dinner?"

*Do I ever*, I think to myself when she bites her bottom lip, awaiting my response. But I already have plans. I bring my hands up to sign, *Can't tonight. I'm sorry. Family dinner.*

Her expression instantly collapses, and I want to kick myself. Then another idea springs to mind. *You could come with me*, I sign. *If you want.*

She tucks her hair behind her ears and lifts one shoulder. "I don't know. I don't want to crash your family dinner. Especially since I might be depressing company tonight."

*You're never depressing,* I reply. *Don't let what Stefan said ruin your night.*

A small smile forms at the edge of her mouth and she shifts on her feet. "Okay. If you really want me to come, I will."

I nod, then rub my hand in a circular motion on my chest in the sign for *please*. Relief washes over her features. Like always, we exit work together and she tells me she's going to go home and change before she comes over to my parent's house at five p.m.

I go home too, but don't even bother to change my clothes as I sit down and type out a scene for my fantasy novel while I've got some time to spare. Twenty minutes before five, I text Jamie the address, hop in my truck, and head to my parents'.

I've never had the opportunity to introduce Jamie to anyone in my family other than Dane, but I'd be lying if I said I haven't mentioned Jamie to my mom. We're a tight-knit family for the most part, and though I don't tell my parents every detail about my life, they know the big stuff. And Jamie is big stuff.

But my mom can be overprotective, especially with me after the bullying I experienced as a child, and maybe that's why I haven't gone out of my way to introduce her to Jamie. She's this feisty little woman who hails from Romania and loves her family fiercely. And to outsiders, she can be intimidating. On the flip side, she can also be over-the-top embarrassing when it comes to girls her boys are interested in.

I shove the thoughts aside as I pull into my parents' driveway fifteen minutes later. Their older one-story home sits on a quiet, tree-lined street in the suburbs of Treemont. We moved here as a family right before my freshman year of high school after Dad retired from the military. I guess you could say my brothers and I were military brats growing up, never really settling into one place. But since we moved to Ohio to be closer to Dad's family, I've never felt more at home.

It's a rainy day and the chill in the air whips through my jacket as I hurry up to the front door. I don't knock when I enter my parents' house, just lumber through the door and kick off my shoes. Before I even make it to the kitchen where my mom is probably hard at work, she comes barreling into the foyer with her tiny arms outstretched.

"*Draga mea*," she says with a toothy smile just before wrapping me up in a hug. Of course, I can't hear the things she's murmuring against my chest, but I feel the rumble of her voice ricocheting through me. It's always the usual, though.

*It's so good to see you, baby boy. Why don't you text me? Where's your brother?*

I pull away and she frowns. "Where's your brother?" Guess I jumped the gun on that one.

Through sign, I tell her he's probably still at the gym. He doesn't have to go back into work for a few more days, and while he's home, he practically lives at the gym down the street from our apartment. I say he's just there to pick up girls, but he claims he's actually working out. I guess his abundance of muscles proves he's at least half-right.

"Fine, okay. Logan and your father are in the den," she says as well as signs, then heads to the kitchen where something I know will be delicious is cooking. The savory smell makes my mouth water.

Before she can scurry away, I grab her wrist. She stops and faces me. *I invited someone to dinner tonight,* I tell her. *Hope that's okay.*

Her dark brows pull together. "Who?"

*My friend Jamie. From the office.*

Her eyebrows raise to her dark curly bangs as a smirk starts on her lips. "I see," she says with a slow nod. "Well, that's wonderful."

I resist the urge to roll my eyes. *It's not what you're thinking, Mom. Don't get any ideas. We're just friends.* Though I desperately wish we were more. But I'm not about to confess that right now. She'll probably embarrass me enough as it is. Or worse, make Jamie and me perform some kind of old gypsy betrothal ceremony her ancestors used to take part in.

You honestly can never tell with her.

She shakes her head and lifts both hands in the air. "What ideas? I'm just happy to see my baby boy make a friend. A girl friend. A girl who is a friend." Her eyes brighten even as she shrugs and saunters away with too much pep in her step.

Second-guessing my split decision to invite Jamie over, I fight the sudden urge to text her and beg her not to come. Maybe I can fake an illness. But that wouldn't be fair to her; we've already made plans. She just doesn't know the wildcard awaiting her that is Alexandra Kent.

Where exactly does my loud, flamboyant mom fall into the plan to make Jamie fall in love with me? I swipe my hands down my face and groan.

This whole thing was a mistake.

I'll just have to be a buffer between the two of them. Maybe I can enlist my oldest brother to help. He's introverted and quiet, kind of like Jamie, but more extreme. If I can sway him to my side, together we can force Mom to be on her best behavior.

I step into the den where Logan and Dad watch a college football game with the subtitles on. They're always on, thanks to me. But no one around here complains; everyone's used to it by now.

Their eyes swing to me when I take a seat on the couch catty-corner to their matching recliners. Dad signs a *Hey, son. Good to see you,* while my oldest brother lifts his chin in a nod with a single wave. Logan's not much for words and keeps to himself mostly, the total opposite of Dane, our mom, and me.

I lean forward and tap Logan's leg, getting his attention again. When he tears his gaze away from the game, I sign, *My friend Jamie is coming over tonight. Can you help me make sure Mom doesn't overwhelm her?*

His lips tip up just the slightest bit as he responds with his hands. "You afraid Mom will try that betrothal ceremony act she did on me that time I brought my high school girlfriend over?"

I curl my pointer fingers and bring my wrists together to sign, *Exactly.*

His shoulders shake on a chuckle before he faces the TV again, signing, "Can't make any promises."

I sigh and lean back. So much for asking for his help.

Dad waves to get my attention. "What's all this about a friend?"

I let my head fall back against the couch cushions. *Just my friend from work, Dad. She's coming over for dinner. That's all.*

Dad dips his chin once, eyeing Logan and then me. "Think your mom will try that ceremony—"

I don't even wait for him to finish before I jump to my feet, watching Mom rush past the den toward the front door. Either Dane or Jamie has arrived, and if it's the latter, I need to intercept her before my overbearing mom does.

# 8

♥

# Jamie

I LOWER MY FACE into the collar of my fur-lined jacket to stave off the cold chill in the air as I wait for someone to answer the door. It wasn't hard to find Parker's parents' house once I typed the address into good ol' Google maps.

The dark brick ranch home is nestled into a cluster of trees, surrounded by similar homes and properties, but this one stands out with its meticulously landscaped front yard, complete with large planters full of yellow and orange mums. The home embodies Midwestern charm, and I can't help but smile thinking of Parker growing up here. It suits him perfectly.

A loud feminine voice sounds from the other side of the door just before it swings open wide, revealing a shoeless Parker with his tie gone, work shirt unbuttoned and showing off the superhero tee underneath. I've seen him in different outfits over the past year, usually his work clothes, but something about the carefree way these hang on him now makes me jealous of anyone else who might get to see him this way.

A hesitant smile lifts his lips as he wedges himself in between the door and the doorjamb.

"Can I...come in?" I ask, letting out a nervous laugh.

"Parker! Move!" The heavily accented feminine voice echoes in the foyer behind Parker just before small, tanned hands yank him backward and open the door wider.

"Jamie!" the little woman cries, holding her arms out to me, fingers wiggling like she can't wait to get a hold of me.

"Uh, hi. You must be Parker's mom." I slide my gaze to Parker, who looks completely mortified. He's covering his face with both hands, head hanging back. Before I can make eye contact with his mom again, she throws her arms around me and squeezes tight.

"It's so good to finally meet you, *fata*. I'm Alexandra, but you can call me Alex," she says loud enough for the entire neighborhood to hear, then lowering her voice considerably, she whispers, "You're even prettier in person." I smile at the curious compliment, but then she runs a hand over my hair in such a motherly way, it brings a sudden tickle to my eyes.

"Come in, come in!" Waving me forward, she beckons me into the house and removes my jacket. "I hope you're hungry because I made stuffed peppers." Her dark curly hair bounces around her shoulders as the gap in the center of her teeth winks at me.

I almost laugh out loud when she hands my jacket to Parker with a disapproving look, then says, "Hang that up, will you?"

As if he's not even there, she loops her arm through mine and pulls me down the short hall into the large open concept kitchen/dining space. I hear football on the TV from the room across the hall, but don't have time to even turn my head in that direction before she's lifting the lid on a cast iron pot and shoving a spoon laden with something savory in my face.

"Here. Try this." Her bright brown eyes gleam as she taps the spoon against my lips. I obey, because what else can I do, and savor the blend of spices that dance in my mouth once the seasoned meat hits my tongue. "These are my special meatballs. They go with the peppers."

"They're amazing," I say, bringing a hand to my mouth. Her responding grin tells me she knows exactly what she's doing in the kitchen.

"I know. It's a recipe that's been passed down through many generations of my family. Of course, I tweaked it a little." She pinches her fingers together, driving home her point. I'm not sure if it's because Parker is deaf that she mostly talks with her hands or if that's just unique to her, but either way, it's adorable.

At that exact moment, Parker enters the room with an uncomfortable look on his face.

"Parker," Alex scolds while swiftly signing with her hands. "The picture you showed me does not do Jamie justice. She's *frumos, minunat*." One dark eyebrow raises over her chocolate eyes as she tilts her chin up in a defiant gesture.

I'm not sure what those two words mean, but I'm completely stuck on the fact that Parker SHOWED HIS MOM MY PICTURE.

Parker's mouth flattens as he responds wildly with his hands, too fast for me to even begin to guess what he's saying, then he takes my hand and tugs me back toward the hallway.

"Okay, but dinner will be ready in five minutes! Don't go far!" Alex calls as we exit the kitchen and head toward where I heard the TV earlier. I want to ask Parker what he said to his mom, but before I can, we're standing in front of a man who I assume is his dad and a younger guy who looks just like him.

Parker motions to me, then introduces me to his dad, Paul, and his brother, Logan. "It's nice to meet you both," I say with a smile. His dad hits the lever on the side of his recliner and gets to his feet to take my hand.

"The pleasure is ours, Jamie. It's not every day that Parker brings a girl home." He winks at Parker who seems to be doing everything he can to avoid eye contact with me while Logan chuckles under his breath.

"Sorry, bro. I tried." Logan shrugs, then directs his attention back to the game.

Parker taps my arm, finally meeting my eyes, and signs, *I tried to tell them we just work together, but they're...* He pauses, seeming to struggle to find the right word. *Pushy?*

The way he winces makes me giggle. "It's totally fine. My pops would be the same way if he were...well, you know. If he knew what was going on." Everyone quiets at my oversharing outburst, probably not knowing how to follow that up. I scrunch my nose. This is why I avoid interaction with humans outside my small bubble of friends. *I'm bad at this.*

"Well, dinner should be starting soon," Paul pipes up, running a hand over his sandy brown hair. "Why don't you show Jamie your old room while we wait?"

Parker eyes his dad, then me. As if it takes all his strength to give in, he lets out a heavy breath and tips his head back toward the hall. We go left this time instead of toward the kitchen and in moments I'm faced with a door that has a blue sign on it that reads *Parker's Room*.

I smile and point it out, but he only shakes his head as he pushes open the door, allowing me inside. It looks like a typical teenage boy space, but with a galaxy type of flair. Star Wars posters line the walls, along with a few intricate drawings of characters from the movies. Instinctively, I move closer to inspect them and I'm awed by Parker's talent.

I turn so he can read my lips. "When did you draw these?"

He hikes a shoulder in the most nonchalant way before answering. *In high school.*

I playfully shove his shoulder with a smile. "You've been holding out on me, Parker Kent. These are *impressive*."

The barest of smiles appears on his face as he moves in closer, erasing some of the distance between us. *I think you're impressive,* he signs. *I don't care what Stefan says, you were so great with those kids today.*

My breath catches at the flirty way he lifts an eyebrow just before he brushes back the hair from my shoulder. My body goes completely still at the contact. I search his eyes, questioning, when a shrill voice echoes down the hall.

"Dinner's ready!" For such a tiny woman, Alex has an astoundingly loud voice. Oblivious to his mom's call, Parker continues to let his gaze roam my face and something a lot like desire fills his eyes.

Or at least, I *think* it's desire? It's hard to tell, honestly. I so rarely see this kind of look from guys anymore that I'm not sure I'm reading it right. But it doesn't make sense that he'd be looking at me that way…we're just friends.

The door to his bedroom whips open, startling us both. "Dinner's ready," Alex says with a wide, toothy grin. "Didn't know if you heard me." She winks, then disappears down the hall and I stifle the urge to laugh.

Something like a growl sounds from Parker as he leads me back into the kitchen. This time, the other two Kent men are seated at the table with another guy I recognize as Parker's other brother, Dane. He resembles Parker more than Logan does with darker hair that's cropped short. He's not as tan as Parker but has the same lighter eyes.

"Jamie," Dane says with a friendly smile aimed my way. "It's always good to see you."

"Yeah, you too."

Parker directs me toward a chair between him and Dane on the end of the table opposite from his mom. When she throws a pouty look his way, I start to wonder if his seating selection was intentional.

In seconds, the large cast iron pot from before along with another are situated in the center of the table with a bread basket to my right. It smells absolutely divine, and I resist the urge to lick my lips in anticipation, remembering how good that meatball tasted.

"Paul," Alex says with an adoring look toward her husband. "Would you like to say grace?"

Paul nods and everyone closes their eyes as they reach out toward the person next to them. Parker grabs my hand without pretense while Dane holds his palm up in invitation with an encouraging smile. *Oh. Okay, we're doing this.*

Now I know why Parker prays every day at lunch. I lower my other hand into Dane's and close my eyes, mimicking everyone's posture. I try to focus on the soothing sound of Paul's voice as he prays, but all I can hone in on is the way Parker's thumb lightly grazes my hand. Each swipe of the calloused pad sends a tingle up my arm, straight to my heart.

Why is his touch suddenly sending my body into overdrive? So many questions begin to form in my mind, and when the prayer ends, I drop Parker's hand like it's too hot to handle. I feel his gaze on me, but I'm not brave enough to meet his eyes after the thoughts that ran through my head moments ago.

Parker's mom plates up everyone's dish in the sweetest, most motherly way and the bread basket gets passed. Conversation flows between the parents and siblings and everyone signs as they speak. It's something I'm grateful for while trying to learn ASL. Hearing the words with the signs makes it easier for me to grasp.

Dane tells a funny joke about the difference between a pilot and a pepperoni pizza, making everyone chuckle. All except for Parker who laughs with abandon. His deep, throaty laugh does something so indescribable to my insides, I don't dare put a name to it. No one else at the table bats an eyelash, like they're all used to the sound.

Warmth creeps to my cheeks against my will as I peer at the guy beside me.

Something feels different about tonight. I don't know if it's his mom's comments or the way he touched me and called me impressive in his old bedroom, or maybe it was the way he came to my rescue while I was having a panic attack over Stefan's disappointment earlier. Whatever it is, I'm nearly convinced there's something tangible between us now—something that wasn't there before.

And as Parker meets my eyes and winks, I'm not sure what to do about it. Not sure if I *should* do anything about it. Old memories resurface in my mind and suddenly make it hard to swallow. If I lost Parker the same way I lost Tyson, I'm not sure I could work another day at the *Gazette*. And if that happened, I'd not only lose my best friend but the chance to land my dream interview with Paris.

---

Once dinner's over, the men linger around the table while Alex darts up to cart off the dishes. I immediately follow, not wanting her to do all the work. When I sidle up next to her, I ask, "What can I do?"

She raises her eyebrows as a slow smile spreads over her face. "Well, aren't you a sweet surprise." Feeling a little timid at her attention, I tuck some hair behind my ear. "I'm just clearing the table, *fata*," she says. "The boys will wash the dishes and put away the food." She nods toward where they're all laughing and talking. "I may have made their plates, but they clean them. I've trained them well."

I can't help but smile at her feisty spirit. She's such an unexpected breath of fresh air. In a way, her boldness reminds me of Daria, but she's an older, wiser version with a distinctly maternal touch. Maybe it's just that I've been missing a mom-type figure for so long, I crave that sort of attention, but part of me wants to move into Parker's old room and claim her as my own.

"You go on and relax in the den," she says, nudging me with her hip. "Parker won't be too long."

I glance back at the table where the men have started to rise. Parker meets my gaze with a reassuring look.

"I should probably get going," I hedge, turning back to Alex. "I don't want to wear out my welcome."

"Nonsense! You will stay and relax in the den." She swipes her hands together like the matter's settled and scoots me toward the hall. "Off with you!"

I laugh at the insistent little woman and do as she says, wondering what it must have been like to grow up with a mom like her. I bet Parker has some great stories he could share. I park it on the large sectional couch in the den, but I'm not brave enough to switch the TV from the sports channel in a house that's not mine, so I wait patiently for Parker.

After a few minutes, *everyone* comes into the den. I straighten. Parker scoots in close to my side, pressing his body against mine from hip to shoulder. His brother Dane sits on the other side of him, while Paul moves to the recliner he occupied before, tugging Alex down onto his lap. It's such a sweet scene, I resist the urge to sigh aloud. Logan takes the other recliner and leans all the way back with his arms extended overhead.

Everyone looks so casual and comfortable, even with my presence here, that it's impossible not to relax.

Alex picks up the remote with a flourish. "It's time for you know what." She sends each of the men in her family a look while she taps buttons on the remote.

Dane and Logan both let out some form of a groan while Parker just shakes his head with a smile. Turning to me, he signs, *My mom is obsessed with this Turkish drama show. The episodes are long, but she'll try to have you hooked if you stay and watch it.*

I readjust my body so I'm a little more comfortable. "Sounds fun," I sign, facing the TV.

I don't miss the way Parker drapes his arm across the back of the couch behind me. The smell of his deodorant and something completely unique to him infiltrates my senses at rapid-fire speed. I so badly want to lean into him and take a deep inhale, but I refrain.

Because that would be weird. We're not dating or even talking about dating. *For the hundredth time, Jamie, you're FRIENDS. And FRIENDS don't cross over that line. You already know what happens when they do.*

The show begins with some of the most beautiful actors I've ever seen. Alex settles into Paul with a satisfied smirk while Logan looks comfortable enough to pass out. Dane scrolls through his phone seeming uninterested and Parker watches with me.

I know he's not a stranger to romcoms because he's watched a few with me and Daria. But never have I been snuggled up into his side quite like this. Since knowing him, he's never shown what I would consider a romantic interest in me. And yeah, I mean, he's objectively hot, but because he was my coworker even before my stint with Mike, I never considered something more with him.

So why does my heart suddenly want to leap into his arms now?

Parker's fingertips graze my arm and I flinch. He bends down to peer into my face, removing his arm from around me for a moment to sign, *You're tense. Relax. We're just watching TV.*

I try for a convincing smile, but inside I'm screaming, BUT THIS DOESN'T FEEL LIKE WE'RE ONLY WATCHING TV. *I'm meeting your family and loving them and you're sending me some weird mixed signals that I desperately want to read into but can't because I've been down this road before and know that it can only end with a crash and burn type of scenario.*

Of course, I don't give voice to those thoughts as I sink further into Parker. His hand comes around my arm more fully than the last time and I rest my back against his chest.

Soon, I'm engrossed in the show that's filled with some of the thickest romantic tension I've ever encountered on television. Halfway through, Logan's fast asleep and Dane excuses himself, saying he's going to head home, giving his mom a kiss on his way out.

I probably should leave too, but I'm too invested now. I have to see if these two beautiful people on the screen are going to kiss or not.

When Dane leaves, Alex pauses the show and hops up with more agility than a woman her age should have. "How about some snacks? Parker? Jamie?"

*Popcorn?* Parker signs. I nod, always up for some snackies at a time like this. Alex disappears into the hall, and I follow, wanting to help. Two minutes later, we're carting bowls of popcorn and cold cans of soda into the den and handing them out to the guys. Well, all except for Logan.

When I go to sit on the couch, I realize Parker has taken my place, leaving me the spot with a better view of the TV without having to crane my neck to see it. *Sit.* He pats the spot next to him and I obey, handing him a soda. He declines the popcorn, so I clutch the bowl to my chest not at all disappointed I won't have to share. Part of me wonders if he only suggested it for my benefit.

Alex clicks the show back on and I go to tuck my feet underneath me, but Parker grabs one of my ankles. I give him a confused look and raise a hand in question. He just smirks and stretches my legs over his lap like it's the most normal thing in the world for me to have my feet on him.

Since when did he become my human footrest?

Then, like I'm in some sort of dream world where Parker lives to make me melt, he starts kneading the balls and arches of my foot with just the right amount of glorious pressure. I try to retract my legs, but he stops me with his surprisingly strong grip.

He holds his palms out facing each other then, tilts them up, making the sign for *Let me*. There's a tenderness in his expression that is impossible to ignore. *You've had a hard day,* he signs. *Let me help you relax.*

A prickling sensation begins behind my eyes, but I will it away and give him a nod. He continues to knead and work on my feet while his eyes focus on the TV screen. He smiles at the appropriate times in the show, so I know my discomfort is all on me. He's probably not reading into massaging my feet the way I am.

Maybe he just feels really bad for the way I reacted to Stefan's lecture, and in his own touchy-feely way, he's doing his best to be a great friend. Either way, I need to get over my reaction to him and watch the dang show.

It's not too hard to do but when Parker hits a particularly sore spot on my foot, something between a needy whimper and a moan slips through my lips. He's completely oblivious to the sound, thank God, but when I feel his family's eyes on me, my head swivels in their direction.

Alex's one eyebrow is cocked in intrigue while she holds a piece of popcorn to her upturned lips. Paul's eyes dart around like he doesn't know where to look as he adjusts the neckline of his sweatshirt. Even Logan is alert now, staring at the way his brother's hands are performing magic on my feet and ankles.

With my face on fire, I slowly extricate my foot from Parker's grasp and worried lines form between his brows. "That's enough," I say as well as sign. "I'm all good." I try for a convincing smile, but he looks skeptical.

Ignoring him and his family, I raise my gaze to the TV and try not to hide in complete mortification. I want nothing more than to sink beneath the couch cushions and disappear until the end of time.

# 9

♥

# Jamie

Just when I think I'll get to sleep in and enjoy my Saturday morning routine, a string of text messages comes in, effectively ruining my sleep schedule. I guess staying in bed until nine thirty before grabbing an iced coffee with Daria and hitting up the local farmer's market will begin earlier than I'd planned.

I roll over in bed and fumble around on my nightstand until I feel my phone beneath my fingers. Tapping into my messaging app, I groan aloud when I see the messages are from Mike. Again.

**Mike:** It feels like you're ignoring me…please tell me you're not ignoring me.

**Mike:** Look, I'm sorry. I can't make things right with you if you won't talk to me.

**Mike:** You're probably grumpy because I interrupted your Saturday morning beauty sleep, but I wondered if I could join you for brunch this morning.

Something twinges in my chest at the thought that he remembered my Saturday morning routine. I shouldn't care. We dated for seven months, of course he would know my routine, but...this level of interest from him makes me feel like he actually *cares*. And that's so unlike Mike that it rattles me. Plus, it sounds like if I don't respond to him, he'll just keep texting.

I blow a frustrated breath through my lips, wishing I was the type of girl who could block and delete a guy when they broke it off. But I'm not that cold. I don't like making enemies and burning bridges, especially when there are so few people from my past still in my life.

And part of me does sort of miss what we had, even if it all went to pot long before I ever guessed it would.

I stare at my phone, debating what to do, when it buzzes in my hand. *Great. Now he's calling.* Taking a deep, bolstering breath, I click the green button and say, "Hello?" as if I don't know who's on the other end.

"Jamie? You answered." Mike's voice is breathy, almost reverent. It has me sitting up in bed, wiping the sleep from my eyes.

"What's going on, Mike?" Even with the breathiness in his voice, there's a bite to my words. I'm not letting him off easy.

"Nothing. Nothing's going on, I just...I just want to see you. I miss you."

Anger swift and hot replaces my curiosity from before. "Mike, what's this all about? You've been texting me more in the last week than you did the entire last month we were together. What's your game?"

"Jamie, there's no game." A pregnant pause. "Maybe a guy like me just doesn't realize what he had until it's gone."

*A guy like him*? Handsome, somewhat charming, with a steady, albeit boring, job as an insurance agent? I take a shuddering breath, then let it out slowly.

"Can I see you?" he asks.

Why is he doing this right now, of all times? Last night I went to sleep questioning my feelings for my best friend...thinking about how nice it felt to let him touch me...how awesome his family is and wishing they were mine.

But I know it wasn't right to think of him in that way. I can't bank on Parker having feelings for me, even with the weird way he's been acting lately. Things have felt different between us, yes, but is that just a part of his touchy nature or is it more? I could be reading the entire situation wrong. It's not like I can ask him and find out. Especially when I already know crossing that line will end badly for us both.

"Jamie? You still there?" The worry in Mike's voice brings me back to our conversation.

"I'm not comfortable having brunch with you," I say honestly. Besides, I'm not going to ditch Daria for our weekly thing just because he wants to see me.

"Okay. I understand. How about I meet you at the farmer's market and just...walk around with you for a few minutes."

I sigh through the phone and it's clear he hears it.

"I could just show up there, you know," he says, a smile in his voice. "It is a public place and all."

"You wouldn't do that." At least, I hope he wouldn't. That's like, stalker level stuff.

"No, not if you didn't want me to."

I relax into the pillows behind me. "Fine. Meet me by the Greg's Nursery stand in an hour."

"Thanks, babe. Can't wait to see you."

I grit my teeth at the pet name he refuses to let go of. "I'm not your babe. And I'll see you then. Bye."

As soon as I press the end button, a knock sounds on my bedroom door. "Come in," I call to the only person it could be.

Daria opens the door and peeks her head inside the room. "Did I hear you talking to someone?" She lifts both eyebrows.

"Unfortunately, yes." I whip the covers off, shivering at the sudden chill when my feet hit the icy hardwood floor.

"Why *unfortunately*? Who was it?"

I stand in front of my dresser mirror, pulling my hair up into a messy bun and glare at her reflection behind me. "Mike."

Her face instantly contorts with horror as she steps further into my room. "Mike? What, why?"

"Exactly," I mumble, opening my dresser drawers and pulling out my favorite pair of black leggings and oversized Shania T-shirt. "Turn around, please, so I can get dressed." She does as I command while I slip off my pink Hello Kitty pajamas and pull on my black clothes. I tug a—you guessed it—black zip-up hoodie over top and pull on a pair of white ankle socks before finishing off my look with my leopard Vans. "*Why* is what I've been asking myself since he texted me a few days ago."

"Wait," she says, turning toward me and holding up a hand. She drops onto my bed with one foot tucked underneath her. "Mike texted you *days* ago and you didn't tell me?"

I roll my eyes. "I didn't want to tell you because I knew you'd get like this." I wave my hand up and down her body. "All defensive and stuff."

She jerks her head at me as if to say, *duh!*, then holds out her hands. "Of course I'd get defensive. You're one of my best friends and he was a jerk. I don't want to see him hurt you twice."

I shake my head. "It wasn't like that, Daria. He didn't hurt me any worse than any other guy who dated me just long enough to figure out I wasn't his type."

She crosses her arms and raises that one, menacing eyebrow again, her signature annoyed expression. "But he was your longest adult relationship. So it hurt worse when he started giving you the cold shoulder. I know it did, don't even try to deny it."

Blowing out a breath, I put my hands in my hoodie's pockets. "Alright, fine. I'll give you that. But I'm over him. I don't want to get back together."

"Good," she says, a spark lighting her eyes. "Because after what you told me about Parker last night, I was kind of hoping the two of you might get together."

A scoff bursts from my lips. "Seriously?" Now I'm regretting telling her about the family dinner with Parker, and the way we cozied up on the couch with each other after. She's seen us together and I guess I just wanted her to confirm that we'd never been quite like that during any of our previous TV hang outs.

I spear her with a glare. "You know we could never work. Tried the dating your friend thing and it went horribly, remember?"

She mimics the look I give her. "That was in high school, Jamie. You can't base what you share with Parker on some immature teenage relationship."

We stare at each other in silent challenge for who knows how many seconds. Finally, she shrugs. "I don't see what's stopping you. You guys get along great. He's hot, you're hot." She waggles her eyebrows, and I laugh. "And he invited you over to meet his parents last night..."

I start to shake my head and object, but she charges ahead. "And you said he was acting out of character...tucking your hair behind your ear, *rubbing your feet.*" She gives me a look. "It sounds to me like he's trying to up his game."

I groan and fall face first onto the bed beside her. "Why does everything have to be a game?" I grumble into the covers.

"What are you talking about?"

"Games!" I cry before sitting up to face her, gesturing wildly with my hands. "Men! Dating! All of it. Everything is a game! Mike's trying to manipulate me somehow, whether it's to get me back simply because he misses me or something else…and Parker's messing with my head—"

"I highly doubt Parker's trying to mess with your head—"

"And Stefan's moving all of his employees around like chess pieces, pitting us against each other just so one of us can come out on top to win this exclusive interview with Paris!"

"Okay, calm down," Daria says, voice like warm honey as she rubs a hand down my arm. "I don't think Stefan is trying to pit his employees against each other. Isn't he trying to bring you guys together with these activities?"

"That's what he says, but—"

"And maybe it's wrong of him to make you guys play nice in order to get this interview, but it could also mean that he's trying to watch and see which of you has the best people skills to be able to handle a celebrity like Paris."

"Okay, maybe, but—"

"And," Daria continues, undeterred, "out of everything you've said, the only thing that really adds up is that Mike trying to win you back right now is sketchy. Even if it is just because he misses you, a guy who doesn't realize that until after you've left the relationship isn't worth keeping around. Trust me." Something flickers in Daria's dark eyes, putting a crack in her stern resolve.

I know she's been hurt by guys in the past, just like I have, but something tells me her hurts go way deeper than mine. She's not one to divulge much about her past relationships, having been raised in multiple foster homes and not wanting to relive that part of her life, but I hope someday she'll be comfortable enough to share.

"Okay," I say. "Maybe you're right about *some* of that."

A proud smile curves her perfectly plump lips. "I know I'm right. Well, at least about Parker and Mike. Stefan, I'm not sure, but I'd like to think your boss has his employees' best interests at heart."

"Yeah, you and me both," I mutter, not at all sure that he does.

"Either way." She slaps the top of my thigh. "It's time for us to get an iced coffee. I promise you'll feel better once you're caffeinated and looking at plants."

My heart lifts at her encouragement and I smile. "You're right. Let's go get some coffee."

---

Everything seems brighter in the world once my hands are holding an iced venti maple pecan latte. My reusable shopping bag with a graphic that reads, "so many books, so little time," is slung over my shoulder with a romance novel in tow, bumping against my side. Usually after brunch, Daria and I sit in silence while I read a chapter or two of my novel, and she peruses the latest fashion magazines.

"I'm upset with you," Daria says, giving me some serious side-eye as we walk toward the farmer's market. Her tone is more flippant than serious, so I keep moving.

"Why? What'd I do?"

She stops and waves a hand over her body. "You didn't even notice my new dress."

I look her over, taking in every detail of the dress she must've whipped up this week. Daria's notorious for sewing a top or skirt, even an entire dress, all in one sitting. "It looks great, D. I love the pin-tucked waist look."

She smiles approvingly as she starts walking again. "Thanks. I actually made it from a men's shirt I found at the thrift store. It's super soft. Feel it."

I reach a hand out to finger the heathered gray fabric at her sleeve. "Wow, you're right. Your skills are impressive." Her lips barely lift any higher, but I know she's inwardly beaming at the praise.

An idea pops into my head. "Hey, maybe you can create a custom dress for Paris Dawson? Then if I get to interview her, I can gift her a totally unique, one-of-a-kind Daria Dantez creation."

She turns toward me with a skeptical look. "Girl. I'm a no-name designer currently working full-time in retail because I don't have enough cold hard cash to start my own business. What would a celebrity like Paris want with something I've made?"

"You're selling yourself short, D. Paris would be lucky to wear something you whipped up. And from what I hear, she's super down-to-earth. I mean, she did grow up not far from here. She'd probably be all about it."

My friend still doesn't look convinced, but when she falls silent, I hope she's thinking it over. Though she can be prickly at times, she's the truest friend I've ever had, and I so badly want to see her succeed at her dream of becoming a fashion designer.

She and I met at our local community college while she was taking business classes and I was getting my degree in journalism. Her quick wit and sarcastic personality instantly drew me, and we've been friends ever since.

When Pops started to lose his memory and checked into the care center, leaving his and Nonie's home to me, the thought of being by myself was overwhelming. I'd never lived alone before and even though the house was paid for, taking care of a house by myself would be a completely foreign experience. It spiked an entirely different level of anxiety when I was faced with that prospect. So Daria offered to become my roommate. Thankfully, her lease was up, and everything fell into place.

It's been amazing sharing a house with her these past nine or so months. She's not as tidy as I am, but she's funny and full of life and we get along great. Even when we don't see eye to eye on things.

Things like the idea that Parker may be into me.

I shove the thought away as we reach one of my favorite vendors, Meta Minerals and More. Stacey, the owner, smiles wide when she sees us approach. "Hey, girlies. How's your Saturday morning going?"

"Great!" Daria answers for both of us. "What's new this week?" Her eyes alight when they take in the sparkling geodes Stacey's artfully arranged on the table.

"Well, we've got these beautiful new amethyst stones in," Stacey replies, her voice fading into the background as I wander to the far end of the table where sparkly white heart-shaped stones catch my eye. The little chalk sign in front of the stones says, *Druzy White Lace Agate* and the price. I pick one of them up and rub it between my thumb and forefinger, inspecting its little divots and imperfections.

"That's a healing stone, you know." The masculine voice has me raising my head.

"Hey, Lionel." I greet Stacey's husband with a smile.

"You look like more of an onyx type of girl," he says before handing me a bracelet with a reflective black stone set in the center.

"Really?" I ask, setting down the white stone and inspecting the bracelet. "How come?"

"Well, every time I see you, you are wearing black."

I laugh, handing it back. "It is pretty." My eyes catch on a set of earrings to my right that sparkle in the sunlight. "Oh, wow. Those pink druzy earrings you've got there are gorgeous."

"They are," he says, picking them up and handing them to me. "Stacey and I actually made these together. It was a team effort."

I lift my gaze to meet his. "You're a dedicated husband, Lionel. Stacey is lucky to have you."

His grin widens. "I'd say it's the other way around. I'm lucky to have her." Considering me a moment longer, he says, "So, those the ones you want?"

Biting my lip, I debate splurging on the earrings I may never even wear. I mean, they *are* pink. Suddenly the memory of the lacy pink underpants resurfaces, and I swallow. "Um. No, not today. Thanks, though."

"You sure? I think they'd look great on you."

I smile, setting them back onto the table and backing up a step. "Not today. I'll think about it for next week, though."

He narrows his eyes like he knows the reason I'm shunning all things pink. "Okay. They'll be here if you change your mind."

"Ooh, are you getting those?" Daria asks, pointing to the earrings. "I'm getting this one." She holds up one of the smooth, pink stones she was eyeing earlier. "Stacey says it attracts men. We'll see." She spears Stacey with her signature raised eyebrow and the shop owner just laughs.

"That's not exactly what I said. But even if it doesn't attract the love you hope to find, it will look pretty on your nightstand." She and Daria exchange payment as we say our goodbyes, and then we're off again, moving toward my favorite vendor, Greg's Nursery. Unfortunately for me, the experience will be tainted by Mike's presence.

Is it wrong that I secretly hope he'll bail on me, and we can finally be done with all this nonsense? Of course, I'm not that lucky. As soon as the green awning for Greg's comes into view, I spot Mike's familiar form next to the tent's opening.

His brown hair is styled, and he looks effortlessly handsome in his dark jeans and hunter green Henley. He's scrolling through his phone with one hand while the other is stuffed in his jeans pocket when we approach.

"Want me to hang back?" Daria's whispered question stops me in my tracks.

"Would you?" I turn to face her, and she nods. "Just don't go far, okay? I'm hoping this won't take more than twenty minutes."

"For your sake, I hope you're right." She gives me a knowing look, then puts on her sunglasses and saunters away toward the aisle of fresh veggies.

Taking a deep inhale and releasing it slowly, I walk forward. "Hey, Mike."

As soon as he hears my voice, his head whips up. "Jamie." His smile is mega-watt. "Man, you look great. It's so good to see you." He pulls me into a lung-crushing hug, and I resist the urge to push him away. He must feel my stiff posture because he backs up with a grimace. "Sorry, it's just been too long. And you look even better than when I last saw you." As if he has the right to do so, he sweeps his gaze over me from head to toe.

"I'm wearing leggings and a band tee," I deadpan. "If you think I was dressing to impress, you're wrong."

Even my sarcastic ire doesn't trip him up. "You don't need to dress to impress. You're beautiful as is." The way his smile refuses to dim is disconcerting.

"So," I say, shifting my weight from side to side. "Want to…look around?" I motion inside Greg's tent, hoping to at least see if I can find a friend for Beatrice. She's getting lonely on my desk all by herself.

"Yeah, sure."

I move forward, eyeing this week's plants as Mike trails behind me. As much as I can, I focus on the green leaves, the different species of houseplants Greg carries, as well as the discounted fruit trees he's trying to unload before winter. But with Mike looming over me like a heavy storm cloud, I find it hard to focus.

"How Fluffy?" I ask, sneaking a look at Mike. He winces, probably because his cat was a sore spot in our relationship.

"Fine." We say nothing more as I try to enjoy plant shopping, but with Mike here, I just can't.

Chalking it up to a loss, I completely skip over the succulents and silently promise Beatrice that I'll go friend-hunting next week. We leave the tent, and I whirl on Mike. "This is weird."

His face falls a little, but he doesn't lose that infuriating smile. "I know, I just...I just want to be with you. Hang out."

My breathing turns rapid, and I can feel my nostrils beginning to flare. "You said you wanted to make things right with me. To apologize."

"Yes, I do."

"So do it."

He pauses a beat before straightening his posture, his brown eyes locking with mine. "Jamie, I'm sorry for not treating you like you deserved to be treated. I ditched you when I should've been a better boyfriend. Commitment is something I've always struggled with, but I realize now how childish I was being" His shoulders sag with the admission and I'm stunned by the genuine regret in his eyes. "Will you please forgive me?"

His apology is so sincere it almost breaks my resolve to cut him out of my life. "I...yes. I forgive you." *There. That wasn't so hard.* I swallow and avert my gaze.

"Thank you," he breathes. Taking my hand, he places it on his chest. "I'd like you to give me another chance. Please."

I meet his eyes, bristling at the contact, unsure where to go from here. His eyes are pleading, but I don't think I can give what they're asking. I truly don't want to hurt him when he's being so vulnerable. This is exactly the kind of thing that would've had me melting in his arms a month ago. If he'd have shown me this softer side then, maybe I would've stuck around even when he started to blow me off for his cat.

One thing I know for sure—I can't go any further until I know his motivations. Is it really that he misses me or is it something else?

"Why?" It's a simple one-word question. But how he answers matters.

"Why?" he repeats like he doesn't understand.

"Yes," I reiterate. "Why do you want another chance with me."

His brown eyes bounce back and forth between mine as he licks his lips. "Because I miss you, like I said. I realize now how good for me you were. And..." His quiet confidence falters as his eyelashes flutter.

"And what?" I set my jaw, biting the inside of my cheek.

"And there's this thing coming up. This...work dinner that's really important to my boss." He waits for me to respond, but the moment I shake my head and start to pull my hand away, he tightens his grip and rushes on with his explanation. "Please, just listen for five minutes, okay?"

"I don't owe you anything," I bite out, enraged.

"No, no you don't. You're right. I was an idiot to let you go, I see that now. And you don't owe me anything, but I'm asking you to listen. Just for five minutes."

His words puncture my steel resolve once again. Why can't I be as hard and unyielding as Daria is when it comes to exes?

"Fine. Spit it out."

His shoulders relax and he swallows, his Adam's apple bobbing. I take advantage of his relief and pull my hand away, crossing my arms under my chest.

"Family is super important to my boss," he says, stuffing his hands into his pockets. "His agency is a pillar in the community, a family-oriented business."

I start tapping my foot when he beats around the bush.

"And he's holding this big family insurance dinner where all of the clients and their families are invited to attend. It's at the Marshall's mansion on the edge of town. Have you heard of it?"

I nod. Almost everyone in Treemont has heard of the mansion-sized family home that was turned into a wedding venue a few years ago.

"Well, my boss, John, sort of gave me a…a talking to." For the first time since knowing Mike, pink tinges his cheeks and he looks embarrassed. "He basically said that it was time for me to take my work seriously and settle down with a family. That I'm twenty-nine and I'm not getting any younger. And he wants to turn the business over to me someday, but he needs to know I hold the same family-oriented ideals that he does before he does so."

My brows pull together of their own accord. "Mike, you shouldn't let your boss call the shots when it comes to your life." As soon as I say it, I cringe. Am I letting Stefan do that to me?

He dips his chin and rocks back on his heels. "I know. And I'm not, really, it's just…after he said all that, I got to thinking. I realized that the only woman who ever made me even consider settling down was…well, it was you. And I was too stubborn to see it at the time. It took you breaking up with me and completely ignoring me to see that we could really be great together."

I take a moment to consider everything he's telling me. His regret seems sincere, but if all this was spurred on by some lecture he got from his boss, how can I trust that it's real? And even if it is real, do I want to give another chance to a guy who couldn't see my worth while we were together?

# 10

♥

# PARKER

I'M SITTING ON THE couch, coffee in hand, with my laptop propped on my legs when Dane shuffles into our shared living space. His head tilts my way for half a second and he flashes me a peace sign. I lift my chin in acknowledgment and go back to my novel, trying to work out a plot hole.

I'm so engrossed in the task, I barely notice when Dane lowers himself to the other end of the couch, his own coffee near his lips. He takes a sip, then holds up a finger like he wants to keep my attention.

After setting his mug on the coffee table in front of us, he signs, "Heard you had a good night last night." His eyebrows bob up and down like I'm supposed to know what he means by that statement.

*I don't know what you're talking about.*

He cocks his head and narrows his eyes. "I think you do."

I take a deep breath and close my laptop. *Who have you been talking to.*

A slow, sinister sort of smile crosses his lips. "Mom. And Logan."

I purse my lips and look away, thinking over how to address this. Yes, I did, in fact, have a good night with Jamie last night. Introducing her to my family went way better than I expected. But something changed while we watched Mom's favorite drama, something that made her pull away from me—physically and emotionally.

She seemed embarrassed when she left, refusing to meet my eyes, and scuttling toward the door as soon as the show was over. Maybe it had to do with the way I pulled her feet into my lap. Making her uncomfortable was the very last thing I ever wanted to do, but if I did, I should apologize. Then Logan kept sending me weird looks while Mom beamed as bright as the sun. I had to get out of there almost as fast as Jamie.

*What did they say?* I finally sign to my brother, hoping they said more to him than they did to me.

He hikes a shoulder and picks up his coffee again. "Oh, just that you two got awfully cozy on the couch last night. Apparently, she *really* likes your foot rubs." He winks and I have the sudden urge to slap the coffee mug right out of his hands while simultaneously punching him.

*Whatever goes on between me and her is our business*, I sign, defending Jamie in the only way I know how. He quirks an eyebrow and goes back to his coffee before turning on his phone and scrolling through what I assume is the day's news.

What would make him, or Logan or Mom for that matter, think she really enjoyed what I was doing to her feet? She didn't give off those vibes when she pulled them off my lap, a blush coloring her cheeks. Had she said something I didn't catch?

Feeling the need to speak to her, I pull my phone out of my pocket and send her a text. I know she's at the farmer's market right now looking for a sibling for Beatrice. Or maybe it was a friend... Anyway, she always peruses the portable shops every Saturday until they close down at the end of October. So she may not see my text until she sits down for brunch with Daria. Either way, I want to check on her.

**Parker:** Good morning, beautiful. Thanks again for coming to family dinner last night. My mom says that you're the sweetest thing since they invented candy. *eye roll emoji*

I bite my lip, wondering if the addition of *beautiful* will throw her off. I've never referenced her looks before, at least not that I can remember. But if I'm going to make her fall in love with me, I've got to start expressing my feelings—just as subtly as possible so she doesn't outright reject my advances since I've been thoroughly friend zoned.

I scroll through social media when she doesn't text back right away. After a full minute, my phone buzzes in my hand, her name flashing on the top of the screen.

**Jamie:** You have impeccable timing. You literally just saved me from one of the most awkward moments of my life.

My interest piques.

**Parker:** That sounds serious. What happened?
**Jamie:** Can't talk yet. Still with Mike.

Annoyance flares to life in my chest, making it hard to think straight. Why is she with him?

As long as I've known Jamie, she's been a creature of habit. Sometimes I wonder if she likes the predictability of a routine because that's how her grandparents raised her or if it helps to ease her anxiety. Either way, she always goes to the market with Daria on Saturday mornings, eats brunch while she reads a romance novel or blogs, then spends her Sunday afternoons with her Pops at the care center. If I'd have thought guys were allowed to tag along to the market, I might've invited myself.

I blow out a frustrated breath and run a hand through my hair. No, I wouldn't have done that. Because I give her the space she deserves to be herself and enjoy time with her other friends. I'm just teeming with jealousy over the thought that Mike, her tool of an ex, is with her right now.

Maybe they aren't even at the farmer's market. What if she's at his place?

My fingers tingle with the need to text her back and ask what the heck is going on. But what right do I have to ask that question? I'm not her boyfriend. We aren't anything but friends.

Would a friend text her and ask her what she's doing with him, veering from her usual market and brunch routine?

A shove to my shoulder jolts me from my invasive thoughts. "Why do you look like you're about to murder something?" Dane asks.

*Because I feel like I want to murder something.* I don't sign that, but I do think it.

*No reason,* I respond as casually as possible. At that exact moment, my idiot brother swipes my phone out of my hands and jumps up from the couch. By the time I can wrestle him to the ground and pry it away from him, he's already read the text.

"Is Mike her ex?" he signs when I sit back on my heels, out of breath from tackling him.

I could ignore him, but what's the point when he'll just pester me until he gets an answer? *Yes.*

"Why is she with him?"

I rise to my feet, shoving my phone in my back pocket and tugging on the ends of my hair. Dane's questioning makes my initial annoyance flare into outright anger. I don't want to be this guy. Jealous. Overbearing. Insecure.

And yet thinking of Mike putting the moves on Jamie again has panic swelling within me so fast, it steals the breath right out of me. When I spin to face Dane again, he signs, "Maybe she has a good explanation. You should ask her."

I shake my head. *It's not my place. She has to work it out with him without my interference.*

"I get that, but you're her friend—her *concerned* friend—just checking in on her and making sure she's okay. She just said you saved her from an awkward interaction with him. What if he showed up somewhere out of the blue and it made her uncomfortable?"

My brother's words aren't doing anything to snuff out my swiftly rising anxiety.

"Dude, you could be her knight in shining armor right now if you play your cards right," he finishes, looking smug.

*I don't have any cards. This isn't a game.*

He gives me a chiding look. "I know it's not a game, I'm not saying that. I'm saying check on her. See how she's doing and why she's with him. If there's a way you can help, do it."

I consider what he's saying for all of half a second before I park myself back on the couch and text her again.

**Parker:** I know you said you can't talk, but just tell me if you're okay. If he's making you uncomfortable, I'll be there ASAP.

Her text comes through almost immediately.

**Jamie:** I promise, I'm fine. I'll tell you all about it later. Thanks for being an awesome friend.

*Friend.* The word hits me like a brick to the chest. It's what I want to be to her, it's what I *am* to her, but what I wouldn't give for her to let me be so much more.

# 11

♥

# JAMIE

"We won't be going on an outing this week," Stefan says, addressing the room with his hands planted on his hips. "I think we're all still a little bit frazzled after last week's...incident..." Thankfully, he doesn't meet my eyes, or anyone's eyes for that matter, when he says it.

"But we're still going to be doing a team-building activity," he finishes, scanning each of our faces. It almost looks like he's waiting for one of us to put up a fight. If we do, will he put down a mark against us?

Probably.

The Sign Language interpreter stands off to Stefan's right with a bright smile on her face the whole time she signs. I don't dislike the woman. She's pleasant, friendly. But her eyes sparkle when she looks at Parker and for some reason, that gives me indigestion. My intense reaction is concerning, honestly.

As I silently wonder if I should see a doctor about my sudden condition, Stefan waves Jordy forward. She brings over a wooden chair, then sets it down directly in front of Stefan, waving her hands Vanna White style as she backs away.

"Today we're going to be building some trust among our team members," Stefan says, gripping the back of the chair with both hands.

A guffaw works its way up my throat, but before I release it, I bite my cheek to keep it inside. He's literally *never* referred to us as team members before. *Welcome back, Cyborg Stefan.*

"This chair represents the level of trust I expect you all to have for each other." As soon as he says it, my eyes dart to Parker, whose gaze is already fixed on me. His eyes are wide as he blinks slowly. Stefan can't possibly expect us to...

"And each of you," Stefan continues with a gleeful smile in his voice, "will be displaying that trust when you fall backwards into the awaiting arms of the rest of your team members."

My stomach bottoms out. *Noooooo.*

Parker moves in closer to my side, leaning down and making the sign for *Why?*

I hold up my hands with a look that says, *how would I know?*

The interpreter's smile grows tight as if she's as unsure about this little trust fall experiment as we are. Gladys raises her hand, then speaks without waiting to be called upon.

"I can't climb onto that chair. I've got bad knees." She raises one obstinate eyebrow as if daring Stefan to object to her claim.

"Well, you'll still be a perfect candidate to catch your teammates."

She purses her lips, her coral lipstick crinkling into the lines around her mouth. "I've got bad elbows too."

Stefan jingles his keys in his pants pockets. "Gladys, you're participating and that's final."

Her shoulders rise and fall on a deep exhale, but she makes no other moves to argue.

"Um, excuse me, Mr. Sanders?" Lucas interjects. "I'm a little uncomfortable putting my trust in others when my safety is on the line. Is there any way we could cushion the floor before we begin?"

Our boss releases a weary sigh. "I've already thought of that but thank you for admitting that you don't trust your co-workers." Lucas sputters while Stefan motions Jordy over once more. She drags over a long, padded mat that looks like it came straight from a kid's gymnastics class. Maybe he borrowed it from his new friend, Miss Fowler.

At least now that we have a padded fall, I know my boss isn't *completely* insane.

Stefan goes on to explain exactly where he wants everyone to stand while the lucky guinea pig gets to position themselves on the chair and fall backwards. Into the arms of everyone else. Hopefully.

Anxiety buzzes along my skin like an itchy rash as I tune out, utterly dazed after the odd weekend I've had and now this. First the family dinner at Parker's parents' home. It was awesome at first but left off on a weird note. Plus, there's this stilted...something...between us today that I can't quite put my finger on. Then, there was the upheaval of my Saturday morning routine thanks to Mike. And the subsequent conversation and invitation he laid on me afterward.

I still haven't explained it all to Parker. Every time I tried, the words got lodged in my throat. I know he's not going to be happy that I entertained Mike at all, let alone told him I'd consider his offer.

Mercifully, Stefan announces he will be going first to demonstrate his trust in us, his employees. Which honestly feels a little convenient. There isn't a soul in this office that's not going to try and keep him from falling to his death. *Hello, he signs our paychecks!*

We all gather around the kindergarten play mat, as previously instructed, and hold out our arms. Parker takes a spot right next to me and his skin brushes mine, sending little electric tingles spreading through me.

I shouldn't be having these types of thoughts about him when I already know that crossing the line of friendship would ruin us...But he's just so warm and sweet...

"Ready?" Stefan calls out, looking down over his shoulder at us. I swing my gaze over the people standing around me. Glady's arms are barely extended out in front of her, while the sheen of sweat that lines Lucas's brow says he's as nervous as I feel. Eric's tongue is sticking out in concentration and Les stands, legs spread, at the ready. And me and Parker? Well, I think we're just both praying for a miracle.

"Here I go!"

That's the last thing our misguided boss says before falling backward into Les's face, busting open his lip, breaking his nose, and knocking him unconscious.

"I don't even know what to say," I whisper to Parker as I take a sip from my giant water jug. "I mean, I knew it was going to be bad but...*that* bad?" I cringe again, thinking of how blood dripped from poor Les's messed up face while we all worked to get it under control. Parker sits on the floor of my cubicle, legs crossed, with an equally horrified expression.

I guess some mental images just can't be erased.

If Stefan thought that innocent little kid sticking a paperclip into the electrical socket was a lawsuit waiting to happen, he's got to know this is much, *much* worse. As far as the rest of us are concerned, he knowingly endangered his employees with this little trust fall nonsense.

*I feel bad for him,* Parker signs.

"Who? Les?"

*Surprisingly, Stefan. I think he's been genuine in trying to bring the employees together even though nothing has gone the way he planned.*

I lift one shoulder in a half-hearted shrug. "I get that, I do. But if I were him, I'd have taken one look at our group as a whole and known that this team-building stuff would never work."

*That's because you're a realist.*

I scoff a laugh. "A realist or a pessimist?" I shake my head at myself. It's true that I try to look at things from a practical perspective, but it's also true that lately, a certain kind of jadedness has colored my interactions with almost everyone.

I don't want to be perpetually annoyed, but losing Pops as my support system with all the other weird stuff going on lately has sent me into a grump slump.

Parker rests a hand on my knee and his warmth seeps through my black dress pants almost instantaneously. After a moment, he signs, *You are too hard on yourself.*

My lips turn upward a little, but before they stretch any further, a delivery girl skips up to my cubicle with a large bouquet of flowers. "Delivery for Jamie DeFreese," she says in a sing-song voice with a smile aimed straight at me.

"Umm, o-okay. Thanks." I tentatively take the flowers and shoot a quick glance at Parker. His confused expression tells me these definitely aren't from him. Not that I thought they would be. We. Are. *Friends.*

"Have a nice day," the young girl chimes as she takes off back toward the hall.

I scan the flowers for the small card I know is attached and my breath catches when I see who it's from. *Jamie*, the card reads. *I know you're still unsure about us, but please believe me when I say that I've never been more sure. You're the one for me. I'm sorry I couldn't see it sooner. -Mike.*

"Mike sent me flowers." My toneless explanation garners a hissing sound from Parker I've never heard him make before.

Lifting my focus from the flowers, I see that he's annoyed by the tightness in his shoulders and the muscles bulging in his neck. It's then I remember that I was supposed to explain to him what happened this weekend.

I set the flowers on my desk, then sign to Parker, "I saw Mike this weekend." I watch his reaction closely, but other than the slight downturn of his mouth, nothing in his expression changes.

I turn toward Beatrice and run one of her thick leaves in between my fingers while I gather the courage to tell him. "Mike texted and called me on Saturday morning, waking me up," I say while signing, making sure my voice is low enough that no one nearby my cubicle would be able to overhear. Parker leans down, paying attention.

"He begged to see me," I continue. "And before you go getting mad at me for giving into him, I made sure and told him I wasn't comfortable having brunch with him. I only wanted a short meeting where he could say what he wanted to say."

The slightest lift of Parker's lips gives me the courage to continue.

"So, he met me at Greg's tent. And then proceeded to hug me and tell me I looked better than ever, which totally weirded me out. I finally just made him spit it all out. He apologized for not treating me right when we were together and told me he's been thinking a lot about settling down."

I pause before relaying the last part of the story. "And he asked me to go with him to a work party where his boss and all of their clients will be in attendance."

Parker looks down at his shoes, the muscles in his jaw feathering as he flicks the laces over and over. When he looks away, it's his tell that he doesn't want to hear the rest of what I have to say. And knowing this nearly breaks my heart. He's genuinely concerned for me when it comes to Mike. And rightfully so, I guess.

But there's also a hint of something more in his reaction. Something that I weirdly wish was jealousy. Maybe if he was bothered by Mike the way I get bothered by his sweet little interpreter, maybe I wouldn't feel so lousy about the way I feel when she's around.

I gently nudge his knee with my shoe, and he meets my eyes. "I told him I could never go with him to a party like that as his date when I didn't have romantic feelings for him anymore."

Something akin to hope alights in Parker's eyes as he stares at me. It unsettles me so much, I almost forget what I was going to say next.

*What did he say?* he asks.

"He said he was disappointed but that he completely understood. And then he asked me out on an actual date."

Parker gives me a slow nod as one of his dark eyebrows quirks, waiting for more, I'm sure.

"I told him I wasn't interested," I say. "But before he left, he asked me to just think about it. He said he wants me to consider him as a boyfriend again before I outright reject him."

*Did you say you would?*

I shrug. "What was I supposed to say? I'm not heartless, Parker. Besides, we dated for seven months. That's the longest I've ever been with a guy. And if I'm being honest, I miss having someone like that."

*I understand*, he signs with what I know is a forced smile. *You're a good person.*

My heart stutters when he stands and pulls me into a tight hug. If I'm such a good person, then why does telling Parker about Mike make me feel so...wrong?

# 12

♥

# Parker

The past week at the office has flown by. After the trust fall disaster on Monday, Stefan locked himself in his office for two days. That was until he sent us the email about our next excursion. I really thought after what happened with Les, he'd get off this employee morale boosting thing, but it seems to have only been a hiccup.

In the email, he explained that he'd already booked this activity, and he felt as if it was safe for everyone to take part and enjoy a little time out of the office. But then he went on to tell us what we'd be doing.

I almost choked on my coffee when I read that we'll be visiting an outdoor safari, complete with live animals. And in true Jamie fashion, as soon as she read it, she popped over to my side of the cubicle with a horrified expression. *"A safari?!"*

I guess it would be one thing if said field trip related to our jobs at the paper, but much like the pumpkin patch fiasco, this excursion, in no way, pertains to writing and reporting. Unless we're going to record the eating and pooping patterns of giraffes, I'm pretty sure it's a moot point.

Now the day of the field trip has come, and I'm starting to lose faith that these excursions will help make Jamie fall in love with me. Yes, we've been getting more time together, but her feelings seem all over the place when it comes to Mike and me.

It's clear she misses having a boyfriend, but it also looks like she sees Mike as more of a prospect than me. Can she envision what a romantic relationship would be like between us? I thought we shared a few charged moments in the past few weeks, but maybe I'm just reading what I want into our interactions.

It's hard to tell at this point.

Especially when Jamie's head rests lazily against my shoulder as we bump along in the tour bus Stefan rented out for this little excursion.

I crane my neck to see if Jamie has dozed off, but when I look down, she turns her head toward me. For a split second, our faces are just inches apart and her warm breath fans over my neck. It sends an unexpected tremor through me, but when she feels it, she pulls way. Instantly, I regret my body's reaction.

"Sorry," she says as she tucks a stray piece of hair behind her ear with a timid smile. "Your shoulder was just more comfortable than the window."

*Any time,* I sign to her, meaning it.

Before we boarded the bus, Jamie explained that she'd been studying up on animal signs that she could practice today. I laughed it off like a joke, and she swatted my arm. I might have made light of it, but knowing she makes an extra effort to learn Sign Language warms my heart.

I'll just have to make an effort of my own to teach her the proper signs for each animal we see today, in case her research was lacking. It's easy for me to imagine just the two of us wandering around alone today. Me, showing her how to make signs with her hands, her speaking to me with her full, pouty lips...

An abrupt stop sends my forehead slamming into the seat in front of me. I make a face and rub the spot, feeling heat creep into my cheeks.

What kind of loser embarrasses himself in front of a girl because he was daydreaming *about* that girl?

Jamie places both her hands on my face and turns my head toward her. "Are you okay?"

*No. Not even a little bit,* I think. How can I be okay when her brow puckers with such sweet concern and her hands are holding my face so tenderly?

I simply nod, because the more I think about it, the longer I stare into her eyes, the more I realize how hard it's going to be to tell my best friend how severely she affects me. It will inevitably affect *us*. And do I really have the courage to blow past the line of friendship we've safely built over the past year?

Something or someone at the front of the bus grabs Jamie's attention and I follow her gaze. Stefan stands, addressing everyone. He's too far away for me to catch what he's saying, but by his gestures, I kind of get the gist. I definitely caught the word *partners* and he's holding a clipboard in his hands. Is he going to let us choose our partners again?

Jamie's expression has fallen considerably. She looks like someone just sentenced her to an afternoon of cleaning toilets. I nudge her shoulder and try to offer her an encouraging smile.

She turns toward me with a frown. "He's splitting us up today. We will each have an assigned partner that we're tasked with getting to know better throughout the day."

I'm sure my expression mimics hers as I face Stefan. He offered to have the ASL interpreter come with us today, but I insisted she not. I'm more than capable of taking in the sights and reading signage. Don't get me wrong, I'm grateful to have a job that makes accommodations for my deafness, but sometimes it feels good to just mesh into the crowd. I don't need someone following me around all day reminding me that I see the world through a different lens than the rest of my co-workers.

Besides, I assumed that I would get to be with Jamie all day and I have no problem staring at—I mean *reading*—her lips.

People around us start to stand and everyone begins to exit the bus. Jamie turns to me signing, "I'm sorry to tell you that you're with Lucas." Her stare goes cold as she finishes with, "And I'm with Les."

It's a miracle that Les is still at work with what happened earlier in the week. I would've thought he'd be a least a little bitter about getting accidentally beat up by our boss, but he legit returned to work the next day with a bandage on his nose and a smile on his face.

I wrap my arm around Jamie's shoulders and give her what I hope is a bolstering squeeze before rising and following everyone else off the bus. My assigned partner isn't my favorite person, but it could be worse. I could be stuck with Jordy, the girl who slaps my arm every five seconds to show me something or get my attention.

The only good thing about being stuck with Lucas is that I won't feel obligated to be polite to him. And since I can't hear him speak, I can easily tune him out by turning my head away from him.

When I make it off the bus, I wrinkle my nose at the distinct smell of animals living nearby. My partner—an unwilling partner by the looks of it—is waiting for me toward the rear of the bus with his arms crossed. He looks as excited as I am that we're assigned to each other.

I make my way to him and raise my chin in greeting. He grimaces in response.

When I turn around to make sure Jamie is taken care of, my foot catches on something hard and I stumble, falling to my hands and knees. Lucas quickly jerks back his foot as I catch myself. The hard gravel of the parking lot digs into my palms and knees. I quickly jump to my feet and glare at the man I'm sure intended to make me look like a klutz a moment ago.

Lucas holds his hands up in mock surrender. "It's not my fault you don't watch where you're going."

Really? So that's how this day is going to go? Perfect.

Instead of watching my feet, I'd rather watch my fist slam into Lucas's smug face, but I also don't want to get fired, so I refrain. Besides, my dad taught me a long time ago that violence is never the answer. I release a frustrated breath as I swipe my gravel-peppered hands on my pants legs.

A soft hand on my arm guides my attention away from my annoying partner. "Are you Okay?" Jamie asks for the second time in the last fifteen minutes.

*Yes, you?*

She nods and hooks a thumb over her shoulder. "Better get back to my partner."

*Let's meet later.* I turn my gaze to Les, who's already snapping pictures of the signs in the parking lot with his smartphone like a tourist. I stifle a laugh for Jamie's sake, then give her an affectionate chuck under the chin before walking off to join Lucas.

I'm not sure how this day is going to pan out when it's all said and done, but I'm already over it.

---

One excruciatingly long hour later, I find myself not knowing a single thing more about my partner. And that's just the way I like it.

Everything I've witnessed of Lucas today proves that he's a shallow, self-centered guy who makes no qualms about ogling women. And not just overtly attractive women, either. I'm talking women of all shapes, sizes, and ages. It's like he can't help himself.

So, I guess I did actually learn one thing about him. His type is *all* types.

Thirty minutes ago, when we were in the albino alligator exhibit, I caught him trying to strike up a conversation with a young mom who had three kids in tow. Her wide eyes darted between me and Lucas, silently pleading with me to promptly remove him, which I did, much to Lucas's dismay.

But the incident didn't stop him from cozying up to the middle-aged staff worker at the eagle exhibit, who was sharing facts with us about the bald eagle. I couldn't hear her giggle but judging by the way her shoulders shook and her eyes danced as Lucas sidled up to her, she soaked in his flirtations like a sponge.

Of course, my *partner* took it upon himself to announce to anyone who spoke directly to me that I couldn't hear them. Each time he'd narrow his eyes my way with that infuriating smug smirk of his too. I don't mind when a friend or family member does it if I can't see a person who's trying to communicate with me, but to go out of his way to tell people I can't hear them when I'm already paying attention is annoying.

I know Lucas thinks he's better than me because he has use of all of his senses, but I don't care. My sensory difference has no bearing on my ability to read a situation. I'd rather have self-awareness—something that Lucas clearly lacks—any day.

I reluctantly follow Lucas into a large aviary that houses birds of all kinds, according to the sign outside, careful to put some space between us. I don't want any of his poor, unsuspecting victims thinking that I'm with him. I wish I wasn't.

When we enter the aviary, clusters of people mill around the space, looking up into the tree branches, eyeing the different small birds. I lift my gaze to where a cardinal sits on a branch, cocking its head from side to side as its mouth opens and closes rapidly with each chirp.

What I wouldn't give to be able to hear the sound a bird makes.

Before I trip into a pit of melancholy, I make my way further into the aviary and see a familiar figure at the edge of one of the groups of people. *Jamie.*

I make my way over to where she stands, but she doesn't see me coming. She turns toward a bird feed dispenser and places two quarters into the slot. When she turns the knob, bird seed pours into the metal cup at the bottom, and I wait as Jamie collects it into her palm.

When her hands are full, I step behind her and cover her eyes with my hands. As soon as my hands touch her face, I remember petting that sloth a while ago and hope that my hands don't smell like a wild animal. I made sure to use hand sanitizer afterward, but still.

Jamie spins around and when she sees it's me, her face lights up. "I knew it was you. I'm glad you found me."

I smile wide, beyond glad I found her too. And not just here at the wildlife park, but in life. Just having her around makes everything seem better.

"Here," she says, lifting the bird seed in her hand.

I hold my palm out, and she pours some inside. I watch, enraptured, as she lifts her hands into the air and a small bluebird lands on her palm. It feverishly pecks at the bird seed, then flits away before another small bird replaces it.

I follow Jamie's lead and raise my own palm into the air. But instead of a bird gracefully lighting onto my hand, a disgusting squirt of grayish-white liquid plops on the center of my wrist.

I frown at the offending bird poop while Jamie tosses her head back and laughs. The way her shoulders shake sends a bittersweet feeling coursing through me. As much as I wish I could hear the chirp of a bird, I'd give almost anything to hear the sounds coming from Jamie's beautiful mouth right now.

The sight of her this amused is so lovely it *almost* makes getting pooped on worth it.

Almost.

---

Another hour later, I'm walking up to the camels beside a beaming Lucas. Apparently, one of the staff workers in the petting zoo gave him her number and he's floating away on cloud nine. I, on the other hand, am sweaty and irritable from having to be Lucas's social buffer all day long.

As we approach the camels, a small group of people fills a platform to my right. When I spot Jamie and Les talking to a worker, I step closer. Jamie keeps nodding at the worker, while Les rubs his hands together like a man with an evil plan. If his shiny face wasn't exuding boyish excitement right now, I might be a little worried.

After the worker finishes speaking, he steps toward Jamie and helps her into a saddle on the camel's back.

*What? Is she really going to...*

I quickly glance around and find a sign that reads *Camel Rides, $10*. When I look back, Jamie's already seated on the camel and Les is planted behind her looking happier than a kid at an amusement park. Jamie's face, however, doesn't hold the same excitement. In fact, she looks terrified. Her white knuckles grip the saddle horn in front of her, her body stick straight.

I step up to the railing that separates onlookers from the camel corral and whistle to get her attention. She immediately turns her head my way. I wave, offering her an encouraging thumbs-up. Her responding smile is apprehensive and she doesn't wave back.

Just then, the camel starts ambling forward, making Jamie and Les's bodies sway from side to side. Jamie's eyes grow wide as she keeps a tight hold on the saddle horn. The worker leading the camel wears a carefree grin that eases the discomfort I feel from watching Jamie struggle with fear. Even though she clearly doesn't seem to be enjoying this ride, the worker at least appears capable.

As the camel makes a turn around the paddock, Les waves an arm up in the air like he's riding a bull. Something about the way he moves must disrupt the camel because it stumbles to one knee, forcing Jamie and Les to lurch forward.

On instinct, I jump the fence and start toward them, but quickly get detained by another park worker who I didn't see standing off to the side. All I can spare him is a brief glance. I know he's probably telling me to keep a safe distance from the animals, but that's not easy when Jamie needs me.

I helplessly watch as their worker frantically tries to right the camel, but the animal struggles to remain upright. By some miracle, Jamie's rigid body remains in the seat, even though Les is pressed up against her from behind, arms caging her in.

I can't make out her expression from this far away, but I imagine this situation is doing a number on her anxiety. I struggle against the park worker's hold, wishing I could be by Jamie's side to help. When the man detaining me seems to get more upset, I pull out of his grasp and walk backward to the fence, raising my arms in surrender.

A shove against my back draws my attention away from the camel and onto Lucas. His mouth is flapping up and down while he tosses a handful of popcorn into it. He points toward where Jamie is straining to keep hold of the camel. The only word I can decipher between his obnoxious chewing is the word *girlfriend*.

Deciding to ignore him, I turn back to see if the worker was able to help Jamie and Les. My chest constricts as the scene with Jamie takes a frightening turn. The worker, still trying to pull the camel upright, yanks too hard and Jamie loses her grip and tumbles forward.

Without thinking, I bolt past the worker who kept me back a minute ago and rush toward her. She rolls on the ground as Les hangs on the back of the camel for dear life.

When I get to her, I gently shift her onto her back and take in her dirt-covered face. I quickly run my hands along her body taking a mental assessment of her legs and arms, assuring myself that nothing is broken. She meets my eyes with an intensity I've never before seen on her beautiful face.

With shaky hands, I quickly sign, *You OK?*

She nods and reaches for me. By the time I've righted her, Les has safely made it to the ground while a worker leads the uninjured camel away.

I wrap my arm around Jamie and steer her back toward the railing when another worker rushes up to us. Jamie waves him off, but I know better than to think she's unaffected by what just happened.

It shook her, I can tell. She's quivering in my arms and leaning her body into mine like she's depending on me to hold her upright.

When we reach the gate next to the platform, the rest of our work group has assembled to check on Jamie and Les. I loosen my hold as people crowd her, asking if she's okay. At least, I assume that's what they're asking. Most of their mouths are moving so fast, it's hard for me to keep up. I ease away from everyone and stand back.

I need to make sure she's not more injured than she's letting on. But before I get my chance, a woman who looks like the park manager approaches with Stefan and a man holding a medic bag. They direct Jamie to a nearby bench and look her over.

While the medic checks all of Jamie's vital signs, Jordy scoots in beside her and holds up her phone screen for Jamie to see. Her face drains of all color as her lips part before her hand flies to the bridge of her nose, pinching it tight. I can only guess what Jordy's showing her, but if it's what I think it is, it's not going to be good for Jamie.

After she's been thoroughly checked, she makes her way to me with a sickened expression. "She got the whole thing on camera, Parker."

*Are you OK, though?* I ask. *No injuries?*

She grabs my shoulders, giving me a shake. "No, I'm not *okay*. Didn't you see what I just said? Jordy recorded my very public, very *embarrassing* brush with death. My camel debacle. My fall from grace. The single most humiliating moment of my life. Yes, I'm injured. My pride will never again be intact." Her head falls into her hands, and she shakes it back and forth.

I place my hand on her shoulder and squeeze. She peeks up at me and I sign, *Did Jordy also record my rescue?* I'm hoping to ease her anxiety with a little humor. I can only pray it works.

She flashes me a small smile and rolls her eyes. "Yeah, I suppose she did. Lucky you." She pokes me in the chest. "In your fifteen minutes of fame, you get to look like a real-life Clark Kent. Pretty soon, we'll have lines of ladies waiting outside the *Gazette* wanting the handsome Parker's autograph."

Her little lecture does nothing to stop the grin as wide the Ohio River from spreading across my face.

Jamie thinks I'm handsome.

# 13

♥

# JAMIE

On the evening of the most humiliating day of my life, I lay slumped on the couch in my Hello Kitty robe, wondering where I went wrong. Was it when I started working for the *Gazette* two years ago or somewhere in between?

Maybe it was when I decided to be a hero and give Les Jenkins the thrill of a lifetime. I had no idea when I agreed to ride the camel with him that I'd be thrown from the animal, eating dirt in the process. It looked perfectly safe at the time. I watched another couple ahead of us ride without a hitch.

Sure, I was apprehensive, as anyone who is boarding a larger-than-life animal would be, but I never would have suspected that things would take such an embarrassing turn. It was bad enough knowing Parker and my other co-workers were watching, let alone finding out all of Jordy's ten thousand Instagram followers had too.

Who knew she had that many followers, anyway? I mean, it just seems excessive. And another thing, who goes live on Instagram while their co-worker is being *thrown* from a camel's back? *Who*, I ask, *who*?!

"Are you going to sit there all night and sulk?" Daria's unsympathetic voice jerks me out of my self-loathing.

I send her a stern glare. "Possibly." Picking up the remote, I scroll through the romantic comedy options on Netflix. "Don't you have a date tonight?"

Daria plants her hands on her slender hips and stares me down. "Yes, I have a date. But I also have a best friend who got thrown off a camel today, so if you're going to pout and want someone to whine to, I'm here. If not, I'll go. You decide."

Leave it to Daria to get straight to the point. I love that my friend is blunt and brutally honest, but sometimes I wish she'd be gentle and coddle me like I'm five. I sigh. Just because I'm miserable doesn't mean she should be too.

"I'll be fine. I'm just going to water my plant babies and watch something funny while eating a pint of Rocky Road." I tilt my head from side to side. "I may even listen to some Shania. She always puts me in a better mood."

Daria's lips tick upward into a small smile as she crosses her arms. "Why don't you text Parker? Maybe he can keep you company while I'm out."

My stomach flip-flops and I pull my robe a smidge tighter. "Uh, no. I won't be texting Parker. He witnessed that whole debacle today. The last thing I want is to rehash what happened and see the pity in his eyes. Plus, I think I scared the poor guy to death."

Daria laughs. "Oh, I know you did. Don't forget, we all saw how he raced to get to you when you went tumbling. In fact...," Daria swipes her phone off the kitchen counter and scrolls through it. "It looks like fifty-six *thousand* plus people saw Parker rush to your aid today."

I groan and plant my face into the couch cushion. I have a love/hate relationship with social media. I love how easy it can be to connect with people, especially through writing and blogging, but I also hate how everyone is *so* connected. My embarrassing moment from earlier has reached viral status in just a matter of hours.

"Don't remind me," I mumble into the cushion. Daria's laugh echoes down the hall.

"I probably won't be long tonight, anyway," Daria calls from the bathroom. "This is a first date, remember? If the guy lasts past the first twenty minutes, I'll be surprised."

Sometimes, I don't understand my friend. She's stunning and fun and has no trouble finding dates. But she can also be as prickly as a cactus when it comes to men. She's not lying when she says that most of the guys she dates don't make it past the first twenty minutes. It's like Daria makes it her personal mission to run every interested guy off. If they do manage to last past one date, they never usually make it more than a couple of weeks before she's naming every single one of their flaws and moving on.

I'd like to put all the blame onto my friend for her serial dating ways, but I can't. Her hard exterior and verbal armor seem to be products of never having anyone to rely on in her younger years as she was passed from foster home to foster home. Plus, her cheating ex in college didn't help soften her any to the opposite sex.

The clacking of her heels across the hardwood floor draws my attention. When she does a little spin in front of me, I whistle. "Dang, girl, you look hot!"

"Thanks! It was my first time sewing an off-the-shoulder top but I kinda like it."

"Me too! I guarantee your date will last more than twenty minutes once he sees you like this."

She shakes her head, adjusting her armful of bracelets. "We shall see." Grabbing her purse from the coffee table, she heads for the front door. "I'll see you later, alligator." She opens the door, then stops and turns. "Just promise me you won't order the popcorn shrimp from Pow Kow tonight, okay?" She gags then finishes with, "Last time you mixed shrimp with ice cream, it wasn't pretty."

I wave her off. "Don't worry, I won't. I have no desire to wake up tomorrow in a pile of my own—"

"Ew! Stop! I'm leaving." Daria shoves her fingers in her ears as she walks out the door, slamming it shut behind her.

I laugh and snuggle deeper into my robe. Pulling a fuzzy blanket off the back of the couch, I scoot into a more comfortable position, lying on my side. As I scroll through Netflix, my phone buzzes underneath me. I grumble, shifting to reach it. When I tap the screen, there's a text from Parker. My stomach immediately takes an odd little dip.

**Parker**: How's it going, Camel Whisperer?

I roll my eyes. I want to be mad that he's making fun of me, but I can never be mad at him.

**Me**: Never been better. Not only am I internet famous now, but I also have a goose egg the size of Ohio on my left knee. I think I should probably ice it. So, ya know, I'm just living the dream over here!

**Parker**: Aw, I'm sorry, James. I shouldn't have made fun of you. Want me to bring you an ice pack? Or snacks? I think we're due a movie night, anyway.

Once again, my stomach takes a dive like I just crested the hill of a small rollercoaster, especially at his use of my nickname. I shift from my side and sit up, hoping the change in position will get me off this ride.

**Me**: No, that's OK. I'd rather wallow in my shame alone tonight.
**Parker**: :(

**Me**: No, seriously. I'm fine. I'm just sitting on the couch about to turn a movie on.

**Parker**: I can be there in ten…

**Me**: Stahhhpppp. I don't need you to coddle me tonight. I'm perfectly fine questioning all of my life choices by myself, thank you.

**Parker**: K. Be there in 10.

I sigh and fall back against the couch cushions. Let it be known that I did try to thwart his attempt to baby me. Not that I wouldn't love to have his company… I'm just still so embarrassed after today.

Against my better judgment, I watched the little incident that was plastered all over social media an hour ago. And let me tell you, if I hadn't been the one falling off the camel, I would have seen it and instantly laughed my head off. It was hilarious. I get why it went viral so quickly. But I'm finding out that being the butt of a joke isn't all it's cracked up to be.

In the two hours that I've been home, I've received dozens of messages on my social pages asking if I'm okay or if they can get my hot rescuer's number. Not to mention the frantic call from Mike that said he saw the whole thing online and wanted to make sure I was okay.

It took five minutes to convince him I was fine and didn't need him checking up on me. Yet again, he insisted he still has feelings for me and urged me to think about giving him another chance. Like I need to deal with that right now. Ugh.

My phone buzzes again.

**Parker**: Should I bring Rocky Road or Mint Chocolate Chip?

I smile at the way he knows me so well.

**Me**: I'm already locked and loaded. Thanks though. Just make sure you bring an extra blanket. I don't feel like sharing tonight.

**Parker**: :( Alright. If you insist.

I stare at the frowny emoji for longer than necessary. If I didn't know better, I'd say he was being a tad flirty with me. He would never normally make a sad face at a comment like that. Was he hoping to share a blanket with me?

Suddenly feeling self-conscious, I run to the bathroom to make sure I look presentable. My reflection in the mirror above the sink reveals my top knot is a little lopsided, so I tighten it and run a makeup wipe over my face. I don't need to add smudged makeup to the list of things Parker can make fun of me for.

As of right now, he's got quite the list. Falling out of my chair at work and flashing him my one and only pair of lacy pink undies? Check. Being a co-conspirator to the accidental electrocution of a minor? Check. Falling off a camel's back in front of all my co-workers? Also check. Having said incident recorded live for everyone on the interwebs to witness? Quadruple check.

I lose the Hello Kitty robe, thinking it's not exactly movie-watching-with-your-boy-bestie attire. Thankfully, the pink sweatpants and gray T-shirt I have on underneath don't have any stains or holes, so I don't need to change. I hurry and tidy up a bit so Parker won't think Daria and I live like slobs. There's not much to clean up, but there are a few dirty dishes on the counter and a bra hanging in the bathroom.

As soon as I get ready to plop back down on the couch, the doorbell rings. I answer it, totally unprepared for the vision of sexy comfort that is my best friend. Parker looks even better than he did earlier. He's freshly showered, wearing gray sweatpants with a white T-shirt that stretches taut over his chest and conveniently hugs his biceps. He smiles down at me with his fluffy blanket in one hand and a bag of pizza rolls in the other.

I give him an appraising look. "I told you I was locked and loaded."

He simply smiles wider and shrugs. I wave him in, and he sets the food on the counter, then immediately turns to me and signs, *Did you eat?*

I shake my head. I wasn't planning to eat real food tonight, just binge on ice cream. Not that I classify pizza rolls as *real* food, but I know Parker does. He turns to the cabinet beside the stove and grabs a baking sheet. After tearing open the bag of pizza rolls, he spreads them out in a thin layer, sets them in the oven, and adjusts it to the right time and temperature.

Turning to me, he signs, *Let's ice that goose egg*, then leans into the freezer and grabs a bag of frozen peas.

When he comes around the kitchen island toward me, I'm stuck in place, my eyes glued to him. He's always been such a good friend to me, but tonight feels different. He's taking care of me in a way that feels *more* than friendly. More like, *boy*-friendly.

As he approaches, he sets the peas on the counter and looks me up and down. *Is pink your favorite color now?*

When I don't immediately respond, he points at my legs. Understanding dawns and he grins from ear to ear. I rush forward to swat his arm, but he's too fast. He giggles as he runs around my kitchen island, evading my reach.

Out of breath from chasing him, I pout and sign, *You're mean*.

He mock frowns with a remorseful look. *I'm sorry. I promise, I'll stop.* Coming toward me, he places his hands on my shoulders and steers me toward the couch. Once there, he motions for me to sit and tosses my blanket at me, laughing when it pelts me in the face.

*The turd.*

After grabbing the bag of peas and gently placing it on my knee, he situates himself beside me on the couch. My stomach tightens when he grabs his own fuzzy blanket and drapes it over both of us. Parker's manly, freshly showered scent wraps around me and I want nothing more than to snuggle up against him, close my eyes and breathe him in while nestling my face into his nicely defined chest.

But I don't. Because friends don't do that kind of thing, right?

Instead, I grab the remote and scroll through our viewing options for the evening, double checking that the captions are on.

After asking him what he feels like watching, and him just shrugging in response, I go to my usual favorites. When he spots *My Best Friend's Wedding*, he taps my hand and points. I click on the movie and sink further under my blanket. This one is a favorite of mine, but I'm kind of surprised that Parker chose it. He almost always just lets me pick.

When the buzzer on the oven sounds, I start to rise, but Parker grabs a hold of my wrist. *Let me. They're done?*

At my nod, Parker hops up and goes into the kitchen. A minute later, he returns with two plates loaded down with pizza rolls and two flavored sparkling waters tucked under his arm.

I smile as he hands me one of each and sign, *Thank you*.

Neither of us tries to make conversation as we eat and watch the movie together. But I love the way Parker chuckles when something strikes him as funny. His laugh is so genuine. He never tries to stifle it to keep from disturbing someone else, he just is who he is without caring what others think of him.

He turns and meets my gaze, a question in his eyes. *Ready for ice cream?*

I shake my head and pat my stomach. "I'm so full, I don't think I can right now."

Parker feigns shock and falls back against the couch cushions. I playfully bump his shoulder and he returns my smile. Then he does something so unexpected, I don't know how to properly respond. He sprawls out onto the opposite end of the couch and motions for me to lay beside him.

I trail my eyes over him, confused. But that doesn't deter Parker. He just leans toward me and tugs my arm until I fall against him on my side, facing the TV, bag of peas forgotten. He readjusts his body, giving me a bit more room, and pulls me close against his chest, his arms snaking around my stomach.

Butterflies swoop in my midsection when his thumb moves back and forth against my side. I wish I found this position uncomfortable, but I don't. In fact, I'm now *so* comfortable that I find myself leaning my head back against Parker's solid chest. We fit together perfectly, like two pieces of a puzzle that were designed to snap into place.

Parker's steady, even breathing soothes my frayed nerves and my eyelids begin to droop.

Who knows how many hours later, there's a tug on my foot, jostling me awake. Groggy, I open my eyes to find that I'm still snuggled up against Parker and the room is completely dark aside from the faint glow of the TV. I have no idea what time it is, but it's clear that we fell asleep a while ago. Parker is quietly snoring, half-underneath me from behind. I smile to myself as I close my eyes again, breathing him in.

But then I remember that *someone* woke me up.

Daria stands at the end of the couch, staring down at us wide-eyed. I blink up at her, afraid to move and wake the man beside me. I realize how this probably looks...Parker and me tangled up together on the couch...But I don't want to have to be the one to wake him.

Daria crosses her arms as her eyes drift between me and Parker. "What happened here?" she asks in a hoarse whisper.

"We fell asleep watching a movie. No big deal." We probably don't have to whisper while Parker gently snoozes, but it feels necessary.

"I see that," Daria says. "But I thought you didn't want him to come over tonight. Something about you not wanting to see the pity in his eyes." Daria sends me a look that says she's on to me.

But she's wrong. She's not onto anything. There's nothing going on between my male bestie and me. Nothing more than comfortable, easy-breezy friendship that is currently manifesting itself as a strictly platonic boy/girl sleepover.

Parker starts to stir, and Daria hightails it from the room, apparently not wanting him to see her. I close my eyes and pretend to be sleeping. Parker lets out a heavy sigh, his warm breath rustling my hair.

His head jerks from side to side, like he's trying to remember where he's at, then stills. My body thrums with fanciful, girlish sensations when Parker turns his lips into my temple and presses the gentlest of kisses there while pulling me tighter against him.

I'm stunned.

Shocked.

Every inch of my body is frozen while the spot where his warm, plush lips touched me burns hot, seared as if from a branding iron.

Parker shifts again until he lifts off the couch. I roll onto my side, facing the couch, still pretending to be asleep. There's no way I'm letting him know I was awake during our little head kissing sesh. The next thing I know, he's laying *his* blanket over top of me and tucking it around my shoulders. My insides twist and turn into a big pile of jelly.

I want to simultaneously scream and swoon and jump for joy.

And I don't even know why.

When Parker opens and closes the front door, I slowly turn and stare into the darkness, hoping he really did leave. If he caught me awake, my ruse would be up.

The next second, Daria tiptoes out to the living area. "Is he gone?"

I bolt upright on the couch, still in shock that my best friend kissed me and snuggled me while I slept. I send a silent thanks to God for not letting Daria witness that little moment.

Daria stalks toward me with a devilish smile on her face. "And here I thought I'd be coming home to cheer up my sad friend with a cautionary tale of why not to date guys from dating apps, and instead, I find her cozied up to her work husband on our couch. And she didn't seem sad at all. Nope, she was blissfully asleep on his chest."

"He's not my work husband," I say, trying and failing to defend my now impossible-to-define relationship with Parker.

"Mmhm. Sure. Then what is he?"

I avert my gaze and fiddle with the edges of Parker's fuzzy blanket as I mentally sort out my feelings. "He's my best friend. He's basically you, as a guy."

Daria's loud laugh echoes through the room. "Honey, if what I walked in on tonight is what having a guy best friend looks like, then sign me up!" She saunters back down the hall and closes her bedroom door, signaling an end to our conversation.

I sigh and fall back on the couch. My mind spins with everything that's transpired in the last few hours. In truth, I don't look at Parker the same way I look at Daria. How could I?

Sure, he's my friend, but I'm also ridiculously attracted to him.

Which is wrong. Probably the worst, most despicable thing I could do. Visions of Daria and Briar choosing to stay friends with Parker over me when we eventually crash and burn flit through my brain, but I squash them before my anxiety runs away with them.

I can't let my trauma from what happened with Tyson run my life—and I definitely don't want it to ruin this moment.

I turn onto my side and pull Parker's blanket up to my nose, burying my face into it and breathing in the masculine scent that's so uniquely him. I let out another satisfied sigh and close my eyes. Maybe just for tonight I can pretend that being attracted to my best friend is totally normal. Okay, even. Because there's nothing I'd rather do than dream about being wrapped up in Parker Kent's arms all night long.

# 14

♥

# JAMIE

When Sunday rolls around, I'm feeling all the mixed-up emotions. Which isn't ideal considering it's the one day a week I set aside to visit with Pops at the care center. Not that I don't want to come and see him more throughout the week, it's just that when I do see him more than once, it seems to agitate him.

The nurses in his unit kindly explained to me that with patients like Pops, routine is everything. On the days I randomly showed up because I had time in my schedule, he would usually end up telling me to leave or asking me to take him home. It breaks my heart to see him in that state, so I dutifully follow the routine the care center set in place, limiting my visits to Sundays.

Dementia is a tough illness. One day, Pops will be completely lucid, excited to see me and prattle on about the comings and goings at the nursing home, while other days, he'll talk to me as if I'm his sister or mother, not understanding that they've both gone on to Heaven.

He never mistakes me for Nonie, though. And whenever he mentions her, it tugs on my heartstrings like nothing else could. I so desperately wish he had her to hold on to during this time in his life.

The patterned wallpaper in the care center's hallways peels along some of the edges and the carpet is worn thin in places. The staff is friendly as they pass by me in the hall with their tired smiles. It must take a lot out of them with so many patients like Pops to care for. I wish I could afford to put him in a facility that allows for more personal care, but this place was the one he'd chosen.

Just thinking of the day Pops pulled me aside and told me he wanted to go into assisted living brings tears to my eyes. *James Gang, I want you to have the house,* he'd said as he scratched the white scruff lining his jaw. *It's all paid for, and all the legal work has been taken care of. My lawyer's coming over today, and we'll sign everything over in your name. Loretta's dying wish was to leave everything to you.*

Nonie told me as much when she was alive, but it pained me too much to hear it. I didn't want their things, the house, or Pop's extensive tool collection. I just wanted, and still want, them.

Only them.

As I step into Pops's room, he's seated in a chair by the window, his gaze set on something outside. I take a tentative step into the room and wait. He doesn't take his eyes off whatever is holding his attention, so I slowly move closer and sit in the chair across from him.

Gradually, his gaze strays from the window until it finally lands on me. He smiles a warm, welcoming smile, the kind that wraps around me like a hug. "Hey, Janessa. They told me you were coming to see me today."

*Janessa*. My mom.

It's not uncommon for Pops to mistake me for Mom, but it hasn't happened in quite a while. Unfortunately, she's no longer earth-side, either. She died when I was six from lupus. My mom and dad never married, and I've only seen him three times in my entire life, the last time being my high school graduation. The only two constants in my life since childhood have been Nonie and Pops.

"Hi, Pops," I say, hoping that the sound of my voice will remind him who I am. "How are you today?"

His smile falters a little as he turns back to the window. "I'm okay. Just lonely."

My chest tightens. "I'm sorry, Pops."

As if he knows exactly who I am, he faces me and leans forward in his chair. "I miss Loretta."

Reaching for his hand, I clasp it between both of mine. "I miss her too, Pops." My eyes mist over, and I blink quickly to ward off the threatening tears. Pops must sense my rising emotions because he places his wrinkled hand over our joined ones and gives me a reassuring pat.

"It's okay, honey. She'll be back soon. She just went to the store an hour ago."

I smile at the way his words completely contradict what he just told me a minute ago. "I know, Pops. I know."

For the next hour, we converse as much as he's able, and I make sure to tell him that I took care of the bill for the care center. I don't know why I always feel the need to tell him that, but it makes me feel better knowing I'm carrying out his wishes. It's his money, after all, and I want him to know, as much as he can, that I'm being a good steward of his things.

When it's time for me to leave the nursing home, Pops waves goodbye like he sees me every day. My heart breaks a little knowing that things will never be the same for either of us. We both have to live and carry on without Nonie and Mom.

As I pull out of the care center parking lot, a wave of emptiness crashes over me, threatening to take me down in one fell swoop. Tears prick the backs of my eyes as I turn onto the main road headed back toward Treemont. In a matter of minutes, tears wet my face and it's a struggle to take deep breaths. I try to slow my breathing by sucking air in through my nose and letting it out slowly through my mouth, but it doesn't seem to be working. I feel as if I could crawl out of my skin and all I want to do in this moment is run away.

As my panic rises, I decide I need to pull over. I find a shoulder along the road and put my car in park. Unbuckling, I jump out of my seat, ready for my feet to hit pavement. I walk with my hands clasped behind my head as I continue to do the deep breathing exercises Dr. Weeks taught me. I try another tactic and shift my focus from the intense feeling of loss overwhelming me to all the positives in my life.

*I get to live in the house that Nonie and Pops shared for the last twenty years. I have a steady job that pays the bills. All of Pop's care is taken care of—at least for now—due to the fund he had set up for it. I have some amazing friends. Daria, Briar, and Parker.*

Parker.

I stop walking and close my eyes, focusing on the way Parker's smile makes me feel. It's warm and bright, exuding light and laughter. Then I think of his brilliant green eyes that always seem to see the best in me. He's not blind to my flaws but accepts them as a part of who I am. I think of his tan hands and how capable they are at expressing his thoughts through Sign Language. I smile as I consider how patient he is with me, even when I frustrate myself.

And just like when he shushed and soothed me at work the day of the tour, a sense of calm washes over me. I open my eyes and realize that the sun has begun to set. The warm glow it casts over the golden corn fields is gorgeous. I take a deep, cleansing breath in through my nose and out through my mouth, wrapping my arms around myself.

I'm amazed at how just focusing on Parker and the qualities that make him special brought me back to a state of calm. At least enough so that I'm able to climb back in my car and make it home without having another panic attack.

"Have you ever thought about going back to that therapist for your...episodes?"

Daria's question hovers in the air around me like an annoying fly I want to swat at.

"No," I say with more force than necessary. "Okay, maybe I have, but...I didn't jive with her personality. She was pushy and...I don't know." I shrug. "I felt like she was defining me by the grief I was experiencing and like I would never be normal unless I took the medication she prescribed."

I walk to the fridge in our small kitchen and grab a can of pop. I try to limit myself to one can a week in the name of health, but when I feel stressed, I find myself reaching for it more often. I pop the tab and take a big gulp of the fizzy liquid, relishing the burn as it goes down.

"I understand. But maybe it just wasn't the right time. Maybe if you went back things would be different," Daria says, in a casual tone. "Or, better yet, maybe you need to find a different therapist who's more gentle and understanding." She takes a sip of her tea, assessing me. She knows I hate it when she brings up the short-lived relationship with my ex-therapist. But after seeing me so torn up after my visit with Pops, I think she just wants to help.

Well, maybe we can help each other. "How about this...I'll go back to a therapist about my anxiety when you also agree to go for your issues with attachment." I take another swig of pop, watching her carefully.

"Touché, my friend," she says as she rises from her stool at the counter, effectively putting a period on this conversation. "All right, I've got to get going. My knitting class starts in fifteen minutes."

I smile while thinking of Daria sitting around in a circle with a bunch of older ladies, knitting. "Oh, please make me a scarf for Christmas," I plead with her. "My current favorite colors are—"

"Whoa, Nelly. Don't get ahead of yourself," she says, interrupting my request with a raised hand. "I'm barely able to knit a three-inch-by-three-inch square. But if I'm good enough by then, I promise to make you something special for Christmas. Maybe a mitten or something."

"Wait, don't you mean *mittens*? Plural?"

"No," she deadpans. "I meant mitten, as in one, *singular* mitten. There's no way I'll have enough time to knit you two in just two months."

I laugh as Daria grabs her purse and heads for the door. "All right, I'll settle for that. See you later."

She tells me goodbye and then I'm left alone with only my thoughts for company. I've already decided to plant myself on the couch and write a blog post about the friends-to-lovers romance I finished last weekend for my book blog. Then maybe I'll curl up with another book and relax. I want to do all I can to settle my mind and refocus on the week ahead.

I've got a cross country meet to cover tomorrow, as well as a wrestling match on Wednesday and a girls' volleyball game Thursday. And, as if my week wasn't busy enough, I know there will be a co-worker camaraderie event smashed in there somewhere too.

At least I've got Parker to entertain me while at work and Daria to keep me company when I come home—most nights, anyway. When she's not sewing or dating or having a social life outside of her lonely roommate.

I blow out a breath as I reach for my laptop and the romance novel I'm reviewing before sitting down on the couch. I still have Parker's yummy smelling blanket, so I unfold it and spread it over my legs as I stretch out. I try to engross myself in typing the story's highlights into a post, but Parker's familiar smell keeps my thoughts circling back to him and our time together Friday night.

I've done my very best not to read into the kiss he placed on my temple while we were snuggled together on this very couch, but my heart refuses to let it go. It's like my subconscious self desires for Parker to see me as more than a friend and my heart is begging for that to be true.

But even if it is true, the thought of ruining my friendship with Parker to take a chance on romance scares me. What if we share a kiss and there are no sparks? Or worse, what if we both fall in love, break up, then subsequently hate each other just like me and Tyson?

I could never forgive myself if I lost Parker as a friend. His steady presence is what's keeping me sane right now. And to me, that's worth more than a few fluttery feelings in my midsection.

Pushing my curiosity for Parker aside, I go back to focusing on my blog post. The friends-to-lovers thing is best left to fiction, anyway.

# 15

♥

# PARKER

I SKIP INTO WORK on Monday with a smile born of sheer happiness plastered on my face. I haven't been able to stop thinking about Jamie all weekend. The way she blushed when I asked if her favorite color was pink, the way her perfect body felt in my arms as we lay side by side on her couch, and the sweet way she smelled when I pressed a soft kiss on her head...

It's all burned into my memory and playing on repeat.

I'm clinging to and savoring those memories probably way more than I should be. I shouldn't be sitting at my desk wondering if my best friend is thinking of me the same way I'm thinking about her. I shouldn't be wishing I was her boyfriend instead of stuck in the friend zone. And I definitely shouldn't be getting excited about the last office activity to boost the overall morale in this dismal place.

Per the email Stefan sent to us this morning, there will be no more outings for the employees of the *Gazette*. And given our boss's penchant for exposing vitamin D deficient adults to activities geared toward children, that's understandable. But we will still be having the Halloween party next week to cap off this thrilling social experiment.

And surprisingly, I'm looking forward to it.

Maybe it's because I get to spend more time with Jamie or maybe it's because Stefan's crazy scheme actually had some merit to it and I'm starting to tolerate my co-workers. It has most definitely allowed me to see a different side to some of them. Either way, I don't have time to figure it out when an incoming text has my phone buzzing in my pocket.

I pull it out and open the message.

**Jamie:** Bad news. I won't be there today. :( I'm. So. Sick. Ugh.

I frown as I stare at the screen. She seemed fine Friday night. I wonder how long she's been feeling poorly.

**Parker:** Aw, James, I'm sorry. What do you need? Cold and Flu meds or some Ginger Ale and crackers?

I raise my head and look over my cubicle to make sure Stefan's not heading my way while I wait for her incoming text.

**Jamie:** I don't need anything but thank you. D's got me loaded down with tissues and Tylenol.
**Parker:** OK. But if you need something, please tell me. I'll be there ASAP.

She texts back a string of smiley emojis and praying hands. I hate that she's not feeling well. An idea forms in my head and I sit toying with it for far too long. Finally, I text Daria.

**Parker:** Hey, I hear Jamie is sick. Is it like a cold or something more serious?

**D:** Hey! Yeah, our girl is pretty pitiful. Coughing, sneezing, chills, fever...the works. She just came down with it last night.

**Parker:** Do you have to work today?

**D:** Yeah, I'm about to head out. Won't be home until late too. Planning on stopping by?

I bite my thumbnail, considering what I'm about to do. Ah, well. Time to take a chance.

**Parker:** Yeah, actually. I want to make sure she's okay and bring her some stuff. Will that be alright?

**D:** Absolutely! I'll leave the door unlocked. ;)

I smile to myself as I type out a quick thanks and pocket my phone. Now to work my butt off and convince Stefan to let me off at lunch.

---

To my sheer and utter shock, it surprisingly worked in my favor to explain to Stefan that I wanted to go and check on Jamie after lunch. Maybe this whole employee morale thing going up in smoke has softened him toward us or maybe he's feeling bad about her run-in with the camel. Either way, I'm grateful and not stopping to ask questions.

I pull into Jamie's driveway and scoop up the bags from my truck's passenger seat. I don't know what all she'll need to make her feel better, but I came prepared.

According to what my family tells me, it's not easy for me to be quiet, but as softly as I can, I open the front door and tiptoe inside just in case she's sleeping. Mom says you should never wake a sleeping baby or a napping woman so I'm taking those words to heart.

Jamie's not in the main living area which makes me think she must be in bed. Moving slowly and still trying to be as silent as possible, I inch down the hall toward the bedrooms. But as I do, I realize I don't actually know which room is hers. It's a small house with one hall and only four doors, so four options. For some reason, the thought of being in *her* room with her *in the bed* makes me pause.

Did I make the right decision to come here and try to take care of her? Part of me thinks like Daria...*yes, absolutely!* The other part wonders if she'll think I'm being creepy by showing up unannounced with all her favorite snacks and drinks. None of it's healthy, either. It's all the stuff I know she loves but denies herself on a regular basis, only saving it for special occasions. I just wanted to do something nice for her, something that would brighten her day.

But now, I'm like a motionless statue of indecision.

Except I'm already here. In her house. Just steps from her bedroom door. Whichever one it is. Blowing out a breath, I shift both bags to one hand and take a step forward.

The door to my left flies open, startling me, and Jamie walks right into me in *just* a towel, her soaking wet hair hanging around her glistening shoulders.

We both jump at the contact, and she nearly falls back as she covers her mouth with her hand. I can't hear the scream that tears from her throat, but I have no doubt it's probably loud enough to have alerted the neighbors.

I grip her still damp arm and right her, eyes as round as I've ever seen them. Her wide, wild gaze darts to the scrap of fabric wrapped around her. Unfortunately, so does mine. Her long legs, dotted with water droplets, peek out under the towel as she shifts her bare feet. And of course, her toes are painted hot pink.

Nope. *Don't think about Jamie and pink in the same sentence right now.* NO PINK.

All at once, her hands are everywhere, trying to cover herself up. I raise the bags to cover my face and wave with my free hand for her to go to her room where she can get dressed. Except I still don't know which room that is, so I just wave my arm around in a roundabout way, hoping she'll get the gesture. Closing my eyes, I silently berate myself for being such an idiot.

Why couldn't I have just texted her to tell her I was coming? That would've kept this little incident from happening. The look on Jamie's face told me she was mortified that I saw her in a towel. I'm hoping it's just because she wasn't expecting me and not because she would *never* want me to see her in a towel. Not that I want her to want me to…

Ugh, I don't even know what I'm thinking anymore.

I bang my head against the wall a few times just for good measure and wait for her to come to me. That seems like the next best thing to do at this point. Leaving would probably just add to her embarrassment, as if I was disgusted by catching her that way or something.

After what feels like an eternity later, she emerges from her bedroom in a pair of sweats and her Hello Kitty robe. It's pink.

I swallow and shove the intruding thoughts away as I walk toward her. *I'm sorry,* I sign, then hand her the plastic bags full of stuff. She offers me a timid smile as she accepts them.

"It's okay. You didn't know."

I frown. *Neither did you. How are you feeling?*

She shrugs and it looks like she sniffles, wrinkling her little red Rudolph nose. "I've been better." Just as she says it, she starts coughing.

It seems to take her a minute to catch her breath and my heart sags. She's really and truly ill.

Taking her shoulders, I steer her into the room she came out of. Thankfully, she doesn't argue. Her bed is in the center of the neat, white-walled room decorated in boxy, sleek-edged furniture. She's got an entire family of plants lining her seventies style dresser and a large macrame wall hanging beside a giant poster of Shania Twain singing on stage.

I move her toward her bed that's been haphazardly made but covered in pristine white covers and scoot a few of her throw pillows aside, then motion for her to get in the bed. As I do, something familiar catches my eye. There's a smaller blanket—*my* blanket—underneath her comforter. I tug it out and hold it up, raising my eyebrows in question.

She begins twirling a strand of hair around her finger like she's nervous. I think she mumbles something about me leaving it here, but she doesn't enunciate or try to sign an explanation.

It doesn't matter, though, because I just caught Jamie using *my* blanket. In *her* bed.

Tucking that little nugget away for a rainy day, I gesture for her to get in bed again. A small smile forms on her pretty mouth as she does as I command, setting the bags on the bed beside her.

She scoots far enough over that there's room for me to sink down too. As soon as I do, I start pulling out things from the bags, making a show of it like I'm some gameshow host impersonator. At this point, I'll do anything to ward off the embarrassment from the hallway.

She laughs and her eyes brighten when I pull out the bags of sour gummies, snack sized-peanut butter chocolate candies, and chocolate covered pretzels. Then I go for the big guns—the ice cream and soda pop.

She signs, *thank you*, but I hold her off with a hand. There are still two more surprises. I show off the last thing from the bottom of the bag with a grin I can't seem to hold back.

"Parker! Is that what I think it is?!"

I nod, handing her the latest new release from her favorite author. It's the last installment of her favorite urban fantasy series, and I know she's been wanting it. But apparently, she's got some rule where she can't buy a new book until she reads everything on her TBR. I do not adhere to such a rule, so I stopped at our favorite indie bookstore on the way over.

"Oh my goodness, thank you!" She leans in and gives me a hug. Her freshly showered floral scent overwhelms me, so I pull back and hold up a hand.

*One more thing*, I sign, then get to my feet. Her bewildered expression is the last thing I see before I'm running out to my truck. When I step back into her room, she's already flipping through the pages of her new novel. A sweet smile blooms on her face as I move closer to present the final gift that I hope will make her day.

I take the plant I purchased from Greg's out from behind my back and hold it out to her. It's not a succulent like Beatrice, but it's got heart-shaped leaves with little stripes of pink that hang over the petite pot's sides.

Her smile falters as she takes the pot in both hands and inspects each of the plant's leaves, running her fingers over them one by one. Her misty gaze lifts to meet mine. "Thank you, Parker. This is gorgeous."

I smile and nod. *I know you wanted a friend for Beatrice. And this one isn't a succulent, but it's pretty and should still be small enough to fit on your desk.*

A giggle or a laugh, I'm not sure which, bubbles out of her and she puts one hand to her mouth. A couple of tears stream down her cheeks, but she's quick to wipe them away. Normally, I might tease her about getting so emotional over a plant, but I don't, especially since she's not feeling the best.

Instead, I gesture for her to lie down. She looks as if she wants to protest, but I repeat the motion and she obeys, still wiping her eyes. Once she's lying on her back, I tuck the blanket around her and lay the back of my hand against her forehead. Fighting off a shiver, she sinks lower under the blanket.

*You have a fever,* I sign. *Where's your Tylenol?*

She points to an array of cold and flu medications that pepper the surface of her nightstand next to her essential oil diffuser. I pop the cap on the Tylenol first, then offer her a couple of pills with the lemon-lime soda I bought her. She fights a smile as she takes them and chugs the soda to wash the medication down.

Next, I put the ice cream away in the kitchen and fill a glass with water to use to refill her diffuser. When I return to her room, her new plant sits in the center of her nightstand, and she's got the bag of sour gummies opened with a wide grin on her face.

"This is so nice, Parker. I can't thank you enough."

*No thanks necessary,* I tell her.

Again, I sit on the side of her bed, right next to her legs. She doesn't kick me off, so I'm guessing she's cool with it. *Hopefully your fever will go down soon,* I sign.

She nods and offers me a sour gummy. I take it from her and toss it up in the air, trying and failing to catch it in my mouth. Her shoulders shake on a giggle and she hands me another. I keep doing it until she's laughing so hard it throws her into a coughing fit.

Feeling like a jerk, I scoot off the bed, taking the sour gummies with me, and make her lie down on her side. I hand her a tissue before kneeling on the floor next to her. She turns toward me, a grateful smile lifting the corners of her lips.

"You didn't have to do all this, Parker. You're missing out on work to be here."

I raise both shoulders in a shrug. *You're more important to me than work.*

Her brow creases and I give in to the urge to run my thumb over the little lines that form there. She goes still under my touch, her entire body seizing up. I slowly retract my hand but don't move away.

I can retreat, or I can hold steady. Almost every part of me is screaming to run away, to hide and not let her see how I really feel. But the part that's been urging me to pursue Jamie these past few weeks grows bolder, ready to face whatever may come after confessing my feelings.

But instead of reading into the moment between us, she gives me a small smile and blinks her heavy-lidded eyes. I brush some of her hair behind her ear and watch as her lashes lower.

Her eyes close completely for a few seconds until she pops them back open. "You should go," she says with a wave. "Get back to work, I'm fine. Especially now." A pink blush fills her cheeks as she bites her lip.

I shake my head and sign, *Just go to sleep. I want to stay in case you need something. Stefan gave me his blessing.*

Her shoulders rise and fall on what looks like a sigh and her eyes close completely. I sit back against her nightstand, resting my hands over my knees, and watch her. As soon as she starts to fall asleep, her lips part, most likely so she can breathe since she's so stuffed up.

I can't help but smile at the achingly pitiful but sweet picture she makes all snuggled in her bed. It sucks that she's sick. But it's kind of cool that she's allowing me to take care of her.

As I soak in the sight of her taking deep, even breaths, my mind starts to throw up images of us together in ten, twenty, even thirty years. In them, I'm still taking care of her and trying to make her laugh. She's still writing and reading amazing stories and taking care of her many plants. But in each of them, we're together and not just as friends.

In those dreams, we're more. I can only hope and pray that someday, they'll become a reality.

Just when I finally think she's dozed off, I rise from the floor and her phone lights up on the nightstand. When it's Mike's name that shows up across the top of the screen, a hard possessiveness roars to life inside me.

I shouldn't pick it up and read the message. I *shouldn't*. But my curiosity gets the best of me, and I tap open the message. It looks like they exchanged another text about an hour ago.

**Mike**: I'm sorry you're sick, babe. Is there anything I can do?

I want to type out, "No, you idiot, leave me alone," but I don't. Pretending to be her would be a whole new level of wrong. And I can't text back as myself or else Jamie would know and wonder what possessed me to do such a thing.

So I carefully place her phone back on the nightstand and peer down at her. All my romance-inflated thoughts from mere moments ago flutter away like they never fully took shape at all.

# 16

♥

# JAMIE

"I THINK I MAY be developing feelings for Parker." Silence greets me as both Daria and Briar stare me down in the middle of our Cider and Stems flower arrangement workshop. "Well? What should I do?"

Daria sets her long-stem glass full of cider on the wooden art table in front of us, a sly smirk blooming on her face. "All I have to say is congratulations."

"Congratulations?"

"Mmhmm," Daria hums. "It's about time you saw what the rest of us see."

"I don't follow…" I say, quirking an eyebrow.

"It's about time you see that he's in love with you," she continues. "That he thinks of you as more than a friend." My eyes fly to Briar, who sends me a placating smile like she might a fussy toddler.

"Do you guys seriously believe that?" I ask.

Briar sighs, picking up the green stem of what we were just told was a peach dahlia and starts poking it into her arrangement. "Honestly…" She shrugs one slender shoulder, avoiding my burning stare. "It does sort of seem like he's into you. I mean, I've only met him a handful of times, but whenever you guys are together, his focus is almost solely on you. It's super sweet, though, because he seems like an awesome guy."

Inwardly, I'm reeling, while outwardly, I'm scoffing. "That's probably just because of the little bit of Sign Language I know. I'm sure he just looks to me because I'm able to bridge the gap between us when we're with others who don't know it."

"I didn't say he looks *to* you," Briar says, finally meeting my eyes. "I said he looks *at* you. In a way a guy would if he was trying to envision what it would be like to kiss you."

My cheeks instantly burn hot as the memory of when my eyes dropped to his lips in the office a couple weeks ago surfaces. And then when I was almost certain his did the same in his old bedroom at his parents' house.

"I think you guys are just reading into our relationship." I lower my gaze to the cut stems of assorted florals in front of me, wishing I'd never brought up the subject of Parker.

"I don't think we are," Daria croons, bumping my shoulder with hers. "You just said yourself that you might be catching feelings. It seems like you both are coming to a startling realization."

I whip my head toward her. "Which is?"

A smile that could rival the Cheshire cat's spreads across her face. "That you guys are meant to be and would make the cutest babies ever." I roll my eyes and push against Daria's shoulder as she laughs. "Hey, don't hate me just because you know I'm right."

Before I can sink any further into my regret, the florist teaching our Cider and Stems class claps. Though the woman at the front of the room is tiny, with silver spiral curls and thick, black-framed glasses, she has no problem commanding the attention of everyone in attendance.

"Okay, everyone. Once you've selected the blooms you wish to use and your foam is placed, we'll begin assembling the arrangement."

"Oops," Briar whispers with a wince. "I already started."

"As you can see here," says Prue, our instructor and owner of the Enchanting Florist in the small town of River Hollow, "I've got a mixture of dahlias, thistle, hypericums, cosmos, Italian ruscus, and daisies. I'll use the larger flowers to frame some of the smaller ones, like so." With professional precision, Prue begins to guide us on how we can replicate one of her beautiful fall flower arrangements.

When Briar had the idea to get together tonight for this little activity, I was hesitant. I mean, piecing together floral arrangements isn't exactly among my skill set. But after mulling over my conflicting feelings concerning Parker when he helped nurse me back to health, I needed to get out, to get my mind focused on something else.

Ever since he came to my rescue with treats and gifts I in no way deserved, I've been replaying our every interaction from the past few weeks. My heart seems to want to believe that something has shifted between us, but each time I entertain that idea, my mind swoops in to bat the thought away.

What happened between Tyson and me was excruciating. And maybe it was partially our immaturity that made us hate one another, but I'll never really know if it was that or the fact that we never should've crossed the line of friendship to begin with.

Prue's voice has me pushing my worries aside and focusing back on our task. Once she finishes explaining exactly what we're supposed to do, we begin to follow her instructions. I grab a white daisy from our work space and poke it through the foam, followed by another.

"I don't understand why you're having such a hard time believing that Parker likes you, Jamie," Daria says, eyes focused on the arrangement in front of her. "I mean, you're single now. If he's had feelings for you all this time, it would make sense that he would be trying to win you over now."

My brows pull together. "Does it though? This isn't the first time I've been single since we've known each other. I was single when we met too." I pick up another flower, I think this one is called a thistle, and stick it in the foam beside the daisy.

"That's true," Briar pipes up. "But maybe he didn't want to ask you out at first because you worked together. Or maybe he was shy. I can certainly relate to that." A faint pink blush rises on Briar's cheeks as she ducks her head and goes back to her flowers.

"I don't know why you'd be shy around guys, Bri," Daria says with a laugh. "You're basically the real-life version of a fitness model."

"Looks aren't everything," Briar mutters, seeming to ignore our blatant stares as she toys with the arrangement in front of her.

"Anyway," Daria continues, "She's right. He might've been shy or concerned about the company policy when it comes to dating." She pauses. "What is the company policy when it comes to dating?"

I lift both shoulders. "I honestly have no idea, but I can't see Stefan signing off on something like that." I clear my throat. "Not that I'd *want* him to. I mean, I'm just speaking hypothetically." I roll my bottom lip between my teeth as images of what it might be like to date my best friend scroll through my head like a movie reel.

In each one, we're laughing and playing around, just like always. Except there's more flirting. And touching. And longing looks at each other's lips.

"Okay, but wouldn't it be weird?!" Both of my friends' heads swivel in my direction at my outburst.

Briar cocks her head. "Wouldn't what be weird?" It's at that moment I realize both my friends have most of their arrangements done while mine sits almost untouched. How long was I daydreaming about dating Parker?

They blink at me, still waiting for a response. I clear my throat. "Dating Parker, my friend. Wouldn't that be weird?"

"Well, that depends," Daria says before taking a sip of her cider. "Are you attracted to him?"

I pick up another daisy and twirl it between my fingers. "I do *think* he's attractive. Like, I can understand why Jordy practically fawns over him. He's nice to look at."

"So then...what's the problem?" Daria's raised eyebrows tell me she thinks I must be loose a few screws.

"I guess I've just never allowed myself to think of him in a romantic sense before. Like, for instance," I say, shifting to face them. "He's always tickling me or touching me to get my attention, and until recently, I've never thought a thing about it. Any electricity I felt was always brushed off and not acknowledged, ya know?"

"Yeah, but you're not really a physically affectionate person," Daria says. "Not like Briar, anyway." She bumps my friend in the shoulder while Briar tosses up her hands.

"I can't help it, okay? I'm just naturally a hugger!"

"Okay, but do we really need to be greeted that way at the beginning of *every single* yoga class?" Briar rolls her eyes at Daria's question, then focuses back on me.

"Anyway, back to *your* issues...You really don't think you're attracted to him?"

"I didn't say I wasn't. But it's hard to tell. Daria's right. I've never really been physically affectionate, especially with guys, and I never kiss a guy until after we've dated for at least a month or so. It's always been more important to me to connect on an emotional level first."

"That makes total sense," Briar says. "But think about it this way...you already know that you and Parker connect emotionally. You even know you guys have a great time together. He gets you, you understand him and his weird obsession with Star Wars." I laugh. "So, why not give the physical stuff a try just to *see* if you're attracted?"

"I kind of hate how everything you're saying makes total sense." Daria and Briar both share a laugh at my expense. "Okay, but what about what happened with Tyson?"

Daria groans. "Oh please don't go into that again." With a shake of her head, she pins me with a look. "Girl, that was a *high school* relationship. And I didn't know Tyson, but I can almost guarantee he's nothing like Parker." Before I have a chance to respond, Prue claps her hands to get everyone's attention.

"Okay, everyone!" she chimes. "It's time to finish up those arrangements!" Each of us goes back to our work, determined to go home with the best one. "Now, for your homework," Prue says as she passes us each a piece of paper." I want you to look over this sheet with the care instructions for your flowers. They'll last longer if you follow the instructions listed."

Daria leans closer and whispers in my ear. "And your homework, Jamie, is to put the moves on Parker and see if there's any of that sizzling attraction we've been talking about."

I gulp so loud she must've heard it because she's giggling as she leans back in her seat. Can I do what she's asking? Can I make a move on my best friend? I guess we'll just have to see.

---

When I walk into work the next day and find Parker's cubicle empty, my stomach sinks. I look around the break room, the rest of the main room filled with cubicles, and even the hallway. He's nowhere to be found. Setting my stuff down at my desk, I reach into my purse and pull out my phone.

**Jamie**: Hey, where are you?

There's no response for several minutes, so I boot up my computer and settle in at my desk. Maybe he's just running late. Just as I start to open my emails, my phone buzzes.

**Parker**: I'm not saying you got me sick, but...I seem to be experiencing the same symptoms you were a few days ago.

I slap a hand on my forehead and wince.

**Jamie**: Parker, I am SO SORRY!!! What can I do?
**Parker**: Please don't be sorry, it's not your fault. My mom literally came and shooed me out of my apartment so I'd come and stay in my old room while she has the ability to nurse me back to health. *eye roll emoji*. So really, I'm good.

I lean back in my chair, my shoulders sagging in relief. At least he's got his mom to take care of him. I smile, thinking of how his determined mom must've done exactly as he described and forced him to go home with her.

A small ache forms in my chest when I think of how Nonie used to do those things for me too. I will the feeling away before the tears start and focus on my work. I may not be able to leave work early since I missed two whole days, but I can at least stop over and see Parker after work before I have to go and watch the girls' volleyball game I'm tasked with covering.

A knock on my cubicle wall has me spinning and facing Gladys. She's not smiling, but she's not scowling either so I hope that means she's not the bringer of bad news.

"Hey, Gladys. What's up?"

She raises an eyebrow and leans back, peering into Parker's cubicle. "Where's tall, dark, and handsome at today?"

Normally, I'd smile at her way of describing Parker, but I can't while knowing he's ill. "He's sick, unfortunately. I think I'm going to stop over and see him after work."

She gives me a slow nod, then takes a step forward. "Well, I wanted to stop in and talk to you about helping me plan this Halloween party next week."

"You're in charge of planning?" I do my best not to sound surprised, but I have to admit, I kind of am.

"Of course I'm planning it. You think I'd leave planning a party of this much importance to some inexperienced young thing like Jordy? She'd probably order pizza and cake and call it a day." Gladys shakes her head and crosses her arms over her burgundy velour tracksuit. "No. This is Halloween we're talking about. It needs to be done right."

My brow scrunches as the mental image of Gladys knocking out Dracula pops in my head. "I thought you didn't like Halloween after what happened at the corn maze?"

"Hah," she laughs. "Of course I like Halloween; it's gimmicky attractions I despise. And also work field trips."

I smile. "Yeah, same. Okay, so what do you need help with?"

She clasps her hands in front of her, peering at me over her glasses. "Well, I was hoping you could do the decorations and I'll take care of the food. When people walk into the break room, I want it to feel like they've stepped into a haunted house. But you know…without the scares."

I nod. "I think I get what you're saying. Has Stefan signed off on this idea?" I hate to ask because I probably sound like a suck up, but I really don't want to do anything to upset our boss, not with this interview on the line. And not with how gracious he was about me missing a couple days of work.

"He did. Since this is to be our last activity, he told me to go all out." She leans in and lowers her voice. "Between you and me, I think he's feeling a little wounded after the past few…mishaps…with his little employee camaraderie thing."

"Yeah, I could see that."

"So." She claps. "You'll help?"

I smile, thinking of how much I've come to tolerate my surly co-workers these past few weeks, maybe even come to *like* some of them. "Absolutely."

# 17

♥

# JAMIE

By the time I'm rolling out of work, a weird sort of giddiness has me jittery. My plan is to head straight to the store to get Parker a few things like he did for me, then head to his parents' house.

I don't have his mom's number to call her and warn her beforehand, but something tells me she won't mind my showing up there unannounced. Alexandra Kent seems like the type of woman who lives and breathes for entertaining company with her warm personality and excellent cooking.

Daria's charge from the other night rattles around in my brain as I walk into the drugstore and begin perusing the aisles. *Your homework is to put the moves on Parker and see if there's any of this sizzling attraction we've been talking about.*

My cheeks heat just thinking about being so bold, even with how sweet he's been to me lately. Refocusing on my task, I grab all the junk food I know Parker will like, as well as his favorite pop. Then I go in search of anything spaceship related. Unfortunately, Walgreens doesn't carry much space paraphernalia so I'm out of luck there, but I do manage to grab a *Men's Health* magazine as a kind of joke.

It's almost laughable how fit he looks with the way he eats, but hopefully he'll find it funny.

I grab some cough drops and a few other things I hope will help him fend off the sickness, then I'm off to his parent's house. When I step up to the front door, I'm feeling ready to give my bestie the same kind of treatment he gave me when I was sick. *Without* putting any kind of moves on him.

Mere seconds after ringing the doorbell, Alex swings the door wide. "Jamie!" she cries in her lilting accent just before wrapping me in the tightest hug in human history. "It's so good to see you!"

"It's good to see you too." I hold up the bag of goodies. "I just came to drop these off for Parker and to check on him."

"Aww," she croons, holding a hand to her chest. "That is so so sweet of you, dear. Please, please, come in."

I do as she says, and she practically flies around me, taking the coat off my shoulders. "Come into the kitchen for a minute," she all but commands as she takes my hand and tugs me forward. "I made some tea. Parker's favorite. You'll take it to him."

I can only nod in response as she ushers me into the kitchen where a sultry, woodsy smell permeates the air. She moves to the stove and lifts the teapot, pouring hot water over two teacups where looseleaf tea leaves are held suspended in metal strainers. "I was going to have tea with him, but I think he'd prefer for you to bring it to him." She sends me a suggestive wink.

"Uh, thank you," I say, dipping my chin and waiting patiently for the tea to steep. As quickly as I can, I change the subject. "What's that lovely smell?"

She raises her gaze to meet mine, a slow smile spreading on her lips. "That's my homemade soup. It's a mixture of beef, herbs, and some vegetables. It's good for the soul when a person's sick." She completes her description with a kiss to her fingers, then removes the strainers from the teacups. "Now, you take this to Parker. He's in his bed, but I don't think he's asleep."

She places both teacups on a small antique tray and hands them over. I scoot the bag of goodies to my arm and accept the tray. "Yes, ma'am. I will."

Alex nods her approval with an encouraging pat, then shoos me out of the kitchen with both hands.

I can't help but giggle at how sweet yet forceful Parker's mom is while I take my time walking down the hall so I don't spill any of her yummy smelling tea. Once I reach Parker's door, I knock, then realize how stupid that was. Slowly, so I don't spill anything or surprise him, I creak open the door.

He's lying on his back with an arm slung over his eyes, his chest rising and falling with even breaths. *Great, I'm probably gonna scare him.*

I carefully set the tray down on his dresser, then drop the bag to the floor and move to the end of his bed. I figure keeping my distance will be the best thing to not startle him. Lightly, so I don't jostle him too much, I trail my finger over the top of his bare foot that peeks out from the edge of the covers.

Immediately, he lifts his arm and head to peer up at me. As soon as he sees it's me, a full-blown pearly white smile graces his handsome face. *Hey you*, he signs, then starts to sit up.

I hurry around to the side of his bed and motion for him to lay back. "Don't get up," I say as well as sign. "Rest. I'm just here to check on you."

His smile tips up a little more on one side than the other as he scoots closer to the wall and motions for me to sit next to him. *I'm glad you came.*

I can't help but grin in response. He looks so cute when he's sick with his hair even messier than normal and wearing a wrinkled T-shirt. If it wasn't for the dark circles lingering under his eyes, I'd want to see him like this all the time.

A wracking cough suddenly sounds from his chest, loud and painful, as he turns into his elbow. "Oh, Parker." I cover my eyes with my hands. "I'm so sorry I did this to you!"

He grabs my hands and lowers them to my lap. *You did not do this. We're together a lot, we were probably exposed at the same time.*

I shoot him a look that says *I'm not buying it.* He chuckles but it's barky like his cough. *Don't worry,* he signs. *I'm not mad about missing work. Just mad I couldn't see you.* His lopsided smile paired with the way his thumb grazes over the back of my hand almost has my heart leaping from my chest.

"Well, I brought you some stuff so even if you are secretly upset about me getting you sick, hopefully you'll forgive me." I rise from the bed and grab the bag I'd dropped earlier. Handing it over, I sign, "All your favorites. Plus a little something extra."

He digs into the bag with a husky giggle as he pulls out his favorite snacks plus the cough drops and medicine. When he reaches the *Men's Health* magazine, he pretends to be offended. *Really? You'll never stop trying to get me to eat healthy, will you?*

I shake my head. "It's a grueling task, but someone's gotta do it."

He lets the magazine fall to his lap as he raises his "sword finger" like a threat.

"Don't you dare..." I hiss with narrowed eyes, a finger pointed right back at him. He bends the makeshift sword up and down like he's getting ready to jab it into my side. "Parker, I mean it," I warn, trying to keep my voice low so his mom doesn't overhear.

But as soon as I go to get off the bed, he grabs me with one arm and hauls me back, sword finger jabbing into my ribs and waist. I try so hard to hold in my hysterical laughter, but it's no use when he's laughing hard enough for the both of us.

I try to adjust my body so I can knee him in the stomach, just enough to push him away, but he's too strong. When he turns his head away to cough into his elbow, I take that as my opportunity to tickle him under his arms.

He quickly retaliates by pinning me to the bed by my wrists, his large body hovering over mine. The huge smile on my face falters as his gaze suddenly drops to my lips, before slowly making its way back up to my eyes.

Okay. This time, I know I didn't imagine it. PARKER WAS STARING AT MY LIPS.

Something warm begins to buzz between us, tangible and electric. Parker's breaths fan over me and in a moment of complete and utter surprise, I want nothing more than for him to lower himself on top of me and connect his lips with mine.

Then, as if I'm dreaming, he starts to erase the distance between us, lowering himself to his elbows. I freeze, my body going totally still. His eyes seem to snag on every feature of my face as his hand brushes over the top of my head, fingers tightening in my hair.

Then a harsh knock at the door has me frantically pushing against his chest. "Your mom," I mouth, hooking my thumb toward the door.

His expression turns murderous as he sits back on the bed. I jump to my feet and go to grab the tea from the dresser. It's probably cold now with all the flirting we've been doing.

I feel my cheeks flame. Oh my gosh, I just FLIRTED WITH PARKER.

"Can I come in?" Alex calls through the door just as I hand Parker his cup of tea. My gaze flies around the room, unsure where to situate myself to appear as unsuspicious as possible. Before I can move to the chair at

Parker's old desk, he grabs my hand and tugs me down onto the side of his bed. I pinch my lips and widen my eyes in protest, but he merely shakes his head, his green eyes telling me not to move.

"Come on in!" My voice is too bright and cheery for the moment. I wince, guilt washing over me. If Alex knew the position her son just had me in, she'd probably kick me out of her house.

She opens the door and comes in with another, larger tray full of two bowls of soup and crackers. "I just wanted to bring you two some dinner." Her beaming smile is aimed my way. "I hope you didn't already eat."

I came straight from work, not even taking time to go home and change out of my dress pants and blouse first. "No, I didn't. That sounds amazing, thank you."

She sets the tray on Parker's bedside table. When she places a hand to his forehead, he tries to bat it away, but even that doesn't faze her. "Good, no fever. You'll be right as rain soon enough, my *baiat bun*."

He gives her a terse smile, then signs, *Thanks, Mom*. As wonderful as it would be to have such a loving, caring mom, it's no secret that she tends to get on Parker's nerves at times.

As if we're incapable of grabbing the soup ourselves, Alex hands us each a bowl with a handful of crackers on top. She gestures wildly while going into a story of how Parker got sick one time in the tenth grade and missed school for a week.

"It was awful," she says, clutching her throat. "He had the white bumps on the back of his throat...the skrept throat, they call it." I bite my cheek to stifle a giggle and nod. "Thank God he never got that again."

Parker interrupts her by signing something that looks like, *Let Jamie and me sit and talk before she has to leave,* and Alex holds her hands up in surrender.

"Fine, say no more. I will go, you two enjoy your dinner."

When she leaves the room, Parker's shoulders rise and fall on a sigh. *Sorry, I know she can be a lot to deal with.*

"She's perfect, Parker. Truly. I wish I had a mom like that." I lower my gaze to the bowl of soup in my hands, wishing I hadn't said that. I hate sounding like I'm some pitiful orphan just because my mom's dead and my dad abandoned us. I had two amazing people to raise me, there's really nothing I should complain about.

Parker squeezes my knee. *You'll be a great mom too someday.*

I blink at my friend. "What?"

His lips thin as he swirls the spoon in his bowl of soup on his lap. After a moment, he lifts his hands to sign, *I don't know. I could just see you being a great mom someday. Your Nonie seemed like a great example of how to live and love. I know I didn't know her personally, but everything you've told me points to that. And your Pops seems like a great guy, too. They raised you well.*

My eyes begin to mist over. I stare down at my soup again, blinking away the sudden moisture while I sign back, "Thank you, Parker. That was sweet of you to say."

How had he known that my thoughts have been veering toward wondering what it would be like to settle down with a husband and kids lately? Am I that much of an open book? Or is he thinking the same type of things?

He taps my knee to get my attention. *You OK?*

I force a smile. "Yeah, I'm fine." I fall quiet while we eat, only speaking up to tell him about work and what Gladys tasked me with.

When I spot the time on small digital clock on Parker's bedside table, I frown. "I'm sorry, Park, I've gotta go. I can't be late for the game." It's a championship game too, so it's a big one. He gives me a solemn nod as I take his bowl and set it on the tray. "I'll take these to your mom."

He tries to wave me off, but I insist. "I'll see you in a few days, okay? Get better, Parker."

With a downturned mouth that tells me he wishes I wasn't leaving, he signs, *Thanks, James*. Offering him one last smile, I leave his room, taking the dishes with me.

As soon as I enter the kitchen, Alex walks out of the pantry. "Ah, thank you, Jamie. I'll take those." She removes the trays from my hands and marches them toward the sink.

"It was good to see you again," I say, backing toward the doorway.

"Leaving so soon?"

"I must, unfortunately. There's a game I need to cover tonight."

She spins away from the sink and takes both of my hands in hers. "It was so good to see you again. You are a good girl for Parker."

"Oh," I squeak, then clear my throat. "We're just friends, but that's sweet of you to say."

"No." She closes her eyes and shakes her head, her curls bobbing around her face. "No *just friends*. You two are more. I see it." Popping her eyes open, she points with two fingers at her eyes, then at me.

An uncomfortable, breathy laugh escapes me. "I'm sorry?"

"Sit," she commands, pointing to a chair at the dining room table. I really don't have more than ten minutes to spare, but I obey because as lovely as Alex is, she's also a little terrifying.

"Let me tell you a story," she begins, sitting down in a chair across from me and folding her hands over each other. I wonder if this will be like the one she told us about Parker getting sick.

"When Parker failed his newborn hearing test, I was devastated," she says. "I was determined to do whatever we needed to do in order to help him hear as if you or I do. But after many visits to the audiologist without ever being given much hope, God helped me see that I was going about my son's special ability all wrong."

Her soft smile shows the truth in her words. "You see, Parker *is* different, but not in the way most people see him. He's more in-tune with the way things feel. He experiences the world through sight and touch, through vibrations. And I think because of that, he's a more sensitive individual. It's not his deafness that sets him apart, it's his intuitiveness."

I nod, taking in all she's saying. I could never understand what it's like to be Parker, but I do understand *him* and everything she's saying resonates with what I know of him.

"But it's no secret that my second son has always struggled with making friends. It's partly because of his sensory difference and partly because we moved a lot during his childhood. We enrolled him in different schools and determined to learn Sign Language for ourselves to communicate with him better, but he still struggled to maintain relationships. He withdrew from us, and it broke my heart."

My own heart tugs at the mention of Parker's lack of friends growing up.

"But when he was in junior high, he met a girl named Ella at his school for deaf youth. She was such a sweetheart. But she wasn't well. She had cancer."

I gasp, unable to stop myself.

"Parker and Ella became very close over the two years we were stationed in Idaho. He saw her in a way others didn't—focusing on who she was as a person and not her illness. But her health took a wrong turn…" Alex's voice thickens with emotion as her gaze falls to where she's running her finger over a groove of wood in the table. "As she neared the end, Parker refused to leave her side. Her parents, God bless them, understood and allowed him to stay during her final hours. But when Ella took her last breath, Parker took it very hard."

My sudden emotion boils over and a tear rolls down my cheek. Quickly, I swipe it away.

"He fell into his father's arms, weeping. And then, two months later, we got orders to move again. The move might've been just as hard for him—to leave the place that carried Ella's memory." She sighs, long and sorrowful. "Since then, he's never allowed himself to get close to another girl. Not in high school, not college." She pauses. "Not until he met you."

My breath hitches.

"You should see your face," she says, a smile curving her lips. "You look like I just told you he's going to propose."

"Is-is he?" I sputter, not knowing what to do, what to think.

Her grin widens. "No, dear. Not that I know of. He says the two of you are *just friends*." She gives me a sly wink, then reaches over and pats my hand. "But I'm his mother and I see what he doesn't. He cares for you, Jamie. And if you care for him, all I ask is that you give him a chance."

Her brown eyes are warm and filled with unshed tears. "I'm not trying to put any pressure on you. But if you don't feel the same about him as he does you, tell him before he falls too hard. Because when Parker loves, he dives in deep."

Alex's words stick with me the rest of the night. I barely have the mental wherewithal to record any of the stats from the girls' volleyball game. And when I'm lying in bed hours later and receive the sweetest text from Parker, thanking me for the things I brought him and telling me that he already feels healthier just holding the men's magazine in his hands, I can't help but wonder if I should take her advice to heart.

# 18

♥

# Jamie

Being back at work and finishing up a report on the volleyball game fills me with a comforting sense of control. Lately, my world seems tipped on its axis and I'm grasping at everything—anything to keep me upright. It feels good to be back at my cubicle of safety.

But even though Stefan didn't give me any grief for missing those days of work, Lucas couldn't let it skate by without making a ridiculous comment about how it must have been nice to have a two-day vacation with my boyfriend. As if Parker and I weren't sick.

Maybe if Lucas showed a little kindness to his fellow co-workers from time to time, Stefan would give him the afternoon off too.

A text makes my phone vibrate on the desk and I pick it up.

**Parker**: So. This Halloween Party. Want to wear matching costumes?

I glance toward the cubicle wall that separates my office from his and smile. He's not at work today, but I texted him earlier and he said he was feeling much better.

**Jamie**: What did you have in mind?

**Jamie**: If you say you want me to go as Princess Leia, I'm gonna do the celery thing with your mini chocolate candies again.
**Parker**: You can't threaten me with celery. *celery emoji*. Ok, so no Han Solo and Leia...what about that couple from your fantasy book?

Something that feels an awful lot like birds taking flight in my midsection makes my stomach quiver. Is he seriously suggesting we go as a...*couple*? To a work party?

**Jamie**: You mean Aris and Kat? Well...he's a long-haired fae who rides a motorcycle. *elf emoji*. LOL You sure you're up for that?
**Parker**: I may have trouble procuring a motorcycle on such short notice, especially since I don't have a license, BUT I could definitely make the long hair work. Just give me a list.

I bite my lip to keep a goofy smile from breaking out across my face. He's seriously willing to dress up like part of a fictional couple for me? I have the sudden urge to dance around in my seat like a giddy little kid but worry someone walking by might see me. Instead, I just smile like a fool and imagine Parker dressing up like some leather jacket wearing fae man.

**Jamie:** OK. If you think you can pull it off... Here's what you'll need.

I proceed to text him a list half a mile long because I want him to know what he just signed up for. I laugh as I type out the last item and hit send.
Feelings I never thought I'd have the right to feel for Parker start to burrow their way into my heart. With each text, each touch, each secret smile he saves just for me, I'm beginning to hope that he sees me as more than a friend.

*But where will we be if he doesn't?*

I shove that unwanted thought aside and go back to work. For now, at least, I'll allow myself to relish the flirtatious attention he's giving me and pray that we both don't crash and burn at the end.

---

Walking through the mall doesn't give me the warm fuzzy type of feelings it seems to give Daria as she flutters at my side, moving from rack to rack *oohing* and *ahhing* like each article of clothing she sees is somehow unique and exquisite. Even Briar appears completely in her element as she walks beside us, taking everything in with a satisfied smile.

It's not that I dislike shopping at the mall, but it's always stuffed full of people. At least when I go to the farmer's market, it's out in the open air where we can breathe easily without bumping into hordes of giggling tweens.

"You said plaid, right?" Daria asks, holding up a purple plaid shirt with sequins on the pockets and fringe around the hem.

I resist the urge to grimace. "Uh, could we go for something a little more...subdued?"

"You're not wearing black," she deadpans.

I tilt my chin and raise my eyebrows. "I wasn't suggesting that. I only meant something with less sequins and fringe." She shrugs and hangs the shirt back on the rack.

"How about this one?" Briar says, holding up a gray and black plaid shirt with thin maroon stripes running through it.

"Now that I can work with." I take the shirt from her and hold it against my torso. "I think I'll need a medium," I say, switching out the one I'm holding for one that's the right size. "Okay. I think the only other thing I need is a tiny backpack. Kat wears one on the night she and Aris go hunting for clues about her attacker."

"Ooh, this story sounds like a good one." Briar's eyebrows dance as we make our way to the teeny bopper accessories shop in the center of the mall.

"It really is. I can loan you the books if you want. Parker just got me the most recent release." As soon as I say it, a smile forms on my lips. I can't even go a day without thinking about all the sweet things he's done for me lately.

"Parker got you a romance novel?" Briar presses both hands to her chest. "That's the sweetest thing I've ever heard!" Her eyebrows crinkle over her big doe eyes, and I swear they almost seem to water.

"Yeah, yeah. We all know Parker's amazing," Daria says with a sarcastic bite. "He's the cinnamoniest cinnamon roll man I've ever met in real life. If only he had a twin." She crosses her arms under her chest, looking mildly annoyed.

"Well," I hedge, drawing the word out. "He does have brothers."

"Hm," Briar hums as if she's actually thinking over the possibility while Daria keeps her posture rigid and her mouth closed.

"They seem like really nice guys too," I continue, unfazed. "And I can attest to the fact that they all come from a great family. Parker's parents are the sweetest." Alex's face comes to mind as does the heart to heart we shared at her kitchen table.

"You know," Daria says, interrupting my thoughts. "It almost seems as if you're already considering you and Parker as a *couple*."

*Am I?*

I feel a flush creep up my neck, but thankfully, I'm saved by Briar. "That's not the vibe I'm getting," she counters in the sweetest voice she possesses. "To me it seems like you're just excited about the possibility of more with him. And you have every right to be because he's amazing."

I smile at my friend and squeeze her hand.

Daria stops, forcing us to do the same. "I didn't mean that like it was a bad thing. Jamie already knows I think she and Parker would make a great couple. I'm just saying...make sure he admits his feelings before you do. I don't want to see you get hurt." A haunted look fills her dark brown eyes before she shrugs it off with sarcasm. "I want to know he's as invested as you are before you go all Jack and Jill down the hill over him."

I let loose a nervous chuckle. "Seriously, D, you've got nothing to worry about. Parker and I are friends. Friends who have just recently started flirting and toeing the line between what we are and...what we could be. I wouldn't exactly say I'm *all in*."

What I don't tell her is that Parker's mom all but confessed he has feelings for me that he hasn't yet come to acknowledge.

She raises one dark eyebrow; a typical Daria move. "That's what you *say*. But I've also had to listen to your Shania love song playlist on repeat the last few nights. I'd say you're teetering off the edge of the friend cliff, ready and willing to fall in a pit of ooey, gooey love."

I shake my head and look away, unable to bear her scrutiny any longer, and almost sag with relief when I see the accessories store on my right. "Oh, there it is." Not waiting to see if my friends follow, I head for the store and make quick work of picking out a cute little lavender leather backpack. It's not really my style, but maybe I can gift it to Briar after Halloween. She's totally into girly, pastel accessories.

Once I've paid and the conversation from before appears to be long forgotten, the three of us head to the food court. "I'm dying for some orange chicken and rice," Daria says, holding a hand to her stomach. "I accidentally skipped lunch again."

"How do you accidentally skip lunch?" I ask her. "That's like saying I forgot to brush my hair. I could do it, but it would make the entire rest of my day miserable if I did. I may eat healthy most of the time, but my meals are planned and prepared way in advance because this girl gets hangry."

My friends share a laugh. "Girl, me too," Briar says. "I once skipped breakfast when I was running late for a college class, and I got so hungry by ten a.m., I ended up begging the person seated next to me for half of his granola bar."

"That's not *that* embarrassing," I say.

"No, you don't understand." She points out a nearby table where we each take a seat. "The guy already had half of the granola bar eaten and I begged him for the rest of it. He looked at me like I had three heads."

"Okay, point taken." Daria laughs, flipping her long hair over her shoulder. "Neither of you babes can miss a meal. In that case, let's decide where we're going to eat."

All three of us pick Panda Moon when a very familiar masculine voice calls out my name. My stomach drops. I turn to see Mike approaching with a shopping bag in his hand.

"Hey, Mike," I call back with an awkward wave, hoping the bright smile on his face isn't solely meant for me.

"I seem to be bumping into you everywhere lately," he says, sidling up to the table with a wink aimed straight at me.

I give my friends a tentative smile and Daria glares at Mike, narrowing her eyes. "Is that so? I seem to remember you *crashing* our farmer's market date. It didn't seem so…coincidental…to me."

I shoot my friend a scolding look, but she merely raises that judgy eyebrow of hers and sits back with her arms folded in front of her.

Mike huffs a tight laugh while rubbing the back of his neck. "So, Jamie…you got a minute?" He tips his head back, motioning away from the table. "To talk?"

Swallowing hard against the quickly rising lump in my throat, I glance between my friends, looking for an answer on what to do. Dealing with weird ex-boyfriend situations ranks right up there with having to deal with Stefan. Both dreadful experiences overall, even with Mike's apology last time. Daria stares me down with an undecipherable look, while Briar offers me an encouraging nod.

"Sure," I tell Mike, rising from my seat. "Just a minute though because we're about to grab lunch."

"Absolutely." He steps back, leading me away from the table. We start walking without any real destination, meandering around the center aisle displays at a snail's pace.

Finally, he clears his throat and faces me. "So, how have things been going lately?"

I blink up at him. "Mike, you just texted me the other day."

Another forced smile and he's back to rubbing the back of his head. "I-I know, it's just…you've barely responded to my texts, and I wasn't sure if you've been thinking about what I said. You know…thinking about me and you."

Placing my hand on his arm, I pull us to a stop. "To be honest, Mike, there's not really much to think about."

His expression shifts from confused to almost irritated. "Not much to think about? Jamie, we dated for over half a year. I was with you for longer than any other girl before you. And now you're telling me that you can drop me? Just like that?"

I open my mouth to speak, but he starts in again, moving a step closer. "How many times do I have to apologize for being a horrible boyfriend before you'll believe me?" He's close enough now that the warmth from his body stretches to me. "I've tried to give you the space you need while still showing you that I'm not giving up on us...I've texted you, sent you flowers, tried to spend time with you, even though it's clear you'd rather watch paint dry—"

"If that's clear to you, then why don't you just move on, Mike?"

His face falls, but I soldier on. "Look, it's not that I think you're a bad guy, I just think you weren't present enough in our relationship. It felt like you liked the idea of me more than you actually liked *me*."

"Jamie, that's not true," he says, shifting his shopping bag to his arm and taking both of my hands. "I liked—I *like*—you a lot. So much so that I'm ready to settle down with you. And I'm not ready to give up on us. Not yet." His gaze lifts to something behind me, then drops back to my face. "Jamie, look where we are."

My brow furrows as I spin around. We unknowingly stopped right outside of a jewelry store. Big, sparkling diamond rings are plastered all over advertisements on the windows. Large, warm hands grip my shoulders as Mike whispers into my ear. "Jamie, I know I was wishy washy about us before, but I'm ready to *commit* to you now. To be a *husband* to you. Isn't that something you want?"

I take in the beautiful engagement rings and envision one of them gracing my finger. It's a promising image he paints, bringing with it visions of white dresses and veils, vows and first dances, but when the picture materializes to a fully formed image, Mike isn't the groom at my side.

It's a guy with dark, unruly hair, tanned skin, and light green eyes. It's a man signing his vows, not speaking them, and we're surrounded by his sweet, fun family, not Mike's stuffy parents who always seemed to look down on me for not having ones of my own.

I slowly turn and try to give Mike a smile, but I know it falls flat. "Mike, I'm sorry. But I can't do this with you. I've moved on."

He doesn't say a word at first, only flits his eyes from the jewelry store to me. "I still think you should think about it." He says the words so quietly, I almost don't hear them over the din of people walking past us.

I sigh because what else can I do at this point, aside from making a scene. "Goodbye, Mike." I turn and walk back toward my friends, hoping and praying that when Parker envisions his future, it's me he sees too. Because if he doesn't, I might have just turned my back on my one and only chance of having my white picket fence kind of life.

# 19

♥

# Parker

Looking around at the tastefully creepy break room, I'm amazed that Jamie and Gladys pulled this off. Black and orange streamers hang from the ceiling while black balloons flank a table filled with food. Black ravens perched on black branches hang over the table with a gold pennant banner that reads *Happy Halloween*. There's even a smoking cauldron filled with who knows what bubbling beside the drinks.

Thankfully, Jamie didn't include any spiders or webs in her decorations. For that fact alone, I determine she's a keeper.

All my co-workers stand around talking, holding plates full of the festive Halloween-themed treats Jamie and Gladys prepared. They bought most of the food from O'Malley's subs, but I know Jamie made some of the Halloween-themed ones. It should probably weird me out that Les is biting into what looks like a bloody eyeball, but knowing it's made out of white chocolate and peanut butter makes me head toward the table to grab one for myself.

Just as I take a step, someone taps my shoulder. I turn and Jamie stands before me looking adorable in a short dark red wig, a white T-shirt, and jeans with a plaid shirt tied around her waist, completed by a little backpack hung over her shoulders.

*Very cute*, I sign as I smile down at her. *Or should I say, very Kat.*

It looks like she's fighting a smile when she reaches inside my leather jacket and pinches my side. I grab her hand, holding her back, and for the first time, she takes in my getup.

"And you look very...Aris." She smiles wide, flashing her teeth and biting that lower lip.

The long, dark wig I bought paired with the thick leather jacket Dane loaned me is so hot, sweat's dripping sweat in places it has no right to drip. But it's all worth it if she's going to look at me like that.

*Would I pass as a motorcycle riding fae?* I ask before tucking the sides of the wig behind my ears to expose the pointed ones I found online. Her mouth parts, and she reaches up to trace her hand over my ears. When her fingertips graze my neck, I resist the urge to shiver at the slight touch.

"You totally would," she says with a smaller, more intimate smile. "Wait." She trails a finger over the fake scar on my eyebrow that I worked tirelessly on for a half hour. "How did you—Parker, did you read the books?"

I shrug, then sign, *I wanted to make sure I really grasped his character.*

Her beautifully full lips part in surprise as she stares at me with a kind of wonder I know I don't deserve. All I did was read a few books.

*Let's eat before it's gone*, I sign before ushering her toward the food table. Both of us pile our plates with a sub and some ghoulish treats. Once we're settled in the corner, I scarf down the food faster than I probably should. But it's hard to communicate with her while my hands are full, and I'm determined to be a good, conversational date tonight.

Jamie might not be looking at this like we're on a date, but I am. It's why I suggested we go as a couple from one of her favorite series. I figured if I wanted her to start seeing us that way, I needed to encourage it. I offered to pick her up, but she had to be here early to finish some last-minute decorations and said I wasn't allowed to help. She insisted it needed to be a surprise.

I'll admit, after tending to her when she was sick and seeing that text from Mike, I might've gone down a dark hole of depression during my own sickness. But then she showed up. For me. Just like I had for her. And it renewed my will to want to fight for her—for us.

I toss my plate in the trash while she finishes the rest of her food and return with a smile on my face. *Everything looks great. You and Gladys did an amazing job. And the food? Fantastic.*

Her lips tip up in a shy smile as she signs, *Thank you.*

At that precise moment, Lucas approaches and looks at us like we're from outer space. "And who are you?" he asks Jamie, not even deigning to look my way. I already know the guy seems to think I'm the scum on the bottom of his shoe, but for whatever reason, it irritates me more than usual.

He turns in such a way that I can't see his lips and my rising irritation almost boils over. Especially when I see Jamie's lips tighten and her eyes take on a deadened appearance.

"We're characters from a book, Lucas," she says, through gritted teeth.

He tosses his head back and laughs, then shakes it as he walks away like we've somehow lost touch with reality.

As soon as he leaves, Jamie rolls her eyes and takes a sip of her drink. "He's such a jerk," she mouths for only me to see.

*Who did he think we were?* I don't know that he asked her anything, but I'm guessing he did by her response.

"He asked if you were a washed-up rockstar and if I was your groupie."

I bite my tongue to hold in a PG-13 word my mom wouldn't approve of. Jamie's right. Lucas is a jerk without any real cause. He thinks everyone is beneath him and I don't understand it. If Stefan doesn't see through his façade and offer Jamie the interview in the end, I'm going to seriously consider whether or not working here is worth it.

Over the course of the past few weeks, I've seen a different, softer side of my boss. But it'll all be a moot point for me if he gives the exclusive interview to anyone but Jamie. She works so hard at her job and takes each assignment seriously. Not that Eric and Lucas don't, but the quality of her storytelling far surpasses theirs. She's able to weave a tale that anyone would want to read, not just local sports enthusiasts. She does investigative work into the players, even at their junior levels, by getting in touch with the families and highlighting their personal strengths. She's personable and makes everyone she comes in contact with feel special, just like those kids from Miss Fowler's class.

"Anyway, let's not focus on him," Jamie says and signs at the same time, pulling me out of my thoughts. "Let's try and have some fun." She points to where Eric is trying to bob for an apple, then puts a hand to my arm to get my attention again. "Gladys insisted on having some old-school games."

I turn back to the tin bucket full of floating apples. Eric dunks his entire head into the water, trying to chase and catch one. A few people, including Les, look to be cheering him on. When he comes up for air, he resembles a drowned rat. Yeah, I don't think I'll be playing a game where I'm bobbing for apples in Eric's leftover spit.

*Maybe something else?* I ask, then point to the Alexa on the table that's playing music. *How about a dance?*

Jamie tilts her head, an amused smile curving the edges of her mouth. *You like to dance?*

I rear back with an expression that says, *duh, of course I do,* then take her hands in mine. She laughs, pushing me back and setting me away from her.

"But no one else is dancing!" Her hands grip my forearms like if she keeps me at arm's length, I somehow won't get my way. "And it's Halloween music!"

I shake loose of her hold then sign, *Turn on something we can dance to. Fast or slow, your pick.*

Her expression turns curious, and I can already tell she's going to give in. I can only hope that the curiosity brimming in her eyes is because she wants to know what it would be like to dance with me and not wondering how or if I'll move in time with the music.

Of course, I can't hear it, but I can *feel* it through the vibrations in the air, the floor, the pulsing of the bass. And I want to show her there's a romantic side to me she hasn't yet seen.

She takes a few steps toward the little black puck with lights, says something, then walks back over to me. "Okay," she says, putting her hands on her hips. "I kept to the theme and put on a different rendition of 'I Put a Spell on You.' It's a slower one." One eyebrow curves upward like she's daring me to do this. But she doesn't have to, I'm the one that put her up to it. There's nothing I want more than to slow dance with Jamie, even if it is in a room where all our co-workers are hanging out.

I raise my eyebrow right back and hold out a hand. Her lips quirk up just the slightest as she lets me pull her close. She rests one hand on my shoulder, while I hold the other secure and begin to sway us back and forth. Her face alights with surprise when she sees that I actually *can* dance and not just bumble around. To her credit, she tries to mask it, but I know all of Jamie's expressions by heart. There's very little she could hide from me.

Shockingly, Lucas begins to guide Jordy in a dance next to us and another couple who delivers papers begins to join in too.

Jamie turns and takes in the people moving around us, then looks up at me with her big, quartz-like eyes. There's something like awe, respect, and maybe a little surprise hidden in their depths. Whatever it is, she doesn't resist when I tug her closer and move her hands to my neck.

Running my hands down her arms, her skin pebbles. I try not to smile at the way her body reacts to my touch, but it takes effort. Gently, I press my chin against her temple, closing my eyes and breathing her in. We're still moving to the vibrations of the bass, but it feels like we're floating, like the entire world has fallen away and it's just us—together.

I'm so spellbound in this moment with her, totally consumed by the way she makes me feel, that it stuns me in place when she leans back the slightest bit and presses her lips to my jaw. My eyes fly open, but I don't dare move.

As if sensing the way my entire body has tensed in response to her *lips being on me*, she lowers her head to my chest to hide her face. But I'm not letting her get away that easily.

She just *kissed* me.

I grab Jamie's hand and lead her out into the main room that's crowded with cubicles. No one's out here, but it's still not private enough for what I want to ask. Moving until we're out in the hall by the elevators, I stop and whip her around to face me. Her chest heaves and her eyes are wide.

*You kissed me,* I sign. Not the most eloquent of ways to start this conversation, but I need her to confirm. It almost feels like a dream, something my mind conjured up to satiate my own desperate longings.

Her eyes immediately drop to the floor between us, and she tugs her bottom lip in between her teeth. Shifting on her feet, she wrings her hands like she's a child being scolded by a parent. I place my hands over hers to still her movements and calm her down. Spiking her anxiety is the last thing I want to do.

Her watery gaze rises to meet mine. "I'm sorry," she mouths. "Please don't hate me."

All at once, oxygen leaves me. How could she ever think that I'd hate her for making a move? This is what I've been waiting for—praying for—dying to have happen for who knows how long.

I hook a finger under her chin and tilt it up. Looking into her eyes, I realize the best communication I can give her wouldn't be spoken, signed, or written. It should be shown, given, said in a language that doesn't require words.

I tentatively lower my mouth to hers, but just as I make contact, she startles and steps back, her eyes searching mine. For a moment, I wonder if I've read this all wrong—if I've pushed her past what she thinks is acceptable.

Maybe it's just that I'm a terrible kisser. After all, I'm probably the least experienced person in that area. But then she signs, "You want this?" before motioning between the two of us.

I can't help but smile as I lift my hands to say, *More than anything*.

She doesn't respond. Only stares at me like she can't believe this is happening.

*I want you,* I sign. *Your kiss, your smile, your laugh…everything.*

Her mouth parts and I advance toward her, backing her up against the wall next to the elevators. *If you don't want me, you need to tell me now before I do something we'll both regret.*

We're chest to chest now, so close my body buzzes with the need to touch her. Gripping the sides of her face, I stare into her eyes and wait. All I want is to kiss her, to get lost like we were while we danced, to float off to a place where it's only the two of us.

But if she doesn't want this, what I want doesn't matter.

It'll shred my heart to pieces, but one word from her and I'll back away and do everything I can to repair our friendship.

Her lips quirk up the slightest bit on a timid smile. "I want you, Parker." Her body shivers on a quivery sigh the moment she says it like it took all her energy to release that bit of truth.

Without waiting another second, I tilt her face to meet mine and lay claim to her mouth like I've dreamt of doing for months. I'm slow at first, taking my time, praying she doesn't see through my inexperience and hate me for it.

But when her lips part under the pressure and I deepen the kiss, a vibration from the back of her throat spurs me on. My hands are suddenly moving everywhere at once. Over her shoulders, down her back, gripping her hips...

Sinking into the kiss, I lose myself in her taste, her warmth. But she's doing something with her hand that distracts me. I pull back, out of breath, and look down. The button to the elevator lights up under her fingers. My brows come together as my eyes flick to her face. A wicked sort of smile curves her lips as the elevator doors open, and she grabs the sides of my leather jacket, walking us backward and dragging me inside.

# 20

♥

# Jamie

I can't believe this is happening. I CAN'T BELIEVE THIS IS HAPPENING.

I'm *kissing* my best friend. And boy, can he *kiss*.

Yes, I know I started it. But something about being in his arms while we danced tipped me over the edge. The tension between us rose to new levels, new heights I didn't even realize existed. Parker's smell, his touch, it all overwhelmed me to the point that I couldn't be near him a second longer unless I gave in to the urge to kiss his chiseled jaw.

And then he looked so shocked—so taken off guard—that I instantly regretted it.

I'd convinced myself that I'd been reading him wrong these past few weeks, that everything we've shared was simply done in the name of friendship and nothing more. Until he dragged me away from the party and kissed me *again*. Intentionally. Purposefully. Deliciously.

I had no choice but to be honest about my feelings.

Kissing Parker is an experience unlike any other and I never want it to end. Which is why the need to be alone with him overtook me, and I pounded on the elevator button until the doors finally opened.

Grabbing his leather jacket, I pull him inside, push on the button that closes the doors, and press my lips against his again. My enthusiasm seems to take him by surprise, but it doesn't take him long to catch up.

Electricity sparks and sizzles between us as his mouth moves over mine. Someone who could hear might try to rein in their heavy breathing during a kiss, but Parker can't be bothered. His breaths are erratic and wild, mimicking the desire in his touch.

Once again, my back's against the cool metal wall, but this time, Parker hauls me up higher by my legs. I squeak in surprise, but instinctively wrap them around him anyway. He doesn't miss a beat as he kisses me again, then whispers his lips gently down my throat.

I whip the wig off his head, needing to run my fingers through his real hair, then I'm clinging to his shoulders, his arms, his back, loving the feel of him under my hands.

How could I never have realized that things would be like this between us? How could I have ignored this crackling tension for so long, almost missing it completely?

He meets my mouth again with a deep groan that sends warmth zinging through my entire body. Then the elevator doors open, and I pull back, hoping that's not what I think it is.

But of course, my worst fear is confirmed.

Stefan, Gladys, and Lucas stand at each other's sides, taking in the view with contrasting expressions. Gladys's is mildly impressed, while Stefan's flashes between anger and embarrassment, and Lucas smiles with a maniacal glee that turns my stomach.

Parker releases me and I adjust my top, pulling the sleeves of the plaid shirt around my waist tight. "Um," I start, then clear the gravel from my throat. "We were just…uh…" Any sort of valid explanation escapes me.

"Sorry to interrupt," Gladys says, changing the subject and saving me from having to say, *we were just making out in the elevator.* "But it's time to play pass the pumpkin. And you won't want to miss it because I shoved a fifty inside." She wiggles her eyebrows like fifty bucks is akin to winning the lottery.

"Yeah," I say, running a hand over my wig, making sure it's not totally disheveled. "Um. We'll be right there." Out of the corner of my eye, Parker picks up his wig and tries to fit it back on his head.

"I thought I saw them come this way, Mr. Sanders," Lucas says, his sick smile widening. "Guess I was right." Without another word, he stalks off and leaves us to our fate, whistling while he goes. Clearly, he orchestrated this interruption.

Gladys sends me a knowing smirk with a wink, then saunters off back to the break room while Stefan doesn't so much as budge.

Silence permeates the air, heavy and thick, while his expression gives nothing away. Finally, our boss sighs and says, "We'll need to discuss this in my office on Monday morning." My stomach roils at his pronouncement, and he leaves without another word.

I release a deep exhale and turn to face the man I'm not sure I can still look in the eyes. I'm so afraid of what I'll read in his expression after what just happened between us. Regret? Shame? Disgust?

But when I meet Parker's eyes, they sparkle with amusement as he runs a hand over his mouth. "We're in so much trouble," I say with a groan.

He laughs and shakes his head. *It'll be alright.*

"Are we...OK?" I sign.

His wide smile nearly blinds me as he hooks an arm around my waist and pecks me on the lips. *Never been better*, he signs, then tips his head toward where we should be. *Ready to pass the pumpkin?*

Blinking the kiss-induced haze of the last few minutes away, I nod. Parker leads me back to the break room like what we just did together wasn't completely unexpected and more than a little bit taboo for a couple of people who insist we're *just friends*.

By the end of the night, I'm exhausted. Even with more of my co-workers helping me and Gladys remove the party decorations, it was still tiring. Plus, my emotions have officially been overextended. First with my warring feelings for Parker, then giving in to them, then being caught with him in the elevator by none other than my *boss*.

Ugh.

Thankfully, Stefan never said another word to me or Parker before he left the party early. But that doesn't erase the ball of anxiety that's knotting up my insides even as we speak. All weekend long I'll worry about what our conversation will be like on Monday.

*I guess I can kiss that interview with Paris goodbye.* Bosses don't take kindly to employees who make out with their co-workers at work parties, I'm sure.

Warm hands press down on my shoulders. Parker's easy smile works to loosen a bit of the tension eating me up as he motions for us to head out.

I grab my little backpack, promising myself I'll grab the boxes of decorations on Monday when I'm not so tired. I take a deep inhale of the cool evening air once we make it outside. The wind's bite makes me shiver, but Parker must notice because the next second, he drapes his leather jacket around my shoulders.

He's being so sweet and tender, I almost can't take it. But then again, Parker's always like this. He's always gentlemanly and kind. Why couldn't I ever see those things as boyfriend material before now? Why did it take me this long to wake up to his attention?

Then like a light bulb flickering to life, I remember why I refused to see him as more. *Tyson.* All the ugly memories of our breakup float through my mind, unsettling me. What have I done? Did I doom Parker and me to the same fate by making a move on him?

Before I can question myself too much, we're at my car. I turn to face him and he grips the lapels of his jacket, pulling me closer. He kisses me again, soft and sweet, totally unhurried, as if we have all the time in the world. When I taste the punch and candy from the party on his lips, I smile against his mouth. It breaks the kiss and he pulls back, searching my eyes.

Lifting his hands, he signs, *What's so funny?*

I shake my head. "Nothing."

He tilts his head, not believing me. *Am I a bad kisser?*

A laugh erupts from me so forcefully, I double over. When I straighten, Parker's arms are crossed, his expression unamused. "You are *not* a bad kisser," I insist, then wrap my hands around his trim waist and bring him back to me. "How could you even think such a thing?"

He pulls his lips into a thin line, then licks his bottom lip like he's mulling over what to say. Finally, he signs, *You're my first.*

My brow furrows. "Your first what?"

*I've never kissed a girl before. Besides a peck.*

My mouth parts as I blink up at him. I'm sure my eyes are as big as dinner plates as I take in this bit of information. Parker's mouth twists to the side as he reads my reaction. I tighten my hands around him. "You're an amazing kisser, Parker. Like, out-of-this-universe amazing. And that's not why I was smiling."

His lips tilt into a boyish half-smile as he shrugs like he's waiting for more.

I lift an eyebrow. "I smiled because you *unsurprisingly* taste like candy."

Laughing, he throws his head back and wraps his arms around me. I nestle into him, joining in, and soon we're both shaking with uncontrollable laughter. I'm thankful we're alone and that no one is around to witness this. Hysterically laughing in a parking lot at close to midnight might look weird to anyone else, but for me and my best friend, it feels as if we were always meant to do this.

# 21

♥

# Jamie

Because this Saturday is unlike any other day in existence because I KISSED MY BEST FRIEND last night, I insisted Daria and I forego the farmer's market and go straight to brunch with Briar.

She's been shooting me weird looks all morning, even after Briar showed up with her sweet disposition. "So, what's this all about?" Briar asks before taking a sip of her iced coffee. "You never skip the farmer's market."

I pull my lips in, shifting my eyes from one friend to the other.

"Spit it out, Jamie!" Daria's wide eyes as she leans into the table toward me are my undoing.

"Parker and I made out last night!" I bring both hands up to cover my mouth as I take in my friends' reactions.

Daria purses her lips, fighting a smile, and sits back in her chair. She points a perfectly manicured finger at me accusingly. "I knew it! I knew this was why you came home so late and had 'When You Kiss Me' blaring when I woke up this morning."

Briar squeals in delight. "This is so exciting!" She starts slapping my arm over and over. "Tell. Us. Everything! Was it *amazing*? Was it all you hoped it would be? Gah, he just seems like he'd be *such* a good kisser." She presses both hands to her chest like she's about to faint.

"It was so good," I say, letting my smile break free. "Like, I can't even explain it with words."

Briar squeals again while Daria covers her ears. "Okay, we get it, you're excited." D chuckles. "Now, let's get the nitty gritty details." She zeroes in on me with her signature intimidating look. "Who started it? You or him?"

I fold and refold the napkin on the table. "Well…I *may* have started it."

"I knew it." Again, Daria smirks like she's privy to everything. "I knew you wouldn't last long as soon as you admitted your feelings to us."

I throw up my hands. "I couldn't help it! The man dressed like a character from my favorite book for me, even reading the series to get fully into character, then asked me to dance at the Halloween party, in front of everyone, mind you," I add, turning toward Briar, who practically faints at that detail, "and I just got swept up in the moment. Besides." I skip my eyes to Daria. "You're the one who told me to put the moves on him. You got in my head!"

She flashes me a satisfied smile while her eyebrows dance up and down.

"But there's more," I say, biting my lip. "After I kissed him, he froze and I feared I'd royally messed up."

"What happened?" Briar whispers, leaning in like she's hanging on my every word.

"He pulled me out into the hall by the elevators and asked me if I kissed him."

"How could he not have known?" Daria's voice rises with skepticism.

"He knew," I say. "I think he just needed me to…I don't know…admit it. Besides, I only kissed his jaw."

"Aww," Briar simpers, "his *jaw*."

Daria rolls her eyes with a smile. "Okay, so what did you say?"

"Well, at that point I really did think I messed up, so I begged him not to hate me. And that's when he told me he wanted me and pressed me up against the wall."

"Ahhhhh!" Both of my friends squeal now, gaining the attention of people walking past our quaint little table by the sidewalk. I purposely chose outdoor seating at our favorite café for this exact reason, but apparently it wasn't enough. Now we've got literal passersby thinking we're nuts.

"Shhh," I shush my friends. "Keep it down. People are staring." They immediately school their expressions. "Okay, so we're kissing, and then I suddenly get the urge to drag him into the elevator where we continue making out until Stefan opened the elevator doors and caught us."

Both my friends' mouths fall open.

"Your boss caught you?" Briar asks while Daria winces.

I sigh and fiddle with the straw in my coffee. "Unfortunately, yes. And then he proceeded to tell us that we needed to discuss it in his office on Monday."

Briar scrunches up her nose. "Yikes. That can't be good."

"I'm just resigning myself to the fact that I've lost my chance at the interview with Paris. I figure if I tell myself that now, it'll soften the blow once he actually delivers it." I'm keeping my tone light, pretending like the situation doesn't bother me as much as it does…but inside, I'm reeling with the possibility that kissing Parker might've lost me the most important assignment of my career thus far.

Daria reaches over the table and squeezes my hand. "I'm sorry, Jamie. I know how badly you wanted it."

I offer her a reassuring smile. "It's really okay. I don't regret kissing Parker, even if it was the final nail in the proverbial coffin for me."

Briar giggles as she opens her menu. "Well, let's order and you can give us all the juicy details about that kiss," she says with a wink.

For a moment, my heart lightens. Because what I said was true. Even if kissing Parker made me officially lose this interview, it was still worth it. But I can't deny that there's a twinge in my chest that still wishes things could've turned out differently, especially when I'm not even sure I'll have a job after our meeting on Monday.

# 22

♥

# JAMIE

I'M ON MY OWN for the evening since Daria chose to work some overtime at Gail's Department Store. That means I'll be wearing the rattiest clothes I can find while also doing a glittery black charcoal face mask that burns like Hades' hair when I rip it off, and dancing around the house listening to Shania's new album.

And since I ate super healthy all day, I *might* even indulge in the tiniest bowl of ice cream while I sit and blog for a bit about the new book Parker got me.

*Parker.*

I've practically floated around on a cloud all day thinking about what we shared last night. In truth, I'm not sure where we're going to go from here, but I'm trying not to be as afraid of it anymore. There's still a low-level anxiety that settles under my skin anytime I remember what went down between me and Tyson…but Parker and I have already crossed that line. There's no going back now.

And it's clear that our feelings are mutual, what with all the delicious, mind-blowingly good kissing we did.

But that's not even the best part. No, that's been the sweet and flirty back and forth texts all day. My phone buzzes on my nightstand again and I practically squeal in delight when I pick it up and toss myself onto my bed, belly first.

As soon as I read the text, I smile from ear to ear. The mask on my face instantly begins to crack, so I school my expression.

**Parker**: So if you're home alone tonight…does that mean I can come over?

I release a love-sick sigh and roll over onto my back.

**Jamie**: I would say yes, but…I'm already in my pajamas.
**Parker**: The pink ones?

I bite my lip against a giddy smile.

**Jamie**: Since when do you memorize my pajamas?
**Parker**: Since I come over when you're sick.
**Jamie**: *eye roll emoji*

I lay my phone down on the bed and close my eyes, instantly bringing up the memory of that day. I'm still so embarrassed he caught me in nothing but a towel and saw me hack my lungs out afterward, but I should've known then how deep his feelings ran. That was a total boyfriend move.

When there's no immediate response from Parker, I rise from the bed and turn on my playlist, popping in my earbuds as I go. As much as I'd love to have him over and continue with where we left off last night, the thought of doing so makes me feel like a needy girlfriend.

And if there's anything I've learned from the dating scene this past year, it's that I need to let a guy make the first moves. Every time I tried to press Mike for more, it only got me less of what I wanted.

So even though I think Parker is different, taking things slow is probably in my best interest. For once, Daria's advice doesn't seem so silly. I'm content to continue our flirty texts all night if he is.

Besides, tonight is the perfect opportunity to deep clean the kitchen. I need to do something that will distract me from the looming meeting with Stefan on Monday. And I'm not left with a ton of time during the week between my job, blogging, and covering local sporting events, so I've got to get it in while I can. Plus, I'm multitasking with the face mask.

I get to work cleaning, belting out the lyrics of the song I'm listening to as I go.

In minutes, I've got the cupboards wiped down and the kitchen island cleared. I'm dancing around with the mop, using the handle as a makeshift microphone while trying to reach a particularly high note in the song, when I spin around and scream bloody murder at the sight of the man standing in front of me. I drop the mop and jump onto the counter like that would ever save me from an intruder.

Parker's eyes are wide, an apologetic smile on his face as he holds one hand out to steady me like he might a frightened horse and the other holds a two cartons of ice cream—Rocky Road and Mint Chocolate Chip.

"Parker!" I screech, yanking the ear buds out of my ears. "You scared the living daylights out of me!" I don't know how to sign living daylights, but I definitely signed the part about him scaring me.

He sets the ice cream down on the island, then takes slow steps toward me. *I'm sorry. I just wanted to surprise you. But you didn't answer the door when I knocked...I was worried.*

As my erratic heartrate begins to come back down to normal, so do my thoughts. "It's okay. I was just listening to music." I hold up my earbuds, and he nods. The closer he gets to me, the more he looks like he's trying his hardest not to smile. "What is it? What's so funny?"

He purses his lips, then lifts a finger and points at my face. *You look a little bit like a swamp monster.*

My hand flies to my face as I remember the glittery charcoal face mask that's probably cracked and dried to bits by now. Groaning, I hop off the counter and run to the bathroom to wash it off before I can embarrass myself more.

Once it's gone and my face is dried, I skulk back into the kitchen area where Parker casually leans against the island with that perfect half-smile of his. He looks so right standing there, almost like he belongs here. With me. Forever.

I shove the needy thoughts away and walk straight for the ice cream beside him. "My two favorite kinds," I say as well as sign. "Thank you."

*You're welcome.* His eyes drift down my body then back up to my face. *You're not wearing the pink ones.*

I shove his arm and he laughs before his expression turns serious. *Sorry to interrupt, I...* he shrugs. *I just missed you. Wanted to see you.*

I suck in a deep breath, then release it. "I missed you too." It feels good to say and even better to see those words come from him first. It gives me hope that his feelings really are as deep as mine. Maybe we won't end in disaster, after all.

I move closer and set my hands on his waist. "So...do you want to stay for a while and hang out?" Cleaning can be left for another night now that he's here.

A slow grin works its way to his tanned face when he signs, *Thought you'd never ask.* His gaze drops to my lips, then flicks back to my eyes, questioning. I offer him one solitary nod before he wraps his arms around me and gives me a sweet and slow kiss.

I'm not sure how it's possible but kissing him now feels even better than it did last night. Like a precious keepsake, a promise of something more. Something real and deep and right.

I pull away before either of us can get too carried away like we obviously did in the elevator and ask, "Want to watch a movie?"

He dips his chin while licking his lips and it takes a great amount of effort not to kiss him again. *Is it okay if I use the restroom first*, he signs, then points down the hall.

"Oh, go ahead." As soon as he leaves, I grab the soft blanket he left here plus my own and throw them on the couch, then head straight for the ice cream he brought. But before I reach it, my doorbell rings.

"What in the world," I mutter to myself as I trek to the door. Tossing it open, my breath hitches. "Mike? What are you doing here?"

"Jamie," he says on a swallow. "I'm sorry to just show up out of the blue like this, but after how we left things, I knew you'd say no to seeing me."

Anger and annoyance swirl together in my gut at his boldness. "If you knew that, then why did you think it was a good idea to show up at my house unannounced?"

His face pales the slightest bit, but he doesn't retreat. "Because you're not taking me seriously. You said you'd give us dating some thought and it doesn't seem like you have. I don't think you really understand how committed I am to you."

He takes a step closer, his eyes searching mine. "And then I realized I used the word like. That was wrong. It didn't—it *doesn't*—fully encompass how I feel about you." He swallows, the muscles in his jaw jumping. "I love you, Jamie."

I shiver, whether from the evening chill or his words, I'm not sure. "It's too late, Mike. It's over for us. I've moved on." His crestfallen face makes me pause, but I can't give him what he wants. "How many more times do I need to tell you before you believe it?"

"Jamie, please," he begs. "I was an idiot, okay? A total and complete idiot to let you go. You were the best girlfriend I've ever had, and I just know you'll make an amazing wife." Without waiting for a reply, he gets down on one knee on my front step and whips out a ring box.

Opening it, he meets my gaze and says, "Jamie, I know it's unconventional for me to ask you like this and it's sudden...I get that, but—"

"Mike, stop. Don't." I back up, completely stunned by the huge diamond ring in the box and meet a very solid chest at my back.

I spin around and the sight that greets me takes me off guard. Parker's expression is murderous as his eyes dart from Mike to me. "Parker," I say, but his eyes aren't on me. I grab his arm to get his attention, but he jerks away at my touch. He refuses to meet my eyes, locking his gaze on Mike.

Slowly, Mike rises to his feet as Parker advances on him. They stand toe to toe for several seconds, Parker looming over Mike's slightly shorter frame. Panic overwhelms me when I think they might get into a fight.

I grab Parker's arm to get his attention and try to explain that I had nothing to do with this, but he shrugs me off again. For too long, the two men just stare at each other, fuming.

I try one more time to get Parker's attention. He briefly meets my eyes, then starts to back away from Mike. I step in between them, hoping to diffuse the situation, and start signing, "I didn't know this was going to happen."

Parker scoffs and shakes his head. *You sure? Because I know you're still texting him. He sent you flowers. What else am I missing?*

I'm taken aback by his reaction. "I am not still texting him."

Parker's expression turns pained, torturous. *Well, he's texting you. I saw it.*

I don't immediately respond because anything I say right now would be said in irritation. He had no right to look at my phone. And he's misconstruing the entire situation.

"What are you guys saying?" Mike interrupts, but we both ignore him.

*What else are you hiding from me, Jamie?* Parker asks. *Do you want to get back together with Mike? To marry him?* His eyes spark in challenge.

Bristling at the notion that I'm somehow entertaining Mike's paltry attempts to get me back, I step forward and look up into Parker's face. "If you don't already know the answer to that question, we're not as close as I thought we were."

He flinches, then backs up. With one last glare at both me and Mike, he prowls to his truck and drives off, gravel flying in his wake.

I'm stunned to silence as my heart breaks. How could he think I'd want Mike after what we shared?

"What was *he* doing here?" Mike seethes.

I whirl on my ex. "He is *allowed* to be here, unlike you. Mike, what makes you think you can come over to my house and propose when I've given you no indication that we are together?" My voice rises with each word as he backs away from me. "You are *not* welcome here, we are *not* dating, and we never will be. Do you understand or do I need to resort to more drastic measures?"

His head drops low, and he pockets the ring box. "No, you don't. I-I'm sorry, I just—"

"You just nothing," I say, slicing my hand through the air. "Once again, Mike, *you* are the one who started ditching *me*. I may have broken up with you, but you gave me no choice. You lost your chance, I've moved on."

His eyes meet mine and there's more emotion in them than I've ever seen from him before. "With Parker?"

I don't offer him a response before I march back inside and slam the door.

# 23

♥

# PARKER

When I storm into my apartment, Dane startles from his spot on the couch. He immediately drops the book he was reading and stands. Signing, he asks, "What's the matter? Something happen?"

I don't stop to give him a response as I stomp toward my room and slam the bedroom door behind me. Pacing back and forth, I rake my fingers through my hair. My mind refuses to release the image of Mike down on one knee in front of Jamie, her hand pressed to her mouth in shock as she backed into me.

I had to leave, I couldn't look at him—or her—another minute without being tempted to do something I'd regret. Something like pound my fist into Mike's face for having the audacity to propose to the woman I kissed last night—then again tonight. The woman I've dedicated these last few weeks to wooing...and for what? Just so Mike could be the one to get down on his knee with the biggest diamond ring I've ever seen and propose?

I mean sure, why not? He's got the better job, the better car, and he's never been friend-zoned the way I have. Oh, and let's not forget, he's *not* deaf! So why shouldn't she choose him over me?

I don't even realize Dane's in my room until I practically run into him. "Don't ignore me," he signs. "Tell me what's going on."

I shake my head, my hands moving erratically. *Nothing. Nothing at all.*

He cocks his head to the side, his expression unimpressed. "Stop being an idiot and tell me."

I glower at my brother and throw up my hands. *Her ex-boyfriend proposed to her while I was at her house. Right in front of me.*

Dane jerks his head back. "What? Why?"

Raising my eyebrows, I give him a look that says, *how would I know?* But I do know. Mike did it because he's pulling out all the stops to get Jamie back. And why? All because his boss told him he needs to settle down or he won't inherit the business?

I grit my teeth, even more frustrated at Mike. He's got some nerve...

"Okay," Dane says, moving to sit on the edge of my bed. "Start from the beginning and tell me everything that happened tonight."

I do as he asks and sign the entire story. By the end, I drop down beside him, my elbows on my knees with my head in my hands. We sit side by side for a long time until he jabs me in the ribs.

When I meet his eyes, he says, "Sounds like you need to talk to her and apologize for overreacting."

I bite my tongue, my hands still moving at a fast pace. *Am I overreacting? He's already had a chance with her. He blew it. And now he thinks he can ride in and steal her away from me?*

Dane shrugs one shoulder. "Some guys are just dense, Parker. Or worse, they don't take no for an answer." The thought of Mike pursuing Jamie against her will makes my blood boil. "But what I'm saying is that you overreacted by insinuating Jamie would choose him over you. It sounds like even with all of Mike's attempts to get her back, she's still fallen for you. You said you guys kissed—that she said it was amazing.

A girl like Jamie wouldn't do that if she was planning on giving her ex a chance."

Blowing out a breath, I scrub both hands down my face. I know he's right. I know I messed up with Jamie. But I also know I couldn't have stayed there a second longer without exploding on Mike. He's never treated Jamie right and apparently, never will.

Dane taps my arm and signs again. "You need to talk to her."

Guilt and shame war within me as I hang my head and pull out my phone. I have several text messages from Jamie. Groaning, I fall back on my bed and scrub my hands down my face. Dane pats my leg then his weight lifts from the bed and I know he's left me alone to wallow in my own idiocy.

# 24

♥

# Jamie

"He didn't respond to any of my texts," I whine from my spot at the kitchen island. Jabbing my spoon into my second bowl of sugary cereal, I sniffle while taking a bite. "He just totally ignored me. Why would he do that, D? Why?" Milk drips from my chin with each crunch and Daria looks on with a grimace.

"Honey, he was probably just really upset at seeing Mike here. I mean, I would've kicked the guy in the kneecaps if I'd been here."

I almost smile at my friend and the way she's so eager to resort to violence on my behalf. "But still." I swallow my bite before any more milk trickles down my chin. "He shouldn't have acted like I wanted Mike to propose. I didn't!"

Daria rubs my back in soothing motions. "You're right. He totally shouldn't have. And he should've responded to at least one of your texts." She lets out a soft sigh. "Have you checked your phone recently?"

I shake my head. "No, it died after the tenth message I sent him so I just chalked it up as a lost cause and plugged it in for the night. I can't bring myself to check it. Not when I'm positive he's still furious with me." I poke my spoon in the cereal and swirl it around. "You didn't see his face, D. He was *so* mad."

"At you or Mike?"

I shrug. "I don't know. It seemed like he blamed me for him being here." Staring into the cereal abyss, I mumble, "I knew this was going to happen. This is me and Tyson all over again, but this time it's worse because it's Parker. And I love him!" I raise my gaze to meet Daria's and the uncharacteristic sympathy shining in her eyes makes mine water all over again.

She's silent while she finishes her own cereal and sets her bowl in the sink when she's done. "I think you need to quit worrying about it for now. Go see your pops like you always do on Sundays and just get out for a bit. Leave your phone here if you're afraid to check it."

I eye her for a minute while I think over her suggestion. "Maybe you're right. I do need to see him and maybe it'll lift my spirits." If things go like they did last week though, it won't. It'll only add to my anxiety over the situation with Parker. I guess at this point I can only pray that Pops will be in his right mind and happy to see me.

Daria scoots around the island and wraps me in a hug. "I love you, Jamie. And you're going to be fine. Parker is your friend. Just remember that. He may need some time to cool off, but I have no doubt he'll come around for you."

I meet her eyes and wipe away the last of my tears. "I hope you're right."

She smiles. "I think I am. Now go get ready to see your pops."

I didn't take long to get ready. Not knowing where I stand with Parker has completely ruined my daily self-care routine. Not only have I lost my hot date from the other night, but I've also lost my best friend. The one who I can joke with no matter what, the guy who pranks me as much as I prank him and never gets tired of our antics, the person I feel comfortable enough to tell anything to…and now we're barely speaking.

I turned my phone on right before I left for the care center and the only text I received from him was one that said, "We need to talk."

I couldn't even bring myself to respond. We barely got a chance to explore what a romantic relationship could be like between us and he already wants to break it off. All because Mike showed up at the worst moment ever. When I read the text, I was a puddle of tears all over again so I decided to leave my phone at home.

Daria was right, I did need to get out.

The warm sunshine feels good on my face as I walk down the long sidewalk into the care center. Knowing I'll get to see Pops soon puts a smile in place of my earlier frown. Even if he doesn't know it's me, it'll still be good to see him.

By the time I reach his room, I feel considerably lighter. "Hey, Pops," I say as I knock on the doorframe. He looks up from where he's making his bed and his grin widens.

"Hey, James Gang. Where've you been hiding?"

Tears prick the backs of my eyes as I move further into the room. *He knows me.*

"Nowhere, just been busy with work stuff." I come around the bed to stand next to him and he immediately wraps me in a hug. I squeeze him tight as the familiar scent of musk and spice overwhelms me, bringing the tears I've been fighting to the surface. *He's here*. And even though it might not last long, right now, he knows me.

When I begin to sniffle, he runs a hand down the back of my hair. "Aw, what is it, James? Something happen?"

I pull back and wipe a tear from my cheek, nodding. "I just had a fight with my best friend." I can't keep the emotion from my voice, and it warbles and squeaks at all the wrong times.

Pops grabs me by the shoulders and lowers me onto the bed next to him. "Tell me about it, James."

I go into the story of what happened with Parker, from the time he started sending me mixed signals up until last night. Pops even nods at the appropriate times like he's really listening, and it gives me hope that he is. I'm full-on crying *again* by the end, doing my best to swipe away the tears before they dampen the bedspread beneath us.

"Parker is the one you work with, right?" he asks. I smile at the simple fact that he *remembers*.

"Yes, that's him."

He gives me a slow nod. "Everything you've told me about him points to him being a good guy. But even us good guys get our wires crossed sometimes, especially," he says, booping me on the nose, "when there's a beautiful girl in our sights. It sounds like he needed to leave before he took that guy Mike's head off."

I laugh, but it's weak. "You think so?"

"I do. You said before that he got jealous of some messages this guy sent you, so he probably feels like Mike already has a leg up on him. Maybe he wonders if he can even compete for your heart."

"But there's no competition, Pops. I'd always choose Parker."

Pops smiles so wide, the gold cap on one of his molars winks at me. "Then I think you need to go get your man." All at once his smile falters and his brows pinch together. "That reminds me, have you seen Loretta around today? I can't seem to find her."

My heart sags at the question. "No, Pops," I say, my own smile dimming. "Not today."

He nods and pats my leg. "I'm sure she'll turn up soon. She's never gone for long. Besides, it's been good to talk with you."

I reach over and pull him into a hug. "It's been *so* good to talk with you too."

I end up staying for another half hour until Pops's eyes begin to droop while he rests in his recliner. When I pull into my driveway at home, a very familiar guy sits on my front step with a baby plant in his large hands.

I put my car in park and stare at Parker through my passenger-side window. His expression is so pained, it almost makes me want to weep again just looking at him. He immediately rises when I get out of my car and starts toward me.

When we're an arm's length away from each other, I can't bring myself to meet his eyes. Then the cutest little green plant comes into view as he holds it out to me. I slowly lift my gaze to his. A sheepish smile crosses his face as he retracts the plant and sets it down on the front step.

*I'm sorry about last night. Can we talk?*

I pull my sweater a little tighter around my midsection and motion for us to go inside. Though it's sunny, it's still too cold to be hanging out in the frigid air for a long time and I have no idea how this conversation is going to go. If I had to guess, there will most definitely be some crying. From me. Not Parker.

After he grabs the plant, I let us in and lead him to the couch where he sits and faces me, our knees touching. He looks so large, almost too large for my grandparents' retro floral couch.

*May I go first?* he asks.

Trepidation claws its way up my throat. This is it. He's going to say we were better off as friends. That though he's sorry for how things went down, we never should've taken our relationship to a romantic level.

I inhale a deep breath and try to guard my heart against what's to come.

At my nod, Parker begins signing. *I was wrong to get so upset. It wasn't you I was mad at, it was Mike. I...* He averts his eyes and swallows. *Sometimes I struggle with insecurity. Maybe it stems from being bullied some as a kid, I don't know. But when I saw Mike propose to you with that gigantic ring, it made me think that I'd never measure up. Plus, you've dated him. You guys have a history. And you and I have only ever been just friends.*

My heart twists when Parker signs those last words. We might've only been friends up until the other night, but something changed between us then—something significant. And the thought of going back to being *just* friends nearly cracks my heart in two.

"You need to know that I didn't want Mike to propose," I say as well as sign. "He approached me in the mall last week while I was with my friends and basically told me he was ready to propose."

Parker stiffens and his expression turns hard. I rush on before his anger has the chance to boil over. "But I told him that we were over. I walked away from him, expecting to never hear from him again. Which is why I was shocked when he showed up here last night."

Parker looks down and picks at his thumbnail. I tap his knee to get his attention. "I wasn't trying to hide anything from you. Yes, he has been texting me, but I've only been giving him one-word answers. I've tried to make it clear to him that he and I are over. What happened last night was completely unwarranted, I promise."

His green eyes glisten like emerald pools. *I should've stayed. I'm sorry. A good friend wouldn't have jumped to conclusions.*

"You're still a good friend, Parker."

He doesn't respond in sign, just watches me, waiting for something more. He hasn't told me yet that he thinks we're better off as friends.

And he confessed that he struggles with insecurity which means maybe I'm the one who has to stake my claim here—to go for what I really want, without holding back.

I can't keep letting a past high school relationship dictate my future with Parker. It's now or never.

"But I don't want to be friends anymore," I say as I bite my lip and I wait for his reaction.

His face falls. *You don't?*

I shake my head. "No. I want more. I'm tired of being just friends with you."

Nothing happens for a long, breathless moment, until finally, he grabs both of my hands and runs his thumbs over them, leaning in closer. He nuzzles my nose with his before gently pressing his lips against mine. When he pulls back, he brings his hands between us to sign, *I have never wanted to be only friends with you. I love you, Jamie.*

Tears well in my eyes against my will. "You do?"

He nods as he tucks a piece of hair behind my ear. *With all my heart. I'm yours. I've been in love with you almost as long as I've known you.*

Crying, I grab his face and kiss him with so much force, it knocks him back. But before I can deepen it the way I want to, he sets me away from him and with a playful smile, signs, *Does this mean you love me too?*

A grin splits my mouth wide. "Of course I do you stupid man. Now kiss me."

# 25

♥

# Jamie

Today is the day of reckoning for my new boyfriend and me.

Yes, that's right. I said *boyfriend*.

After Parker and I made up, we commenced with some more delicious kissing, then he officially asked me to be his girlfriend. *Cue girlie inner squeal!* But now, it's time to face the music and tell our boss that we're choosing our relationship over our jobs.

Potentially. If it comes to that.

Parker squeezes my hand as Stefan's office looms before us. I meet his eyes and offer him the most reassuring smile I can muster under the circumstances. Parker said he wanted to meet with Stefan alone first, which I tried to argue with, but he insisted. He said there's another matter he needs to speak with him about and I didn't pry.

He kisses me on the forehead before heading into Stefan's office, alone.

Minutes pass and my anxiety rises, wondering how our boss is taking the news of us dating. I don't want to have to quit my job, but that's exactly what I plan to do if Stefan tells us dating each other goes against company policy.

Parker needs his job. And as badly as I want the interview with Paris, I can't let him sacrifice himself for me.

I thought I'd be depressed at the prospect of giving up my job for a relationship, but I already know that what I have with Parker is long-term, especially considering we've already said love words. But it's more than that. Dating my best friend is like already knowing where I'll end up. Because now that we've crossed the hurdle of *what if*, everything else is just...*when*. I no longer wonder if I'll get my chance at the white-picket fence life, chasing our kids around at soccer games. It's just a matter of *when* it will happen.

Finally, Parker emerges from Stefan's office with a tentative smile, the Sign Language interpreter following him out. Not giving anything away, he signs, *Your turn*, then gives my upper arm a reassuring squeeze. I suck in a breath, then move forward, already dreading what's about to come next.

I sink down in one of the two leather seats facing Stefan's desk as he steeples his hands together. "Thanks for meeting me this morning. I'd like to get right down to it if you don't mind."

"Sure," I say while I fold and refold my hands in my lap.

Stefan's eyes land on me, assessing. "Well. I suppose congratulations are in order."

My brows lower. "C-congratulations?"

He nods. "On you and Parker dating. I have to say, I kind of saw it coming."

I let loose a weird, breathy laugh and shake my head. "Um, wow. I feel you're taking this super well. I thought there might be some company policy against dating or something."

Stefan cocks one salt and pepper eyebrow. "There is. But it doesn't apply to the two of you anymore."

I tilt my head and grip the edge of Stefan's desk. "I'm sorry? I...don't understand."

Both of his eyebrows lift this time, and he taps his joined hands on the desk. "Parker is no longer employed at the *Gazette*, so the company policy doesn't apply."

My mouth falls open. "What? H-he doesn't...do you mean he..." Stammering, I whip my head toward the door, ready to leap from the seat and book it to Parker's cubicle. "Did you fire him?" I blurt.

Stefan's chair creaks as he sits back, and I meet his gaze again. "No," he says as he folds his arms over his chest, his suit straining against him as he does. "He quit."

My stomach takes a nosedive. And not a good one. More like you're on a tilt-a-whirl and about to take a hard left, right into the side of the cart kind of dive "Parker quit?!" My voice comes out as a high-pitched squeak.

Stefan nods. "I hate to lose him since he's a hard worker, but he said he feels called to do something else." With a shrug, Stefan knocks his knuckles on the desk. "I don't blame him, really. He's talented and it seems a shame to have him sitting in a cubicle wasting his potential."

I'm so stunned by my boss's words, I momentarily clam up.

"Now that we've settled the matter of you and Parker, there's something else we need to discuss." He grabs the stress ball from his desk and begins squeezing.

I'm still so sick over Parker quitting his job, I don't even know what to think. "Okay," I respond robotically.

"It's about the interview with Paris Dawson." Stefan meets my gaze. "I know things have been a little...intense...lately with these employee morale boosting activities. Truthfully, they didn't pan out like I'd hoped. It was a bust, to say the least."

"I don't know if I'd say that," I chime in, instantly regretting speaking up, but knowing it's too late not to finish the thought. "I mean, I do feel like I know my co-workers better than before."

He gives me a deadpan look. "And has your morale been boosted?"

I pinch my lips together, not wanting to lie, but not wanting to crush his dreams, either. "Well...I mean..."

"It's alright. You can tell me the truth. I already know it was a disaster."

My words to Mike about letting his boss call the shots in his life come to mind, reprimanding me. If Stefan wants the truth, maybe I *should* give it to him, in all its raw unedited glory. I inhale a steadying breath, then release it. "Mr. Sanders, to be honest, I think it was wrong of you to force us to participate in the morale boosting activities if we wanted to be considered for the interview."

He blinks and his mouth pulls tight.

"And I think the activities you chose were better suited for kids, not adults. Plus, you chewed me out when that kid electrocuted himself and that was wrong too. I didn't deserve it."

He blinks. And blinks. Without saying a word.

I roll my lips together and clear my throat, shocked that I just let it all out like that. If there was ever any hope of me gaining the interview with Paris, it deflates the moment I realize I just told my boss off. But Parker already quit, so why not lose the only other thing that gave me hope of a future here too?

"Is that all?" he finally asks.

"Mmhm." I can't manage another word. Not when I know I'm about to get fired for telling off my boss.

After an eternally long silence in which I think he's going to slap me with a pink slip, he releases a long, tired sigh. "I'm sure you're right."

My eyes bug out of my head. "I am?"

He grimaces. "All I wanted was to bring the employees of the *Gazette* together. I realize that we're all a bit different here. We've all got our own ideas of what makes a good story and I'll admit there is a certain...eccentricity about some of the employees."

I smirk, thinking of Les and his love for useless facts, of Gladys and her rhinestone jumpsuits, even Jordy and her bubbly personality.

"But it bothered me when every single person in the office rated the friendliness a one or two on that email survey," Stefan continues. "That's not how I want to run a workplace."

I make a face, gripping my knees. *I knew it.*

"And adding in that bit about you guys participating for the interview was really just to make sure I'd have full cooperation with this exercise. It wasn't to have you and the others compete...it was to bring everyone together under the guise of working toward the same goal."

I nod, still shocked that my boss genuinely cared about our feelings toward the office environment. Then an idea pops into my head. "Um, Mr. Sanders, could I just give one last suggestion?"

He waves a hand, motioning for me to go ahead. "I think the morale of this place would be boosted if you...our boss...praised our efforts a bit more. You know...a little positive reinforcement?" I try for a pleasant sort of smile but fear it's more of a wince.

"It's not that I think you're a *bad* boss, because you're not, it's just that whenever we do something well, it's almost like you downplay it so we don't get a big head or something. But then if we do something poorly, it's always brought up in a meeting as a *learning moment.*" I put those last two words in air quotes for effect. "And having our failures brought to light for others to learn from isn't exactly something employees enjoy."

He sets the stress ball down, leans forward, and steeples his fingers again. "I see." His blank expression gives nothing away, and I can't help but fidget under his stare. "Well, I thank you for your honesty. I'll take everything you've said into consideration."

*Huh?* "You will?"

"Yes. I will. It takes guts to be honest with your boss. And I already know I struggle with affirmations, according to my therapist." Whoa, he sees a *therapist*? "But we're working through it," he says, with a confident smile. "Now, back to what I'd hoped to speak to you about..."

*Oh, right. The interview.*

"I've decided to have you do the interview."

My heart skips a beat. "Really?"

Stefan nods in the affirmative. "Yes. I think you've proven that you have the guts to ask her the hard questions, but also the integrity to write a truthful piece of journalism. Besides, your investigative techniques are on point. You might've used embellishing details in some of your past stories, but they were never false. And you're a woman. It makes sense to have someone with shared experiences tell Paris's side of the story."

My mouth falls open at the praise my boss is giving me.

"Now," he says, a smug smile flitting over his face. "How's that for positive reinforcement?"

A grateful smile breaks across my face. "Thank you so much, I don't even know what to say!"

He eyes me thoughtfully. "There might be one way you could thank me."

My brows lower as I sit up a little straighter. "Sure. What can I do?"

Looking at me over the rims of his glasses, he says, "I can't help but notice that ever since your grandmother passed, there are times at work when you seem to struggle with anxiousness. It's never affected your job, but I hate to see you suffer like I did. And I'm sorry if anything I've ever done has worsened it." His chin drops as he reaches into his coat pocket and hands me a card with a woman's name next to some fancy letters that I know mean she's a doctor.

"This is my therapist, Dr. Gregario. She's helped me through so many things...including my grief."

My eyes snap to Stefan's. "Your grief?"

His eyes follow the movements of his fingers as they tap against his desk. "I lost my wife to cancer eight years ago. It was extremely difficult at first. But with Dr. Gregario's help, it's been...bearable." He meets my eyes, his softening. "Jamie, your work is impressive. You're always on time, always submit your articles in a timely fashion...but if you're struggling with grief or anxiety, talking to a therapist can help." A sour pit lodges in my stomach. "Now, I'm saying this not as your boss, but as a friend."

My lips part as if to respond, but nothing comes out.

"And like I said, I'm not bringing this up because it affects your work...but just speaking as someone who deals with his own issues, seeing a therapist has been life-changing in the best way. Grief is a heavy thing to have to carry alone. And I know you and Parker are close, but..." He lifts one shoulder in a shrug. "Still. It wouldn't hurt to try to see a professional."

I turn the card over in my hands, the sharp edges biting into my skin. "Thank you," I murmur, truly stunned by the offer of goodwill my boss just handed me and equally surprised he noticed my inner struggle these past few months. Raising my gaze to his, I smile. "I really appreciate this, Mr. Sanders. And...I'm sorry to hear about your wife."

His responding smile is dim, weak, speaking to the grief he still carries. "Thank you. Like I said, I'm...dealing with it." He knocks his knuckles on the desk and stands, then reaches out to shake my hand.

"Alright, well, thanks for taking on this project for Paris. She's eager to get her story out into the world."

"Believe me, it's my pleasure. I'm ecstatic to get to work with her." He gives me a few more quick details about when the interview will be as we walk out of his office and hope blooms within me. It's a warm, welcome feeling that has me envisioning a future with way more possibilities than ever before.

When Stefan steps back into his office, I stare at the card in my hands and consider all he shared with me. He didn't have to tell me about his wife…he didn't have to share the name and number of his personal therapist…but he did so as a friend.

I'm beginning to see a less cyborg version of my boss and a more human one the longer I get to know him. Maybe there's hope for the employees of the *Gazette*, after all.

---

Parker is seated in my desk chair when I get back to my cubicle. He spins to face me, a hesitant look on his face. I offer him a smile as I discreetly pocket the business card Stefan handed me. I know Parker has witnessed the grief-induced anxiety I deal with sometimes, but I'm not ready to confess that I might need to see a therapist to overcome it yet.

*Soon, though*, I promise myself.

He goes to get up and offer me the chair, but I place both hands on his shoulders and hold him in place. I get right in his face and speak in a low tone, but make sure to enunciate my words. "You quit your job for me."

His lips twist up on one side in a crooked half-smile as he signs, *Not just for you. For us.*

I rub my hands over his shoulders, squeezing them. "But why? We were supposed to do it together, if it came to that."

He tugs me down onto his lap and brings his hands around me so he can still sign a response. *I have plans for something else. And I have a decent savings. I'll be fine for a while.*

I'm not sure I believe him, but he nuzzles my neck and peppers kisses along my throat, cutting off any more arguments from me. I want to thank him while simultaneously chewing him out for doing something so rash, so stupid without consulting me first.

But with his lips and teeth gliding across my skin, I can do nothing but release a girlish giggle. And then I remember what else I have to tell him.

I lean back and turn toward him. "There's something else."

He gives me a slow nod, as if telling me to continue.

"Stefan offered me the interview!" I whisper-squeal.

A huge smile lights up his face as he twirls us around in the chair. He squeezes me tight from behind and presses a kiss to my temple. I tilt back just far enough to look into his eyes.

"I love you, Parker. I don't know what I'd do without you."

He brushes back the hair from my face as his eyes rove over my every feature. Then, closing the space between us, he gives me the sweetest, most tender kiss. When he holds the sign for love against my chest, my heart melts. Until he swiftly changes it into a sword finger and proceeds to tickle me until I can't take it anymore.

When I'm breathless from laughing, I rest back against his chest, still grinning like a girl who just got a promotion—at her job and in love. A month ago, I'd never have guessed my life would've taken such a startlingly romantic turn, nor would I have believed that my boss was as human as I was.

# 26

♥

# JAMIE

"So what would you say has been the hardest part about going viral as a beauty influencer?"

I push the recorder toward Paris as she adjusts in her seat across from me. We're seated at the small bar-style table in Parker and Dane's industrial-chic kitchen. My amazing boyfriend allowed me to use his downtown apartment for this interview, and I couldn't be happier. Not only is this place immaculate thanks to Dane's obsessive-compulsive cleaning habits, but it's also modern and masculine with an edgy touch.

"I think for me the hardest part was allowing complete strangers a glimpse into my life," Paris says, tapping a perfectly-manicured finger on the tabletop. "With over a million followers, someone always has something to say about how I live my life."

I frown and offer her an apologetic look. "That must be really tough. Especially when you go through a breakup."

She scoffs a little laugh and shakes her head. "You have no idea. It's insane. Everyone thinks they know what happened, everyone thinks they get to have an opinion about the relationship...but no one knows what went on *in* that relationship except for the two people involved."

"Exactly," I say, remembering my own mini-viral moment. I feel for Paris, truly. Seeing her now in person, it's clear she's struggling with the turn her life has taken by the weary lines in her face and the dark circles under her eyes. And I know for a fact she hasn't posted a video to her beauty channel in weeks.

"I just want to set the record straight," she says with a determined set to her jaw. "My ex wasted no time in sharing his skewed side of the story. Now it's time to share mine."

---

"Uh, Parker, you don't even know," I say, as I toss the lavender backpack I kept because it reminded me of a really awesome night onto the sofa and sit down beside it. "That woman has been through the wringer! And to think, she's been painted as this horrible, stuck-up entitled celebrity because of a vindictive ex."

Parker lowers himself beside me on the coach, possibly not catching a word I've said since I'm talking so fast. But in true Parker fashion, he doesn't interrupt. Just takes my legs and drapes them over his lap, removing my shoes as he goes.

I lay a hand on his arm to stop him. "You don't want to do that right now. I've been on my feet all day."

He gives me a lop-sided smile and signs, *That's exactly why I'm doing it, you silly woman. Besides, it's your birthday.*

"But you already gave me my gift!" I push my hair back and show off the gorgeous pink stone earrings that caught my eye from Meta Minerals and More before we were even together.

He shakes his head with a flirty smirk. *Your new pair of earrings wasn't the only gift I have for you. Finish your story first.*

I settle back against the throw pillows and tug Parker's blanket over me. He readjusts it so it's covering my legs but not my feet as he works his magic on every sore muscle in my foot.

"So, I can't share every detail until the story gets published," I say while signing as much as I know, "but I can tell you that she's been through a lot in the last few months. And now she's back in her hometown, just trying to get away from some of the backlash she's experienced."

Parker nods, a line forming between his brows. *Is she OK? Emotionally?*

"She's still working through things, I think. But I shared Dr. Gregario's business card with her just in case she needed to speak with a professional. I know how much she's helped me in the last few weeks so it only felt right to share her name."

Parker smiles and squeezes a particularly sore spot on my foot. I instinctively recoil with a groan, but he doesn't let me go far. In fact, his eyes zero in on my mouth and he tugs on my thighs until I'm right up against him.

*Feel good?* he asks.

A sly smirk curls my lip. "You have no idea." Grasping the sides of his face, I pull him to me and deliver the kiss I've been dying to give him all day long. He instantly responds, drawing me even closer until I'm almost entirely on his lap.

He pulls back abruptly and holds up a finger. *Wait. I don't want to get too carried away.*

I toy with the collar of his shirt. "But maybe I do. And it's my birthday." I pretend to pout and pooch out my lower lip.

He leans forward and kisses me, biting my lip as he goes. *Don't tempt me, beautiful,* he signs just before he reaches over the side of the couch and pulls a stack of papers out of his messenger bag, setting them in my lap. *The rest of your gift.* The boyish smile he gives me sends my heart into overdrive.

My eyes instantly soak up the script typed across the first page.

*A Night of Savage Shadows, By: Parker Kent*

My gaze flits to his face. "Is this something you wrote?" He dips his chin once, a single confirmation. "Like…a book?"

Again, a single nod. His expression remains unreadable except for the slight purse of his lips as he gauges my reaction. I stare down at the thick stack in my lap and start flipping through the pages. Words and phrases stand out like little lights in a dark tunnel, mesmerizing and illuminating.

"Parker, you wrote a book." Thankful he can't hear the breathy edge to my voice, I stare at my amazing boyfriend. He wrote an entire *book*. A novel, by the feel of it. A *fantasy* novel. "Is there romance in this?"

Pink tinges his cheeks and his mouth crooks upward. *Yes. But if it's not good, don't blame me. Maybe you can help me with those parts.*

I gape, completely shocked. "Parker, this is so awesome! You wrote a *book*!" I flip the pages closed and make a show of how heavy it is. "And it's thick!" He laughs and so do I. "Is this the thing you've been working on? Your plan B?"

He nods, eyeing his work.

"Oh my gosh, I can't wait to read it! Thank you so much!"

I reach forward and pull him into my arms, squeezing him tight. It doesn't last long enough when he leans back and starts signing again. *You can only read it on one condition.*

I cock my head in question.

*You can only read five chapters a week. At the end of each week, I want to take you on a themed date that coincides with the story.*

My mouth drops open with a shocked smile. "Parker! Are you for real?"

He grins so wide it shows off all his perfect teeth. *Yes, I'm serious. You have to promise.*

I take my finger and swipe it over my chest in a crisscross pattern. "Okay, I promise. Cross my heart and hope to die, stick a needle in my eye."

He laughs and pulls me back into his arms. I flip open the first page of the book and as soon as I reach the dedication, my eyes begin to water.

*To Jamie: You heard all the words I never said and saw me like no one else did. Loving you makes me a better man. Thanks for being my endless source of inspiration.*

A tear streams down my face and I try to bat it away before Parker sees, but *of course,* the man misses nothing. He puts a hand to my head and kisses my hair, then twirls a strand around his finger while I turn the page and begin reading.

I couldn't say how many nights we do this, but for the next eight weeks, I spend most of my evenings curled up in Parker's lap or by his side reading the words he penned. And to say it's surreal to read our love story woven into an intricate fantasy plot would be an understatement. And it also feels necessary to add that the man. Can. Write.

Not only do Parker's kisses keep me up late into the night, but so do his thoughtfully written words. I always knew he was destined for greater things than the *Gazette*, and this manuscript is proof.

Lady Elyse is a fantastic character who Parker insists is based off of me, but she wields swords and slays dragons alongside her broody, silent assassin, Dandrick. Their love story isn't exactly like ours in that it's more of an enemies-to-lovers tale, however, Parker added so many details that are true to us.

For instance, after they resign themselves to their fate of working together to defeat the evil sorcerer in their world, they become friends.

And Dandrick's attempts to bring a smile out of Lady Elyse are much like Parker's, including tickling with a certain pointer *sword* finger.

And then there's the time they share the horse and Lady Elyse falls asleep on Dandrick's chest like I fell asleep on Parker, plus their steamy kiss against the castle wall bore a striking resemblance to our first kiss...

But the best part about reading through his manuscript has been the dates he's planned for us. While Elyse and Dandrick were fighting off evil enemies, Parker was taking me on an ax-throwing date, then we went to the theater to catch an action movie.

At the point in the story where they had to escape a dungeon, Parker organized an escape room date, even inviting Daria, Briar, and Gladys to come along with us. It was so fun, especially when Gladys figured out the last clue that got us out of the room.

But now, we're nearing the end of the story and I'm almost sad to finish it.

We're sprawled out on Parker's couch, him lying beside me with his arm draped over my stomach, his thumb rubbing circles along my waist. His chin rests on my shoulder as I struggle not to ugly cry at this last scene in the book.

It's so touching with Dandrick confessing his undying love to Elyse in the only way he knows how, begging her not to leave with nothing but hand gestures and silent touches. I'm completely engrossed in the story, but when I turn to the next page, it's blank.

I bolt upright and flip the page back and forth. Whirling on Parker, I raise the thick stack of papers that have curled at the edges from overuse. "Where's the rest?"

A slow smile creeps to his lips and he holds up a finger. Rising from the couch, he heads to his bedroom, then returns with a single piece of paper.

"What," I ask, "did you not finish it or something?"

He shakes his head and hands me the rest. I devour the page as quickly as possible, needing to know how this story ends. Tears form in my eyes at the very last words on the page.

*I'll stay. Yes, Dandrick, I'll stay and marry you. I love you with all my heart.*

I'm a blubbering, emotional wreck when I raise my gaze to see Parker down on one knee in front of me, holding a ring with a gorgeous pink princess-cut stone set in the center of what appears to be a white-gold band glittering with tiny little half-moon shaped diamonds.

I suck in a gasp and drop the paper as my hands fly to my mouth. He mouths, *Will you marry me*, holding the ring up between us.

"Yes!" I scream at the top of my lungs as I fling myself toward Parker. We tumble to the ground, a heap of legs and arms, both laughing, until I realize I might've knocked the gorgeous ring out of his hands.

Helping him to a seated position, I breathe a sigh of relief when I see the ring still between his fingers. Parker takes my hand and slides the ring into place—a perfect fit—just like the two of us. I wiggle my fingers and watch as the pink stone sparkles under the light.

"It's perfect, Parker." I meet his eyes and say, "Thank you. It's breathtaking."

*Just like you*, he signs then kisses me right on the nose. *There's one more thing.*

"What is it?"

He chews his bottom lip for a second before signing, *I sent this manuscript into a writing competition and...I won.*

My eyes go wide. "You won?!" He nods with a smile. "What did you win?!"

He brings his hands between us to sign, *A publishing contract.*

I squeal again, jumping up and down on my knees as I hug Parker close to my chest. I can't believe he won a publishing contract! Pulling back, I ask, "So does this mean you're now a published author?"

He lifts one shoulder. *I will be soon. We're in contract and the book will be published next year. Which means I'm now employed and can provide for a wife.* Shaking my head, I roll my eyes. He should know that's the last thing I'm worried about when it comes to our future. *So,* he continues, *how long do we have to wait to make it official?*

"What do you mean? You just did!"

*No, marriage. When can we do it?*

I laugh, pushing against his chest playfully. "You're ready to get married? Right now?"

His eyes widen as he nods his head up and down emphatically. *Right now. Let's go.* He hops to his feet, pulling me up with him, and makes a show of running toward the door. I tug him back by his hand and give him a stern look.

"No so fast, bestie. I'm making you wait a while." He makes a fist like he's holding a knife and jabs it into his heart. "Sorry, but I've always wanted a big wedding. And something tells me your mom would kill you if we ran off and got married without her there."

He rolls his eyes and signs, *Yeah, you're right. So... summer?*

I smile and run my hands up his chest. "Summer sounds nice. Think you can wait that long?"

He purses his lips and raises an eyebrow in challenge, then hovers his lips over mine. I start to lean in, craving his touch, but he pulls back with a laugh just before I can make contact.

*I think you're the one who won't be able to wait,* he signs with a smug expression.

I go to swat him in the stomach, but he's too quick. By the time I do, we've turned it into a game of tag where we're chasing each other around his apartment until we're both laughing so hard we can't breathe.

And when we finally fall back onto the couch together, my heart is so full, it feels close to bursting. I never could've imagined that my best friend would become the person I get to spend the rest of my life with as my *husband*.

White picket fence, here we come.

# 27
# EPILOGUE

♥

## DARIA

Party planning ranks right up there with shopping for me. It's an exciting experience that gets my creative juices flowing, my fingers itching to get to work, and my feet ready to pound the pavement in search of the perfect touches to complete the aesthetic I've put together in my head.

So when Parker made it official and put a ring on it, I jumped at the chance to throw my two friends an engagement party to remember.

Besides, Jamie's a little like me in that she doesn't have a solid family support system. But she's at least got me, and I won't let her down. If there's anything that's worth celebrating, it's the love that she and Parker share.

Not that *I* plan on experiencing a love like they have in my lifetime, but it works for them and I'm here for it.

Placing the last little spaceship in its place inside the terrarium filled with sand, I stand back and admire my work. When Jamie insisted I add some space-themed elements to the party, I balked. But after spending a ton of time researching on Pinterest, I found multiple ways to add little things in here and there that won't detract from the overall high-end aesthetic.

I'm actually pretty impressed with myself.

White, gold, and black balloons curve upward in an arch along the wall and underneath them sits a table full of little themed treats. The banner under the balloon arch reads, *The force of love is strong with these two.* And boy, is it ever.

I've had to shield my eyes plenty of times after walking in on one of their make out sessions. But I guess when you're in love, that's how things are. I wouldn't know. I've never been in love, and don't plan to be.

When the last guy I got serious about in college cheated on me, I decided to never let myself go all googly-eyed over another man. Sure, I date. I mean, a girl's gotta have a good time now and then, but usually after that first date, I'm kicking the guy to the curb.

Because I'm better off alone. I've got my friends, Jamie and Briar, even Parker, and that's really all I need.

There was that one night where I almost let myself get attached to a guy…he was just too charming and good-looking…plus, he genuinely seemed to have his life together and was a great conversationalist. We met at a party and ended up talking all night long. I felt like we had a genuine connection, and he even gave me his number. But when I tried to text him a few days later, he completely ghosted me. It was then I realized that I should've stuck to my guns from the get-go.

For me, getting attached only ever leads to heartbreak.

The door to Parker's apartment swings open and Parker's mom, Alex, steps inside with her arms full of wrapped gifts. "Oy," she huffs as I run over to try and assist her.

"Here, let me." I take the two gifts off the top and carry them over to the gift table.

"This place looks *excellent*, Daria! You did a wonderful job!"

I smile at Alex's praise as my gaze roves over the industrial-style apartment. It's spotless and decorated and ready to receive guests. I've never met either of Parker's brothers, not even the one who owns this place, but after meeting his mom, I'm excited to see if they're as gregarious as she and Parker are.

"Thank you, Alex. Are Parker and Jamie on their way?"

She nods as she flits toward the gift table and sets down the rest of her gifts. "They should be. Logan too, but Dane will be late." She makes a face like *go figure* at the mention of her middle child not making it on time. I wonder if this is a normal occurrence for him.

Moving to the kitchen to set out the drinks, plates, and napkins, Alex and I make quick work on the party's finishing touches. Soon, the studio-style apartment is filled with people from Jamie and Parker's workplace, Parker's immediate and extended family, and even some mutual acquaintances from our yoga class.

"D, this place looks stunning! I don't know how you did it, but it looks awesome," Jamie squeals as she wraps me in the tightest hug I've ever received.

"Oh, it was nothing." I wink as Parker sidles up next to us, signing what I think are the words *Thank you. It looks great.*

Jamie's been teaching me ASL off and on for the better part of a year, but I still struggle to understand some of the signs. I'm looking into taking an actual class with a professional teacher, but I've been working and party-planning so much lately that I haven't had much extra time to devote to it.

"Well, you both are so welcome," I say with a bright smile. "If anyone deserves to have a memorable engagement party, it's you two. After all, you waited like...forever...to finally get together." I send each of them a sly smirk, but they ignore my ribbing, too infatuated with each other to notice.

When Briar joins us, Parker introduces us both to his older brother, Logan, and his dad, Paul. Both men seem a little shy and not as outgoing as Parker or his mom. After greeting a few more people and mingling a bit, I busy myself with refilling the punch.

I'm so engrossed in my work that when Alex chimes, "He's here!" I can't bother to look up and pay attention to whoever she's referring to. I go to the freezer to get more ice, but when I spin around, I'm met with the face of a man I haven't seen in a year.

He bends down to give Alex a hug and when she puts her hands on his face, his eyes drift upward, snag on me, then do a double take. His expression morphs from happy to…confused? Disgusted?

The plastic bowl that was previously in my hands clatters to the ground. Bending, I scoop it up and avert my eyes, hauling butt to the freezer as fast as I can get there.

"Is everything okay?" Jamie asks, coming up beside me.

"Uh, yeah." I whip open the freezer and grab the metal scoop from the ice compartment to refill the bowl. "I think I might've spilled some water on the floor over there, though. Would you mind grabbing a rag to wipe it up?"

Jamie's gaze flits to where I dropped the bowl, then back to me. "Oh, yeah, sure." She scurries away to do my bidding and I lean further into the freezer, trying to cool myself off.

Why is *he* here? *How* is he here? Is he a friend of Parker's? He obviously seemed to know Alex pretty well…I almost didn't recognize him with the light growth of stubble lining his jaw or the way his hair is shorter than when we first met.

Taking a deep breath in and releasing it, I finish filling the bowl of ice. I have no idea why Charles, the gorgeous, deep conversationalist I clicked with at the random party I attended last year is here, but I'm not going to give him the time of day.

He ghosted me. Left me on read. Never returned the one solitary text I sent.

Doesn't he realize how big of a step that was for me? How much I had to have liked him to even send that message? Ugh, I'm getting disgusted with myself all over again just thinking about it.

I shut the freezer door and take the bowl back to the drink table, determined to avoid him. I doubt he'd try to talk to me with the way we left things, especially since the way he did a double-take has me thinking he's as surprised to see me as I am him.

Still, I intend to keep my distance. This party is about Jamie and Parker, not my issues with the male species as a whole.

But when I spin around, Jamie and Parker are walking toward me *with* the man in question.

*Ughhhh, I've never wanted to disappear more than in this very moment.*

Jamie steps forward and gestures toward the two guys, who now that I'm looking at them side-by-side, seem to resemble each other. Wait. He's not...

"Daria, Parker wanted to introduce you to his brother," Jamie says, taking Parker's hand.

Parker smiles and gestures to Charles, then signs what I think is, *Daria, this is my older brother, D-A-N-E.*

My brows pull tight. *Huh?*

I question my sanity as my gaze immediately swings to the handsome ghost himself, whose complexion has paled remarkably since the first time I laid eyes on him this evening. His lips thin as he locks eyes with me and extends a hand.

"It's nice to meet you, Daria. I'm Dane."

*Ah, so that's how he's gonna play it...*

Parker's brother, the guy who charmed me into texting him, is now staring me dead in the eye and acting like he didn't give me a fake name at a party just to pretend I didn't exist the next day. Part of me wonders if the number was fake too.

Resisting the urge to roll my eyes, I narrow them and accept his lousy handshake. "*Dane*, is it? Nice to *finally* meet you too." I paste the most saccharine smile possible onto my face, but as our hands make contact, I'm overwhelmed with the way his callouses brush against my skin and my smile falters.

Pulling my hand back and wiping it down my designer jeans to rid myself of the feeling, I face Jamie. "I'm going to see if any of the snacks need refilled. Call me if you need me." I make an about face and head for the snack table, which unfortunately is only three strides away, and pick up the one and only tray that looks mildly close to being empty.

Hoping I actually look busy and not just desperate to get away from the lying date that got away, I carry the tray to the kitchen counter and grab the reserve chicken salad croissants from the fridge. I start piling them onto the tray in a somewhat neat and orderly fashion when a man's voice startles me.

"That's not how you do it."

I whip my head in the direction I heard Charles—*Dane*—speak from to find him standing against the counter beside me, ankles and arms crossed, his gaze zeroed in on the tray of sandwiches. "If you do it like that," he croons nice and low, "they'll all get smooshed together and no one likes soggy chicken salad sandwiches."

I cock my head and glare at the intruder. "Excuse me?"

His dark eyelashes flutter as his gaze slowly drifts upward to meet mine. "I think you heard me."

*Who does this guy think he is?* I purse my lips and take a deep breath. "I know what I'm doing. If I wanted your help, I would've asked for it."

I raise what Jamie refers to as my menacing eyebrow, daring him to say another word.

His mouth tips up just the slightest on one side, revealing a perfectly placed dimple. I avert my gaze and finish piling the sandwiches the way *I* want to, not the way the liar beside me suggested, when his hand grasps my elbow. I freeze at the contact and stifle the urge to fling the croissant in my hand at his face.

"Parker tells me you're Jamie's roommate." It's not a question. Just an obvious statement spoken in a husky whisper.

I meet his eyes again. "Yeah, so?"

"Did you know I was his brother?"

I scoff and shake off his hand. "And how would I know that when I didn't even know your *real* name until just now." He opens his mouth to speak, but I don't let him. "Despite what you *obviously* think, I haven't been sitting at home pining for you. You've barely crossed my mind at all." I straighten my spine. "In fact, I didn't even recognize you at first."

A deep divot forms between his brows as he tilts his head. "Look, I know it looks bad, but there's no need for this level of hostility."

I drop the sandwich on the platter and plant my hands on either side of the counter in front of me. "You acted like we'd just *met*. And gave me a *fake* name."

"It's not—"

I hold up a hand to stop him while my teeth grind together so hard, it takes effort to open my mouth again. "I have little patience for arrogant players, so unless you've got something important to say to me, I suggest you get back to the party."

Something like hurt flickers in his eyes for a split second before he schools his features. "I was just curious to know if you'd realized that Parker and I were related prior to now. That's all." The genuinely confused look he gives me paired with the surprise in his voice makes heat creep into my cheeks. I briefly wonder why he seems taken aback, but I'm too proud to ask.

I turn away and finish assembling the sandwich tray. "No," I answer honestly on a swallow. "I didn't know."

I carry the tray back to the table, effectively ignoring the pinch in my chest. It's not that I want to be rude to Dane, but who has the audacity to come up to someone they lied to and ignored, then correct them on the way they're assembling a sandwich tray?

A jerk, that's who.

I'm mostly successful in avoiding Ch—*Dane*— for the duration of the party.

Up until Jamie and Parker stand tall in front of God and everyone to announce that I have been elected to be Jamie's maid of honor and Dane is dubbed as Parker's best man. Everyone cheers and congratulates us like we've been awarded a Golden Globe as I fight a disgusted grimace from taking over my face.

"So," Jamie says, clasping both of my hands in hers. "We originally wanted to wait until summer to get married, but…I don't know if I can wait that long!" Her excitement is precious, but the girl has gone and tumbled face first into the sickeningly sweet pit of love. *Eww.* "Now I'm thinking of having the wedding in April which means we've only got two months to plan everything. Dane says he's got a buddy who owns a gorgeous lakeside estate where we can have the reception, or even the wedding if the weather permits. He's going to work on that for us now…"

She continues prattling off things we need to go over in preparation for the wedding, but I've tuned out.

It's hard to focus on anything when I lift my eyes to the dark-haired, blue-eyed man smirking at me from across the room like he's reading each and every one of my thoughts. Sounds like he's already inserting himself into the wedding planning too. But *of course* he is. He's obviously a know-it-all control freak who can't even trust a woman to assemble a sandwich tray properly.

"So, how's that sound?" Jamie's question pulls me back to the present.

"Um, can you repeat that?"

She smiles. "I asked if you'd be able to go dress shopping with me next weekend?"

I chuckle and flip my hair over my shoulder. "Oh, of course. You know me, I'm always up for a shopping trip."

She grins and pulls me in for another hug. I stiffen at first, but eventually wrap my arms around her. Ever since she started seeing Parker, she's become way more affectionate.

"Thanks for being an awesome friend, D," she whispers into my ear. "I don't know where I'd be without you."

I respond with a smile of my own and tamp down the urge to run as fast and as far away from anything wedding related as I can.

Engagement party stuff? It's fun, cute, and was a blast to pull together. But wedding planning? In two months' time? Having to share responsibilities with a guy who just put himself at the top of my evil jerk list?

Yeah, no thanks.

**To Be Continued...**

# More From Dulcie

♥

**Kissing a Kent Brother**
*Sign Me Up*
*Spoke Too Soon*
*Flirty Little Secret*
**West Coast Slopes**
*Three Days to Forget*
*A Make Out to Remember*
**Dating a Denver Dragon**
*Cross Check Crush*
*Switch and Score*
**River Hollow Romance**
*Not Since You*
*Now With You*
*Next to You*
*Not Until You*
*Not Without Noelle*

SIGN ME UP

## The Honey Legacy
*A Drop in Forever*

# Fun Facts

♥

Hey guys! Dulcie, here.

Thank you so much for reading *Sign Me Up*! As per usual with my books, there are some real-life things I added into this story just because I could. LOL

So, for those of you who wonder which parts I gleaned from actual real-life experiences, keep on reading!

1.) This book is dedicated to my sister, Jamie, who I really did promise to name my child after. Why? Because I used to beg to sleep with her and that was her payment. She's basically just Rumpelstiltskin with strawberry blonde hair.

2.) Though the character was named after my older sister, the fictional Jamie and real-life Jamie don't share too many similarities other than their hair color and love for healthy eating.

3.) "Sword Finger" is a real thing my dad would use on us as kids. He'd wield that thing like a weapon and many a tickle fight took place growing up because of it. He still uses it today when the situation calls for it.

4.) Meta Minerals and More is the name of my brother's business. Check them out on Facebook!

5.) Though heavily exaggerated and fabricated, a similar trust fall incident actually did happen at one of my friends' workplaces. She did not participate. haha.

6.) I may or may not also have a mild obsession with Shania Twain.

7.) A similar "Bobby Hauck" incident really did happen to me in kindergarten. It was mortifying and scarred me for life.

8.) My wardrobe mostly consists of black clothing like Jamie. Sorry not sorry.

9.) And lastly, Jamie and Parker's workplace dance kiss was also inspired by real-life events. I wanted to showcase a couple taking their relationship to the next level by a sweet kiss on the jaw. :)

# Special Thanks

♥

It's hard to believe this is my NINTH book published! I'd love to say that writing stories gets easier as I go, but that would be a lie. It does, however, show me just how fallible I really am and highlights the fact that no story of mine could be complete without the help and input of others.

This story in particular took me a VERY long time to write. My longest yet, I think, at over a year! There were many days I thought it wouldn't ever get finished...that I'd never be able to fully flesh out these characters...but with the help and encouragement of my friends, we made it!

So here's where I take a minute to thank the generous souls that dedicated time and effort to help make this story what it is!

To Jennia, my fabulous, one-of-a-kind editor...GIRL. What can I even say that hasn't already been said? You are my right-hand woman and your advice, professional eye, and constant encouragement are what keep me going on the days I want to quit! I've tucked so many of your words deep into my heart and go back to them often when I'm questioning if being a writer is something I should even pursue. THANK YOU just for being you and being available!

To my VERY FIRST critique partner on this story, Sophie Toovey, thank you for taking the time to read and give me my first words of encouragement, and to my other critique partners, Latisha, MJ, and Annah, THANK YOU for spending so much time reading and critiquing this story in its entirety. Your friendship means so much to me!

A HUGE thanks to my sensitivity readers, Laken and Aubrey. Your advice and guidance was much needed for this story!

To Charity, my eagle eyes, THANK YOU for being SO willing to jump right in and read like a mad woman to get this story out to the other ARC readers. Your friendship is a blessing!

And to my other ARC readers, you guys are awesome. Thanks for taking a chance on Parker and Jamie's story!

To all of my readers, thank you for being loyal and ready to purchase or borrow my books. I count it a privilege to have my stories on your shelves and in your hands.

A big thanks to my sisters and family for giving me so much material for this one, haha. And to my husband and kids, especially, thanks for allowing me the time and space to work. My husband has held me when I've cried tears over this story and soothed all of my doubts when they arose...he truly should get all the praise for this one!

And to my Jesus for always seeing me through. Only He knows the emotional and spiritual struggle I went through to get this book out during one of the most trying times of my life. He's so good and blesses me beyond what I can even imagine!

***Visit small town Ohio in Dulcie's River Hollow Romance series!***
**Secrets never stay hidden in a small town...**

Find a whole lot of heart and a little bit of humor in this found family's story as they learn to navigate through love and loss in charming, small-town Ohio.

# About the Author

Dulcie is a Christian wife and mother, enjoying life in the Midwest with her dogs, chickens, and passel of kiddos.

She writes stories with characters that are quirky, fun, and full of romance! Most of the time, you can find her wandering around her yard-barefoot, playing with her kiddos, or cozied up in a chair with a coffee and a good book. More than anything, she hopes you enjoyed this book and have found peace in a personal relationship with Jesus.

You can find her here:
Instagram: @dulciedameron
Facebook: Author Dulcie Dameron
www.dulciedameron.com

Printed in Great Britain
by Amazon